D0057032

THE
SMALL CRIMES
OF

Tiffany

TEMPLETON

THE
SMALL CRIMES
OF
Tiffany
TEMPLETON

Richard Fifield

RAZORBILL

RAZORBILL

An imprint of Penguin Random House LLC, New York

First published in the United States of America by Razorbill,
an imprint of Penguin Random House LLC, 2020

Visit us online at penguinrandomhouse.com

LIBRARY OF CONGRESS CATALOGING-IN-PUBLICATION DATA
Names: Fifield, Richard, 1975- author.
Title: The small crimes of Tiffany Templeton / Richard Fifield.
Description: New York : Razorbill, 2020. | Audience: Ages 14+ | Summary: After a stint in reform
school, fifteen-year-old "Tough Tiff" returns to small-town Montana to face grief, an overbearing best
friend, her first boyfriend, eccentric neighbors, and the production of a play she wrote.
Identifiers: LCCN 2019036446 | ISBN 9781984835895 (hardcover) | ISBN 9781984835901 (ebook)
Subjects: CYAC: Conduct of life—Fiction. | Friendship—Fiction. | Grief—Fiction. | Family problems—
Fiction. | Montana—Fiction.
Classification: LCC PZ7.1.F532 Sm 2020 | DDC [Fic]—dc23
LC record available at https://lccn.loc.gov/2019036446

Printed in the United States of America

1 3 5 7 9 10 8 6 4 2

Design by Kristie Radwilowicz.

Text set in Apollo MT Pro.

The hardest words I've ever had to write:
For Loretta Jones, 2/10/43–8/19/18.
We were blessed.

Chapter One

THE COURT-APPOINTED ADVOCATE DROPPED ME off at two o'clock in the morning. She didn't even bring me all the way to my house, just left me on the side of the highway. I guess she wasn't worried about my safety, lugging a suitcase without wheels all the way around the loop in the middle of the night. I was the only girl from Dogwood that didn't want to be paroled, but the other girls didn't have to return to Gabardine. I dragged the suitcase across the frozen ruts in the road, the ice sparkling under a thin winter moon, the only light in the entire trailer court. The front door was unlocked, but nobody locked their doors in my hometown.

It was only appropriate that my first day back at high school fell on the first day after spring break. I guess my classmates looked well rested. I had slept for less than four hours, and I'm sure it showed.

David could smell my vulnerability. Before the bell even rang in homeroom, he had managed to set a trap for me, just to watch it spring shut. Eighty-three days, but it was like I never left. I thought he would acknowledge my return, but he looked away and moved his desk closer to the radiator, cold as always. He barely fit in his desk. David was nearly six foot three, the kind of guy who was born with muscles, even though I know the only exercise he got was from arts and crafts. Blond, gorgeous, and this morning, full of evil.

David was my best friend.

That morning, he ignored me, so I knew a plot was in motion. I expected something spectacular, but he just sent over a cheerleader to say something mean. He'd appointed himself in charge of the cheerleaders ages ago, and they all did his bidding. Kaitlynn, Caitlyn, Victoria, and Becky may have been varsity, but they were totally JV when it came to everything else. David fed them the insults, just like he monitored the rest of their diets. Their eyes betrayed them, every single time.

Kaitlynn approached me, as soon as she made sure everybody was seated.

"If we had a yearbook, you would be voted most likely to do a school shooting," said Kaitlynn. She looked off to the side, calculating, double-checking her memory, making sure she had put emphasis on the right words. David even coached their line readings.

"I'm pretty sure that's not a yearbook category," I responded.

"Whatever," she said. "I can just see you shooting up trigonometry."

"It would probably be gym class," I said. "But I'm the only one in our class who doesn't own a gun." Hunting was big in Gabardine. Principal Beaudin actually let kids miss school for hunting season.

"Freak," she said, and walked away. It was a lame retort, but that's how I knew it was her own.

I endured these things, because they didn't mean them, and because this was some sort of gay muscle that David was training.

You would think he would be a target, but he was always the

first to draw his weapon. I guess you could call him the most popular person in our school, but we all grew up together, and there was no hierarchy. David was not popular, he was a glue trap that we all got stuck in before we knew it.

I know it sounded weird, but David was my best friend. I think he threw chaos at me just to keep things interesting. I was the wild card. I was the one that didn't fit his idea of what a high school should be. David read every single Sweet Valley High book, but he thought they were instruction manuals.

When we were freshmen, he tried to convince me to get a makeover. It was not the first time. "When we're old, we will remember high school," he had said. "Even if you end up in prison, you're still going to reminisce."

"Thanks, I guess."

"There's no reason we can't have normal high school things. Drugs, eating disorders, homecoming queens."

"We don't have homecoming," I said. I guess I was wrong about that. After almost three months away, here it was, my own personal homecoming.

During earth science, Kaitlynn appeared in the doorway. She was the office aide, which meant she roamed the halls and sometimes cut holiday decorations out of construction paper.

"Mr. Baker. The sheriff is in the office."

"So?"

"He's here for that girl." She pointed at me. I'd known her for fifteen years. "And he's armed."

I followed her down the hall, but she power walked, so I couldn't keep up. David made all of his cheerleaders power walk, so I had to call after her. "You know my name," I said, and she ignored me.

Outside of Principal Beaudin's office, Kaitlynn sat down in the waiting room, lowered herself into a tiny desk, right next to his secretary's large work station. Piled in front of her were scissors, white printer paper, Elmer's glue, and a vial of green glitter, probably left over from Christmas. These were the same Arbor Day decorations we always had.

"Do these look like trees?" She held up a wonky triangle, the base split by something that was supposed to be a stump. She had outlined the entire thing in glitter. If David was here, he would have corrected her, and the stump would be brown. He hated nature, but he took arts and crafts very seriously.

"I guess," I said and tried to see through the frosted window to figure out who was in Principal Beaudin's office. Kaitlynn glared at me, waved a pair of scissors. The secretary flinched at this.

"Arbor Day isn't even a real holiday," I said. In Gabardine, we already had too many trees. "I'm glad they've got you doing such important work."

"Don't be an asshole," said Kaitlynn.

"Language," warned the secretary. Her phone rang once and did not ring again. "They're ready for you," she said, and returned to her own project, tapping like a bird at her computer keyboard.

I knew what my mother thought of Principal Beaudin because she told me. She didn't trust people with weak chins, and she especially distrusted people who tucked in their shirts. I hadn't seen Principal Beaudin in three months, and although his shirt was tucked in, he seemed to be growing some sort of goatee. I had worried that things would change while I was gone, but the gray ring of hair around his mouth seemed to be the only progress in the entire town.

Obviously, I knew the sheriff. Sheriff Schrader was not an

unfamiliar face. He came to our high school to deliver a speech about the dangers of drugs, although it always ended up being about poaching, which was an actual felony.

Sheriff Schrader smiled at me. I think he liked the fact that our county was boring and what I had done was not. Principal Beaudin pointed at the chair closest to his phone.

"Your mother refuses to come in," said Principal Beaudin.

"She's at work," I said. "Everybody knows that."

"I get my gas elsewhere," said Principal Beaudin. He lived in Fortune, three times the size of Gabardine, and I think their streetlights and sidewalks made him cocky.

"That's a mistake," said Sheriff Schrader. He knew our town, drove at the tail end of every parade. None of my crimes had ever caught his attention, except for the threats. My mother said this was because he got a check from Homeland Security every month. Even though I was never charged for any federal crime, the sheriff wanted that check. He warned my mother that my threat to a federal employee was proof I was being radicalized, even if it was just the Mail Lady.

"We're going to try this through speakerphone," said Principal Beaudin. "It's a little out of the ordinary, but my secretary is a professional, and she knows all the latest technology."

Principal Beaudin didn't see me roll my eyes. He pushed a button on his phone, and the room was filled with the sound of the dial tone. He consulted a piece of paper on his desk, and we all listened as he tapped out the number for the gas station.

Even over the phone, Sheriff Schrader still feared my mother. He removed his hat as we waited for her to answer, held it over his heart.

I had not spoken to my mother in three months. She was not

waiting for me when I arrived last night, even though I'm sure somebody called her. She still wanted nothing to do with me, and it seemed only appropriate to hear her through a small box, at a safe distance.

"What?" My mother sounded the same. Normally, she would have answered the gas station phone with something cordial, but she had obviously been expecting this call.

"Mrs. Templeton, I'm sitting here with your daughter and the sheriff."

"I know," said my mother. "I'm sitting here with eighteen boxes of Hershey's bars that need pricing. Some of us have work to do." Her voice had become a fearsome thing.

Principal Beaudin looked at the sheriff, but he was silent. Principal Beaudin decided to break the silence. "We wanted to meet in person," he said. "It's my job to keep this school safe, and I worry about the path that Tiffany has chosen."

I wanted to tell him that this wasn't a path, and it certainly wasn't a choice. It was a tunnel, and I had to keep moving to survive. The room was silent as we all regarded each other and stared at the phone, like it was a showdown.

Once again, Principal Beaudin broke the silence. I don't even know why the sheriff was there. "We're still waiting for the files from Tiffany's reformatory school. I can assure you that my secretary has requested them several times, because she is a professional."

"Tiffany has been back for less than seven hours," said my mother. "I know how bureaucracy works. You should receive the files in a few years, after she graduates." My mother exhaled, dramatically. I could tell she had lit a cigarette. "You don't need to worry about my daughter," she said. "She completed her rehabilitation."

"Most of it," I said, and I swear I could hear my mother's body tighten over the phone line.

"People grieve in different ways," she said. "My daughter chose violence."

And now Sheriff Schrader spoke, his hat still clutched to his chest. "I'm sorry for your loss, ma'am. But in light of her record, Tiffany's going to need to be extra careful around Mrs. Bitzche," he said. "In fact, I hope she stays away from all federal employees. We don't mess around with terrorism. Before you know it, your daughter will end up in Guantanamo Bay."

"I don't think that's going to happen," said my mother. "But I'm sure she appreciates the warning."

"Last month I went to a training," said Sheriff Schrader. "You never know who is radicalized. There's teenage girls in the Middle East who strap bombs to their chest."

"That's too much of a bother for Tiffany," said my mother. "You'll have to trust me on that."

"Sure," he said. "Teenagers have no work ethic these days. But there's more, Vy."

"Of course there is," said my mother. "I got rid of all the silverware. We have no weapons in our house." I heard her exhale. "Shit. I forgot my razors. That's just great, Tiffany. How am I supposed to shave my legs?"

"Sheriff Schrader has conditions," said Principal Beaudin. "Do you need to find a pen to write them down?"

"Jesus," said my mother. "I'm not in special ed."

Sheriff Schrader leaned down to the phone. "Tiffany is still on probation. She's got fourteen months left."

"She served her time," said my mother.

"Minus eight days," I added.

"It's the court order," he explained. "She's going to need to see the probation officer once a month. Real nice gal. Drives over from Fortune." Sheriff Schrader smirked at Principal Beaudin. "Maybe y'all could carpool?"

"When and where?" My mother had grown tired of this conversation.

"Third Wednesday of the month at city hall," said Sheriff Schrader.

"That's in two days," I said.

"There's one more condition, Vy." He was grim-faced, and his jaw flexed like he was gritting his teeth. "I don't want to issue a restraining order. You need to get a post office box."

"That infringes upon our rights," said my mother.

Sheriff Schrader knew about my mother's politics. He was prepared. "Rural delivery is not a constitutional right. I double-checked."

My mother hissed into the phone. "You cause nothing but sorrow, Tiffany Templeton."

We all heard the boom as she slammed the phone down.

As I walked back from Principal Beaudin's office, I knew she spoke the truth. Even before I was a confirmed juvenile delinquent, I was trouble. My mother used her words to hurt people, but I used my fists. My classmates trafficked in the truth. When they said my dad was fat, it wasn't teasing, just their primal desire to poke. Maybe we were all rats in the same cage, but they were the ones that kept pushing the buttons. They needed their fix, I guess, and so I punched, kicked, pushed them into mud puddles. The brave ones sprang back up, and I gave them a real beating. As a kid, I didn't know why my parents were so fat. It didn't make any sense to me why they were different than the other parents. They were only seen in one dimension, all weight and no depth.

I paused outside of the classroom. I took a deep breath, like I had been taught at Dogwood. I wasn't that girl anymore. I wasn't a fighter. I had plans now.

I would destroy the evidence, and I would stay out of trouble until I could leave this place forever.

When I entered the room, we still had ten minutes left in earth science. I chose to tune out the achingly slow tectonic plates, and instead found my eyes drawn to Bitsy, three seats away from me, who had a motion of his own.

His name wasn't really Bitsy, but we'd all called him that for as long as I could remember. It came from his last name, Bitzche, which was unfortunate for two reasons—first, because it meant he was the Mail Lady's son, and second, because substitute teachers were forever mangling it. "Sounds like beach," he was used to saying. "It's Czechoslovakian."

Bitsy had grown up down the street from me, a few trailers away. I'd watched his dad train him in the yard, windups, sprints, all that. His dad had single-handedly created our high school football team, eight boys strong, the first team Gabardine had fielded in twenty years. Now his father was gone, just like mine. Except his disappeared in the middle of the night with a suitcase and his favorite truck, and when Coach vanished, so did the football program.

For the next ten minutes, I watched as Bitsy tapped his foot, cracked his knuckles, pulled at the hairs on the back of his neck. He cut his own jet-black hair, and poorly. Today, he had combed his bangs forward, and they were so uneven that they looked like the smile of a jack-o'-lantern. He had really long eyelashes, and when I heard him speak, he had a froggy voice that creaked out like he had been talking for days on end.

I'd never found a boy that interesting. I'd been stuck with the same thirty-one kids since kindergarten, but I was unable to look away from Bitsy. It freaked me out, but maybe I was just fascinated by what we had in common. His father was gone, too. But Coach Bitzche ran and left his family behind, along with a puzzled town. As usual, I was unlike the rest of Gabardine. It was no mystery to me.

Most people in Gabardine are easy to figure out. I'm sure his mother caused some cracks in him, just as she had with me. She was like a terrible robot with terrible eye shadow, the same route six days a week, around and around on those perfect legs, even strides. The mail was never a mess. Always aligned on the left side of the mailbox, a stack in descending order of size. Unlike her son, she never twitched, and she never looked exhausted. She didn't even fall apart after her husband left. She just kept walking, and never missed a day of delivery. She was meticulous, but I knew the mess she had escaped. She had reasons to keep walking. Like me, she didn't want things to catch up with her. Bitsy tapped, the mail lady walked, and I lost myself in writing. It might have looked like grief, but the three of us did these things to avoid the truth, because our real stories are dangerous. If I didn't know the truth, I might even feel sorry for Coach Bitzche. When you run away, but nobody chases you, it's the saddest thing of all.

WHEN WE WALKED INTO SOCIAL studies, my older brother Ronnie stood rigid and flush against the wall, wearing his stupid Forest Service uniform. We were accustomed to guest speakers in social studies because our teacher was lazy. But Ronnie wasn't just a guest speaker. My brother was a fanatic. I knew for a fact that he ironed his own clothes, and the creases in his uniform were frighteningly exact. I expected him to salute us or something.

"The Meatloaf," said Becky. "Jesus Christ."

My brother had earned his nickname at age twelve, when he decided he wouldn't grow up to be fat like our parents. A month after he began lifting weights, two weeks after he adopted a terrible grunting noise that accompanied every bench press, he changed his diet. A new protein fanatic, he demanded ground beef at every meal, and so began the saga of the meatloaf. Breakfast, cold meatloaf. Lunch, cold meatloaf. Dinner, freshly prepared meatloaf. Soon enough, he began to smell like meatloaf, too. He sweated garlic and onions and cheap ground round. He stunk. That, combined with the contents of his lunch box, prompted his peers to devise a nickname, one that soon caught on all over town.

Mr. Graff, our social studies teacher, waited for the bell to ring, and didn't bother taking attendance. We sat in our assigned seats, and watched him write across the whiteboard in giant capital letters:

HOW TO SURVIVE IN THE FOREST

David immediately raised his hand. Mr. Graff sighed, and pointed at him.

"What does this have to do with social studies? I stayed up last night reading about Jamestown. Believe me, I would have rather done something else."

"This is important," said Mr. Graff.

"No," said David. "This is our education. We already have enough gaps in this class. You made us skip the Holocaust."

"I'm not having that conversation again," said Mr. Graff. Across the room, I watched Bitsy tap his foot on the linoleum floor. He picked up speed, until his foot was a blur, but he wore sneakers and it barely made a noise. He had always been an anxious and twitchy kid, but nothing out of the ordinary. There was a girl at Dogwood with intermittent explosive disorder, and I wished Bitsy would suddenly freak out and throw a desk at the Meatloaf.

Becky raised her hand.

"Yes?"

"We already know how to survive in the forest," said Becky. "We learned that in first grade."

"Hug a tree," said Kaitlynn. "Hug a dumb tree and stay there until somebody rescues you."

"There's so much more than that," said the Meatloaf, springing from the wall, and to the front of the class. "Too many trees to hug, and not enough people to find you."

Kaitlynn didn't bother raising her hand. "Obviously, you don't know who I am. There would be the biggest search party like ever." All of David's cheerleaders thought they were the center of the universe.

"I don't even go in the forest," said David. "May I be excused?"

"No," said the teacher. "It's a dangerous world. You could be dragged into the woods against your will. Look at what happened to Matthew Shepard."

"That's homophobic," said David. "And another piece of history you have gotten completely wrong."

Ronnie was oblivious to all of this and launched into a speech about moss and how it grew on the north side of the trees, and how you could use this as a compass. In the back row, Bitsy dropped his head to his desk. Ronnie droned on, and tried to sound important. He thought he was a cop, but he was in charge of trees, not people. The forest service made sure of that. He was hired on after high school, but kept getting transferred, because you can't get fired from a government job. At least that's what my mother said. He started as a custodian, but hid all the garbage cans after the secretaries refused to recycle. When they moved him to the garage, his only job was to wash down the pistachio-colored trucks, but within a month, somebody set his locker on fire. His personality was so off-putting that they reassigned him to a ranger position, where he patrolled the Stillwater State Forest, and had no contact with people, except the occasional unlucky camper. He made twice as much money in his new job, patrolling for litter and extinguishing smoldering campfires. In the winter, he watched for avalanches, and delivered boring speeches to high schools.

After the bell rang, I approached him. He smirked, and crossed his arms over his chest.

"The question-and-answer portion is over," he said.

"Nobody asked you any questions."

"I'm not talking to you," he said. "As far as I'm concerned, you're a ghost."

"It's cold," I said. "I need a ride to the gas station."

"Absolutely not," he said. He looked me up and down, and the corner of his mouth raised slightly. "It looks like you could use the exercise." It was true. The Seroquel had made me gain weight, but my pants still zipped up.

"I just want a ride, Ronnie. It's on your way."

"No," he said. "You aren't allowed in my truck. It's still an active crime scene."

I wanted to point out that there was never an investigation, and that I had served my time, but it was useless arguing with him. I would rather walk.

* * *

I KNEW MY MOTHER WAS waiting for me. After school, I walked the highway again, and the asphalt was desolate for the first half mile, until Gabardine revealed itself.

Nine hundred people, but an accurate census was impossible. It was a stubborn place, and nobody trusted government forms. If somebody wanted a head count, all they had to do was ask my mother.

Gabardine had barely changed in one hundred years. In 1910, the Big Burn came close to us. As always, we were a year behind the trend. The Slightly Less Bigger Burn came eleven months later, but barely made the newspapers, even though our entire town burned down to the ground.

Now, as I walked farther into town, all I could see were haggard buildings and a brand-new casino. I passed the DVD rental store, crucial because we didn't have broadband internet. I knew the rest of the civilized world could stream their entertainment. We used to have a pet-grooming business, but it shut down five years ago. My favorite store was also a ghost—I think it must have been a hardware store, but now it only had a sun-bleached sign in the window: *Everything Must Go!* If you turned left at the store, it brought you into our town, where we had a First Street, and a Second Street, but no need for a Third. The highway was supposed to bring us people, but it only brought drunk-driving accidents and Canadians.

Chapter Two

THE READER BOARD OUTSIDE OF the gas station was what I saw first—the gas prices, with the tiles you could flip as the prices rose and fell. Unleaded, Premium, Diesel, and then the fourth number, which anybody in Gabardine knew was my mother's current weight. I'm sure tourists were confused. When she started losing weight to qualify for the bariatric surgery, she added that last row of tiles, because the surgeon suggested she find a team of people who would be encouraging. Instead of a team, my mother had an entire town. After her surgery, the number plummeted, dropping at alarming rates, and she changed the tiles daily.

It had been three months, and I actually wanted to know the number. Today, it was 187.

Next was the Bad Check List. Taped to the front door and replaced monthly, my mother kept a list of customers who'd behaved badly. She believed in public shaming for bouncing checks. When I was a kid, I thought it was a normal part of adulthood, that when you did something wrong, your name was scrawled in Magic Marker and posted in public. My mother caused people to hide from her inside the walk-in cooler at the grocery store, my mother caused one divorce, and my mother caused two families to pack up entirely and move eighteen miles away, to Fortune. Not that it stopped her. She followed them to Fortune to warn the other gas stations, just in case. The Bad Check

List was her leverage. Names were removed after debts were paid, but more likely, after my mother had traded their notoriety for really good gossip or manual labor. Sometimes, both. Regardless, the Bad Check List was the closest thing Gabardine had to local news—read between the lines and figure out pretty quick who fell off the wagon, who gambled away an entire paycheck, who finally got garnished for child support.

My mother said nothing when I entered. She was a short woman, five feet exactly, and when she was at her heaviest, she was a cannonball. After she lost the weight, she was the size of a child who could barely reach the cash register.

I wasn't sure where I was allowed to stand anymore, but my mother answered the question by pointing to the black utility mat where customers stood when she rang up their purchases.

Silently, we watched a woman step down from a giant RV. Alberta plates. Canadians were reverse snowbirds.

"It's so charming here," said the woman.

"Sure," said my mother. The customer was always right, even if they were Canadian.

"Is it a town, or a village, or a hamlet?"

"We have a zip code," said my mother. "That's all I know."

It felt strange to stand in front of the counter, and not perch on a chair behind it, but these were the new rules. The woman paid for a carton of wine coolers, and as my mother counted back change, her words were nearly lost in the sound of my brother's arrival, his stupid diesel engine roaring into the parking lot. As the woman departed, I watched through the window as she coughed in the wake of the black smoke that belched from his truck.

Ronnie pretended to be shocked when he entered the store, even though he'd just seen me.

"Tough Tiff is on the lam," he said. "I never thought she'd be smart enough to pull off a prison break."

"They shut her school down," announced my mother.

"Whatever," he said, and removed his leather gloves. "I'm still not talking to her."

"Understandable," said my mother.

"Are you in any danger?" The Meatloaf whispered this, like he had stumbled into a bank holdup.

"No," said my mother. "I got rid of all the silverware. What do you want?"

Ronnie, the Meatloaf, dug into the back pocket of his pants and removed a rectangle, a stack of raffle tickets, waiting to be serrated, pulled apart. Not this again. The Meatloaf belonged to a weird church, across the state line in Idaho. His church didn't do anything cool like handle snakes or speak in tongues, but he remained devout to the only religion that would have him. The Meatloaf was so hated in Gabardine that he had to worship in a different time zone.

"I don't want the speech," he said. "Just buy five, and I'll leave you alone."

"What's the prize this time? Is it another goddamn quilt?"

"Alpaca wool," he said proudly. "Straight from the flock. Fifty pounds."

"That's not a prize," said my mother. "That's a curse."

"Five bucks," he said. My mother released the cash drawer, and the bell rang out, a sound I had missed. She slid a five-dollar bill across the counter. The Meatloaf began to pull the tickets out of his booklet, but my mother put a hand up.

"No," she said. "Once again, your church raffles something that nobody wants. Keep the tickets, give them to your wife. Maybe she can build a nest or something." This was something I could actually imagine, the Meatloaf's idiot wife, Lorraine, in a giant nest of a hair ball, slack-jawed in the living room, smart as a baby bird, just waiting for somebody to feed her.

Lorraine was dumb and meek, but not enough to join Ronnie's weird church. Sweets rarely crossed state lines, even the Sweets who were legally allowed. When they met, she was just another single mother in a town with a surplus, but I think she looked past his crappy personality and saw government pay and health insurance.

Lorraine came from a clan of white supremacists out by the dump, always on the police scanner. She looked like the rest of the Sweets, squished features, stumpy bodies in sweat suits, their skin darker than most of us. In Gabardine, we all came from Northern Europe, but the Sweets were ruddy and tanned well, maybe from years of passing out in the sun.

Ronnie glared as he backed out of the door, keeping his eyes on me, suspicious as always.

"You can have a hot dog," my mother declared. I guess she was concerned about my nutrition or something, and I was starving. Outside, Ronnie fired up his stupid diesel truck, and the roar shook the metal carousel of the hot dog machine. My mother watched me intensely as I ripped a plastic ketchup packet open with my teeth. Her eyes followed my every move, like I was going to shoplift a bunch of hot dogs, shove them into the pockets of my leather jacket.

She never liked my jackets, black and oversized, hanging to my knees and swinging like a trench coat. According to my mother, each jacket I brought home had its own particular scent, always horrific. My father assured me that they all smelled the same. I honestly thought my mother would be pleased when I brought the first jacket home. Instead, she told me that I looked like a "sailor on leave." I didn't understand the phrase. She only wore black because she said it was slimming. I chose to wear black for other reasons, but to tourists, we must have looked like twins behind the gas station counter. Every July, motorcycle tours came through Gabardine and refueled, and they could eat six hot dogs in one sitting. I didn't care about their appetites, I only saw the jackets, and I knew I wanted one of my own. I saw the uniform as built for travel, built for leaving, armor for tough men who could roar out of town as fast as possible. I wanted to leave, too.

I don't know why my mother watched me so closely. I knew I had to be on my best behavior, that a leash was now yoked around my neck. I could feel it. She would double-check everything after I left. My mother kept an internal inventory of all the merchandise in the gas station, something she could control, I guess. I was the one thing she was unsure of.

I RETURNED TO THE TRAILER park, still hungry. When I opened the refrigerator door, I saw the same things it had contained since my father died: one jar of cold cream for my mother's stretch marks, and a carton of neon-yellow wine coolers. After he died, she stopped keeping groceries in the house, and I think she was relieved. The freezer, as always, was stocked with Lean Cuisines. These were acceptable food, an exact 380 calories. I chose one without looking, and put it in the microwave. I ate it with a plastic fork, and I was halfway finished before I realized that my consequences now included Beef Stroganoff. I carried it to the back porch, and when I opened the door, I could tell nobody had been in there for months. Even though Ronnie moved out years ago, it still smelled like meatloaf. Now, he lived three trailers down, and it probably smelled like frankincense and myrrh. Admittedly, my biblical knowledge was sparse.

Against the wall stood a row of pots, the dirt spiked with the remnants of plants. My father had loved his African violets. We had seven when he died, and it had been an art for him, finding the exact right light to make them flower. We had no other house-plants, and I was fascinated at how his violets had to be watered from the bottom. His flowers did not follow the usual rules, and now they had been punished, abandoned. I could identify.

My family had lived in the trailer park for years, but we had the newest trailer. Although my mother liked to live cheap, she insisted on presenting well. They bought the brand-new double-wide after the house next door exploded. I was four years old, but it's not something you forget. The flames left scorch marks on our skirting, and the smoke stained the vinyl. Instead of repairing the damage, she bought a new house, but had the floors reinforced before we moved in. The weight of her and my father combined caused soft spots, and this time, she was determined to not have the joists replaced every few years

In addition to the new trailer, with the immaculate white vinyl siding, we also had a hot tub that my mother traded from somebody on the Bad Check List. In seven years, we only used it four times, because it was weird to be in the front yard, with all the neighbors watching. My brother drained it three years ago, because it was basically a mosquito incubator. Our yard was planted with Kentucky bluegrass, too, which went against my mother's hatred of things from the South, but it was a variety that nobody else had, and it set our yard apart. Next month, it would chameleon from the yellow of winter into the blue green that made her so happy.

Both trailer houses had the exact same layout. I always got the smallest of the three rooms, even though the Meatloaf had moved out long ago. His bedroom had its own bathroom, but I think my mother was punishing me for my lack of personal grooming. Since Ronnie left, it was supposedly a guest room, but we had never had guests.

My room was dark, the way I preferred it. It had a picture window that looked out onto the island in the middle of the trailer court, but I did not find much solace in staring at a dumpster, especially since many residents had terrible aim, and the ground around it was littered with random trash and broken furniture. I didn't want to ask for curtains, so I thumbtacked an army blanket to block out the view. David had talked me into painting the walls when we were in third grade, and they were still dark purple. This was before he had discovered painter's tape and tarps, so the paint job was sloppy. My bedding had been pink, and I had ruined the guest room bathtub in an attempt to dye all of it black.

After seeing the bathtub, my mother had been furious. "You are so inconsiderate, Tiffany Templeton. You should know better. Take your destruction elsewhere."

I kept my pages locked in my nightstand, and that was all I needed. One of David's cheerleaders, a girl like Becky, Victoria, Kaitlynn, or Caitlyn, might have covered all the surfaces in her room with makeup and jewelry and diet pills, but I left them bare. The only decoration at all was an unframed canvas, a gift from David, a self-portrait, which was typical, the negative space dotted with rhinestones. They were the only thing that sparkled in the room.

In brand-new trailers, every bedroom has a walk-in closet, and mine was no exception. For years, it was a pathetic thing, all of the clothing I owned hung on twenty hangers, leaving room enough for an entire family of Sweets. After my father died, I surrendered to a strange urge. I ripped the clothes from the hangers and jammed it all in the empty bureau drawers. I pulled the gray pillows and duvet inside the walk-in closet, and I slept inside. It was comforting. It was enclosed and dark and I could be alone with my thoughts, pretend that it was a cave in which there was no such thing as Gabardine, no such thing as parents. Inside that walk-in closet, there were no people to lose.

The month before I was sent away, my mother was looking for me all over the house, most likely to yell about something. Eventually, she yanked open the door of the walk-in closet. Needless to say, I was startled. It was not a good way to be wakened.

"What in the hell are you doing in here?"

"I don't know."

"It's creepy, Tiffany. This is the kind of stuff devil worshippers do."

AFTER EATING, I STARED AT a DVD for twenty minutes. I had a collection of horror movies, all of them from the pawn shop, and I mostly kept them on for background noise. This is what happens when things become too familiar. You watch something so many times and you stop seeing it. You watch something so many times, and you count on it being home to cook you dinner, and wave at you from the front porch. You stop seeing it, because it is no longer there.

Even though he was gone, the loss of my dad created an actual space. He was so large he left room, real room for me to grieve in.

Chapter Three

IT WAS STILL NOT DARK enough to check on my box. In March, the sun sets just after six o'clock, and I had an hour to kill before my mother got home from work. She would want to see my face, make sure I wasn't out in the darkness, sneaking around. Even though my mother had not declared any rules, I knew I was on a short leash. I saw it in her face at the gas station, and in the extra bulk of her purse, the phone cord peeking out. Now there was an invisible cord inside the house, and I would not stray. She was prepared to yank me in any direction, a fish on a hook. I knew I could go to David's house, because it was two hundred feet away, and because he was the only person in our town that she liked. And he would be the first to rat me out, anything to gain points with my mother.

David was my best friend by default because he lived with his mother in the next lot over. We grew up together, closest in age, closest in trailers. That's what I mean by default, I guess. David taught me how to shoplift in sixth grade, on a field trip to Fortune to tour the remains of the sawmill, and the stump of the largest cottonwood tree in America. On our lunch break, our un-supervised classmates sought out fistfights with the rich kids of Fortune. They had always been our rivals, and they may have had high-speed internet and computers in all their classrooms, but we had choke holds and upper body strength. David, however, had more nefarious plans and yanked me to the Ben Franklin. That day he only stole fabric glue, but over the next five years, his criminal enterprise expanded. I mostly stole slasher DVDs, but David stole presents for his cheerleaders. I swallowed our secrets, and all the ones that came after. Partners in crime, we had to be best friends. Neither one of us wanted to use the ammunition.

Janelle, his mother, told me to stop knocking on the door a very long time ago, wanted me to consider their trailer my second home. Of course, I did not tell my mother this.

I didn't knock, even though I'd been gone three months, a notorious three months. Maybe Janelle had changed her opinion of me, but I walked into the living room, nonetheless. It was usually cluttered with Janelle's New Age things and David's finds from thrift stores—midcentury modern. You could say it was an interesting juxtaposition of tastes, but today, none of that was visible. The entire living room was piled with the furniture from David's room. He was redecorating again. Stacks of stuff everywhere, but his bare mattress lay in the very center of the room, pristine, and Janelle reclined there, arms folded across her chest like a vampire at rest in a coffin. I knew there was nothing evil here, though. She was meditating. And she was deep inside it; her eyelids didn't even flutter when I walked past and knocked into a set of chimes. The bells rang out, but Janelle didn't stir.

Down the hall, I could see David posed in his doorway, paintbrush in hand. The house smelled like latex paint instead of the usual scent of Janelle's incense, but she loved her son deeply and was used to the smell of redecoration because it happened at least twice a year.

He rolled his eyes when he saw me approach.

"We have sharp objects in this house. I hope you learned your lesson."

The end of his paintbrush was drenched in bright white. A new color, and I had seen them all, had seen all of his redecoration projects.

"No," I said. "I didn't learn my lesson. But I can probably melt a toothbrush with a lighter and stab you to death before you even know it." This was a lie. The only useful thing I learned at Dogwood was how to shape my eyebrows.

"You haven't changed at all," he said. He pointed to the cheap carpet beside him. An iron sunburst clock, the face chipped enough for me to know it was really vintage, the wavy arms that radiated around it pristine. The entire object was bright white, had not faded yellow like most white things that were sixty years old, even the hands that kept time. The second hand was bright red, but he would probably paint it.

"I learned some things while you were gone. Things that changed my life."

"I was only gone for three months."

"It seemed longer. You're my best friend," he said. "If you tell anyone that, I will kill you."

"Okay," I said.

"I learned that you should build a room around one object," he said. "I found this clock, and it was like fate, I think. It called out to me. I know what you're going to ask, so don't bother. No, it doesn't work. If you go away for another three months, maybe I can learn how to be an electrician."

I was used to speeches like this. I was one of the few people that understood David, the other being my mother, and I knew that cruel things came out of his mouth, for good reason. I learned a long time ago that he said terrible things to me because he was practicing for adulthood. David believed that when he finally left this town, he would become rich and imperious. It didn't matter how he got there—he'd never chosen a vocation, or followed through on any of his interests. He had faith, I guess, and around Gabardine, faith was in short supply. Sure, Janelle's chimes and incense were based in some sort of belief, but it sprung from things she had highlighted in yellow from an ever-growing stack of hippie self-help books.

"I'm going to do white on white," he said. "Like a beach house in Miami." I did not question his choice, even though Miami was the absolute antithesis of Gabardine. I knew better.

"White on white," I said. "Like the worst part of winter."

"The snow here is dirty," he said. "All that creeping around, and you don't even pay attention."

"I'm reformed," I said. "No more creeping. No more silverware, either. And my mom took the phone, too. She carries it around in her purse."

"You don't need a phone," he said. "You don't have anybody to call." This was true. "I know about the silverware," said David. "She gave it to us."

"Of course she did," I said. Janelle already had two mobiles on the front porch made of silverware cantilevered on wooden dowels and piano wire. I hoped she had the common sense not to do the same with our family's cutlery. My mom drove slowly through the trailer court, and she would notice something like that.

David took a step back from the doorway to admire his work, and his frame filled the entire space. He was the best-built boy in our class. It wasn't surprising that Coach Bitzche had begged David to join the football team. Our entire freshman year, Coach did everything he could to cajole him, even got on his knees and pleaded. David refused.

"I don't do team sports," said David. He already had a team, and it was all of us, and he was a vindictive and cruel leader. He'd been leading my class since the second grade. When Coach Bitzche wrote David a check for $1,000, about which of course I was sworn to secrecy, David refused the money. In his version of events, he brought the check back to Coach Bitzche, wrote *VOID* across it in huge letters. "There is no amount of money worth risking this face."

Freshman year, David was focused on modeling, and my mother paid for headshots, but it never went anywhere.

I craned around the doorjamb, and my eyes watered—it was so bright, and the paint so fresh. He had used high gloss on the walls, even though he had sworn off high gloss from past redecorating disasters. It reminded me of a laboratory in a spaceship. He waited for my reaction.

"It's a big change," I said. His former bedroom was dark gray, and he had spray-painted the furniture to look like chrome, even sprayed a glass coffee table to make it look smoky. Amidst all the gray and metal and glass, he had chosen citron as an accent color, but the only fabric he could find at the Ben Franklin was closer to a neon green, and he never stopped complaining about it. "I like the white," I said. "When I stab you with my toothbrush shiv, the blood splatter will be fantastic."

"Three months in rehabilitation, and you have nothing to show for it."

"It wasn't rehabilitation," I said. "None of us had drug problems." I stopped myself. "Okay, some of them had drug problems, but that wasn't the point. And I got a lot of stuff done, believe it or not."

"Your eyebrows, obviously. Thank god."

"I wrote a play," I said. "A whole entire play. Stage directions and everything." I slid it from my backpack, but he seemed unimpressed.

"I prefer musicals," he said.

"I know that. Everybody knows that. But I think you'd like this one. It's got death and prostitutes." He snatched it from my hands.

"*The Soiled Doves of Gabardine*? We don't have doves here, Tiffany. We have turkey vultures."

"It's not about birds," I said. I watched as he thumbed through the first pages.

"Interesting," he said.

"I'd like your feedback," I said.

"Everybody does," he said. He pushed past me and returned to the paint tray in the corner, his feet crunching on the tarp, perfectly laid out, corner to corner. I knew this was unnecessary. David never spilled a drop.

Chapter Four

AT SIX THIRTY, I HEARD the crash, as my mother's purse took flight and landed somewhere in the kitchen. In my bedroom, I waited. An hour later, I heard her bedroom door close, and I could unclip myself from that short leash. The box called me, and I swear the voice was distant and full of echoes, just like my mother on speakerphone. I climbed out of my bedroom window.

When my father was alive, I would never have dared to do such a thing. Before my father died, I had no reason to find relief in all that darkness.

At night, the loop of our trailer park seemed to be one whole creature, multiple eyes of windows casting light onto snowy yards. During the day, it was depressing to see. In trailer houses, there are no attics or basements, no places to hide. In the bright light of day, it was a horror movie, all the fear contained in one box, no escape.

Since I'd been back, I'd only entered the trailer park through the entrance closest to town, past the McGurty family, Waterbed Fred (his real name was Fred Hakes, but he was forever known by the name of his long-defunct business), the horrible cheerleader Victoria and her former cheerleader mother, the cursed Bitzches, the sloppy brothers McMackin, and Ronnie, who tried so hard to get away from our family but only ended up next door. We lived in the middle. To the left of us was the burned-out lot, and then David and his mother, but if you kept going left, the loop extended farther to another entrance off the highway. Everything that occupied my mind followed that curve, but it was only safe in the dark.

The tire tracks and ruts had frozen when the sun went down, and I stumbled and slid in my sneakers. I used to be good at this. I used to be stealthy. Tonight, the noise of my shoes was as good as a bell around my neck, jewelry for a girl who didn't even have her ears pierced.

I zipped my jacket up all the way and pulled the drawstrings of my hood tight against the cold. As I passed David's house, the lights blazed in his bedroom window, and Guns N' Roses blasted from the living room, which meant Janelle was doing her sun salutations, always at the wrong end of the day. Next door, the city clerk of Gabardine lived in an immaculate double-wide, a lot of space for a tiny man. Mr. Francine's house was dark, but I could see the glow of a television set from his window that faced the woods behind his home, another shade of blue, always blue, casting against the white barks of the quaking aspens.

I planned to stop at the next house. Betty Gabrian was the only person who wrote to me at Dogwood, and I wanted to give her the script. Instead, David had it, and all I had to show were the blue stains on my fingers from the ancient mimeograph machine, ink still embedded in my cuticles.

I stopped at her front yard, walk unshoveled, a For Sale sign stuck into the snowbank. The windows were dark black squares, and ice clumped in a ring around her house, had slid from her sloping roof. It must have been a stormy winter, and she must have been gone for quite a while. She had spent thousands of dollars improving the trailer, jacking it up and installing a concrete foundation. Real wood siding had been painted to look like stone, until it seemed like a Victorian mansion. She even had a cupola. This had made my mother seethe.

In her letters, she didn't mention moving. The real estate market in Gabardine was nonexistent, so her castle would probably be abandoned for years, and our trailer court could finally have a haunted house, not just haunted people.

In the night, the bluffs of snow glowed, and a wind picked up out of nowhere. The For Sale sign wobbled as it was buffeted by a gust, and my heart was broken.

I had to keep moving. It was too cold to ruminate. In the center of our trailer park, the ponderosa pine that had survived the hits of many drunk drivers swayed in the wind, the lowest branches slapped against the dumpsters. Garbage day was tomorrow, and the wind blew so hard that it whipped the overflowing garbage bags in the dumpsters and sounded like whips cracking.

That was what I heard as I continued on, the night disrupted by trash. Only appropriate, because the next house belonged to Lou Ann Holland, who was my number two archenemy, second only to the Mail Lady. As I ducked my head against the gale, I glanced to my left, at the burning windows. I caught a glimpse of her, and as usual, she stood in the middle of her living room, a gooseneck lamp on the floor firing light across her easel, onto the painting she was working on. Tonight, no blue, and for that I was thankful.

She lived next to the Laundromat, which was the last building on the loop, closest to the highway. She worked there, too, although there wasn't much for her to do. It seemed the location would bring business, but the cinder-block building was always empty. The perfect place to hide something.

In the darkness, I crunched through the ice and stopped when

I found the breaker box and the mountain of a juniper that grew below it. Nobody else dared get close, burrow deep, but my jacket was as good as armor. I barely felt the pricks through my sleeves as I reached deep underneath, near the roots, and removed the typewriter case. Gray tweed that blended in with everything, an aluminum body that could withstand the elements. Most importantly, a lock. I kept the key in my leather jacket at all times. I was sure my mother had gone through everything I owned while I was gone, but the key remained, a tiny thing she had overlooked.

The key shook in my hand, and I didn't know if it was nerves or the cold.

I flicked my lighter and examined my treasures. The pink cinder blocks of the Laundromat held the light, made it seem like something living, breathing. All around me, the quiet of an early spring night, dark so early. I could finally breathe, had been holding my breath since the court-appointed attorney dropped me off on the highway until now.

Inside the case were the things they didn't catch. I was charged with misdemeanors, but this Smith-Corona case was where I kept my real felonies.

Three can openers, silver, brand new; the glow from the lighter made the metal look expensive, even though I knew they were from Shopko. The circular blades had never been used, the turnkey remained at exactly twelve o'clock, frozen from the day it was purchased.

The lighter grew hot in my hand. In the darkness, I waited for it to cool, and I held the case delicately, as if the things inside were breakable. I was the thief, and I knew better than that. These objects were sturdy, solid, unlike the people who had owned them.

I flicked the lighter once more and was comforted by the sheen of a small canvas, an oil painting, brushstrokes so thick that the light dipped in valleys and ridges. A blue man from a deft hand. I sniffed the air, and I swore there was a hint of turpentine, but in a trailer court of wood-burning stoves, I could have been mistaken.

The next item was nearly unrecognizable, wrapped around and around in yards of phone cord, bound tight with the power cable. Unwound, an answering machine would reveal itself, a quarter of a century old. The heart was still inside, an honest-to-god cassette tape, a message captured inside those ribbons for eternity.

I nearly dropped the lighter when it burned my thumb. I knew it would leave a blister, a scorch mark. I couldn't steal lighters from the gas station anymore, so I had to ration the fluid, just in case I fell into a sinkhole or something. That kind of stuff happens around here.

One more flick, and I saw the envelope, so fat it could not close. I had never removed the contents of the envelope, not once, and I had checked the case once a week for the better part of a year. The weight of it assured me that it was all in place. It would be a relief if somebody had replaced what it contained, swapped it out with carefully cut paper. Twenty thousand, one hundred and thirty-seven dollars.

I closed the lid, and tucked it carefully beneath the juniper. I did not need to set a trap. I might have stolen these things, but they were my prisoners. I had my own charges—larceny, assault, intimidation—but the objects in this case were far more danger-ous. I took these things before they could do harm, before they put on their own leather jacket.

* * *

THE NEXT MORNING, DAVID WAITED outside of our house, wearing a coat my mother bought him and clutching the script in one gloved hand and a stack of papers in the other. He had read it all in one night.

"I made flyers," he said. "I want to begin casting immediately."

"Of course," I said. "Thank you for supporting my project."

"This town needs high art," he said. "We also need reliable internet and cell phone service, but I can only do so much." This was a true statement. For the last three years, David had written letters to the public service commissioner once a week, but his pleas for a cell phone tower were never answered, no matter how nice the stationery.

"High art," I said, as we walked through the frozen trailer court, and turned right on the highway. "I never thought I would be capable of creating high art."

"It was a figure of speech," said David. "It's juicy, it's pulpy, it's compelling. But Tennessee Williams, it is not."

"I could add family secrets. Incest. I could add closeted homosexuals," I said, and I immediately regretted it.

Of course, David changed the subject. "I'm going to put these on the locker of every girl in school. Except for those terrible homeschooled creatures." He hated the kids that transferred to our high school after being homeschooled through junior high. They won all the spelling bees, and before they came, that had always been another of David's glories.

At the end of first period, Bitsy stopped me in the hallway, which was unusual. Even after all the years of growing up together in the trailer court and in a tiny town, we didn't chat. Our conversations had only been forced upon us for small group projects. Bitsy wasn't the type for small talk anyway, and I had threatened to kill his mother. That's not the topic for small talk.

"I want to help," he said.

"I'm seeing a probation officer," I said. "And I got lots of therapy. I appreciate the offer, though."

"No," he said. "With the play. I want to do the makeup."

I wasn't freaked out about the makeup part. I was more freaked out about spending time with him. "Talk to David," I said. "I'm just the writer."

"I've learned my lesson with him," he said. "He tried to get me to raise a pig for 4-H."

"I remember," I said.

"We don't have football anymore." Bitsy leaned closer to me, and he smelled better than most teenage boys. "My mom is worried that I have too much free time. I think that's your fault."

"Probably," I said. "I didn't threaten your mother because I had too much free time."

"I'm sure you had your reasons," he said. "She's a fucking nightmare. But I want to make monsters when I get out of Gabardine. For real. I want to move to Hollywood."

"It's a play about prostitutes in the Old West."

"Rad," he said. "I need experience. I'm also good at tackling things, so if you need security or something like that."

"David is directing," I said. "Violence is inevitable."

"Thanks," he said, and walked off down the hallway, unafraid to be seen talking to me. I was still radioactive to most of my peers, and probably on a terrorist watch list because of his mother.

TEN MINUTES INTO SEVENTH PERIOD, the trig/stats teacher was explaining random variables and possible outcomes. It seemed like science fiction to me, until Kaitlynn appeared in the doorway. She pointed at me for the second time, and I knew there was nothing random about it, and only one outcome.

"Excuse me, Mr. French. Principal Beaudin needs to see David and that girl in the leather jacket." She was committed to pretending she didn't know me, even though we'd been stuck together since kindergarten. She was lucky she didn't know my fist.

He was waiting for us. After yesterday, he didn't feel the need for any pleasantries.

"Absolutely not," said Principal Beaudin. His response didn't surprise me. "I saw all of those flyers you passed out."

"This is an impediment to my education," said David.

Principal Beaudin was not moved. "I've let you use school property for science club, debate team, pep club, and Future Farmers of America. All complete disasters. And every single time, you came in here and accused me of impeding your education."

"I've got school spirit," said David.

"I've spent hundreds of dollars on your bake sales, young man. All those fund-raisers for clubs that never went anywhere."

"That's not true," said David. "It's not my fault. I blame it on attention deficit disorder. I can't force kids to be interested in Future Farmers of America."

"You promised you would clone a sheep," said Principal Beaudin. "We don't even have the resources for something like that." He cleared his throat and looked at me evenly. "I read your script, Miss Templeton."

"Really?"

"I skimmed it," he admitted. "I had the secretary read the whole thing, but she took very detailed notes. She's a professional."

"Sure," I said.

"The cafeteria is not the place for avant-garde theater," he said.

"It's not avant-garde," said David. "I don't think Tiffany is capable of writing something like that. We don't have a budget. I don't think we'd need lights or anything. But definitely makeup. I feel very passionate about that. I'm aiming for a November debut. It's such a gloomy time of the year, and I believe theater is the best kind of antidepressant."

"Not in the cafeteria," said Principal Beaudin. "Not in the gymnasium. Nowhere on school grounds. I want absolutely nothing to do with it. I'm sure the school board would agree."

"You don't know that," said David.

Principal Beaudin referred to a single typed piece of paper on his desk. From where I sat, I could tell that it was double-spaced, and I could see the bold dots of bullet points. His secretary really was a professional. "Eight prostitutes," he said. "Three acts, zero moral value. Eight prostitutes sitting around and talking."

"It's like *Waiting for Godot*," said David, even though I knew he hadn't read that. Last year, the month after my father died, Janelle and David tried to cheer me up by getting a free month of HBO. I don't really remember that month, but I'm pretty sure we didn't watch *Waiting for Godot*.

"This is not existentialism," said Principal Beaudin, and I have to admit, I was impressed at the depth of his theater knowledge. "This is unsavory and titillating."

"It's based on the truth," I said. "It really happened. I have newspaper articles and I even have a bibliography. I cited my sources and everything."

"Save it for a term paper," said Principal Beaudin, then reconsidered. "Does this school require term papers?"

This was something he should know. He was supposed to oversee the curriculum. "Yes," I said. "Senior year."

"I've had mine done since I was a freshman," offered David.

"Overachiever," said Principal Beaudin. "As usual." At most schools, this would be a good thing.

"Political subtext in Lady Gaga's oeuvre," said David. "Just the early albums, of course."

"Of course," said Principal Beaudin. "I stand by my decision. School property is not an appropriate place for your play," he said. "I don't want to argue about it. Don't make me send this to the historical society. They might come at you with pitchforks and torches."

"We don't have a historical society," said David. "We've got the opposite. People get drunk to forget everything that happened."

"It's accurate," I said. "If you lived here, you would know that." I hoped that stung. Principal Beaudin kept his home in Fortune, and my mother called him a carpetbagger.

David stood, and I prepared for his speech. Principal Beaudin didn't flinch. He had attended the one and only appearance of the ill-fated debate team, knew a speech was inevitable.

"Colonialism," said David, pointing his finger in the air. "Once again, our real history is being ignored. Controversy! You can't just revise the history of our founding fathers."

"Founding mothers," I added.

"The ACLU would agree with me. This is censorship!" David narrowed his eyes, and I clenched my jaw, just knowing he was about to go too far. "This school should celebrate our past. We should not be part of the whitewashing!"

"All of the prostitutes were Caucasian," said Principal Beaudin calmly. "We're done here. End of discussion. If you want to contact the ACLU, that's fine. Tell them to make an appointment with my secretary, and she will check my schedule."

He waved us out of his office. David was already standing, so he turned on one heel and stomped away dramatically. I was embarrassed, and eased out of my seat, didn't look at the principal as I slunk out of the office. As I passed the aquarium, I glanced at the goldfish, lethargic and fat at the bottom of the tank. I'm pretty sure Principal Beaudin overfed them. He seemed like the type of guy who insisted on feeding the fish but walked away from all the other responsibilities. Typical man, only concerned about dinner. The glass was spotless, because the secretary was a professional.

David was devastated. He never came back to trig/stats.

When I slid into my seat, Caitlyn raised her hand, and immediately offered an excuse for David, out of habit, well trained.

"Asthma," she said. "He had to go home. He almost died."

The teacher didn't really care. I think he knew Statistics was something we would never use. Most of us would keep living in Gabardine after high school, and you could count on my mother to keep track of every number that mattered.

Chapter Five

I PULLED ON MY JACKET and once again headed into town. I stopped in front of Betty Gabrian's house. The For Sale sign had fallen, and I didn't want to prop it back up. I wanted Mrs. Gabrian.

I was in seventh grade when I first became aware of her power. I was at the gas station, perched on top of the safe, and my mother and I watched a Mercedes pull up to the pump and park. The Mercedes was rare enough, but the person inside turned off her car and waited there. For minutes. Finally, my mother decided she was a government agent, threw on her winter coat, and went outside for a confrontation.

I watched the whole thing from the window. It was confusing at first, watching my mother pump somebody's gas, and I ran to the door and peered out, watched a white glove hand my mother a twenty-dollar bill.

"That was a lady," reported my mother, after the Mercedes drove away. "A real lady."

I thought she was being sexist. "Women pump their own gas all the time."

"She moved here from Oregon," said my mother. "Filthy rich and used to full service."

Seventh grade was also the year I stopped wrestling boys.

My body had started to change, which was expected, but after throwing one of the Sweet boys to the ground I felt his boner, which was not. I enjoyed wrestling, much more than punching, because pinning somebody down until they surrendered was a definitive win. Especially if you did it in front of other kids.

I stopped wrestling, and that's when I really started writing, mostly short stories about the people who died in the slasher movies I watched. I gave them backstories. I wasn't satisfied with just letting them be victims. Maybe it was because of how I grew up, where I grew up, everybody in Gabardine flattened into the roles I was accustomed to, and I could only see them in one dimension. I wrote stories about the lives of fake people, what came before they were just a dead body. I kept them to myself, because I knew they were absurdly violent, and because I was traumatized from English class that year and wanted to keep my dangling participles and tense changes private until I could get it right. I always wanted to get it right.

That year, in addition to dashing my creativity by diagramming sentences, our English teacher assigned us a thousand-word essay in which we were supposed to interview our parents about their childhood. I could do the thousand words, no problem, but my sharp-tongued mother and secretive father were not about to reveal anything important or interesting.

I chose the lady who would not pump her own gas.

My mother would be furious that I invaded the personal space of Betty Gabrian, but as I stepped onto the freshly poured cement walkway, I didn't care. In every window, Betty Gabrian had hung curtains, and I knew I had made the right decision. She was the only person in Gabardine who actually pulled her curtains shut, even in the middle of the day.

She was a classy woman and knew how to entertain—even leather-jacket-wearing urchins who asked personal questions. I rang the doorbell (one of the few I had ever encountered) and she answered promptly, without her white gloves, offered me a seat on a leather armchair, and brought me a can of soda and a glass of ice, all before I even explained why I was there.

Betty Gabrian chose to retire in Gabardine, far from Portland, where people never pumped their own gas, and she picked our town because of the history. She'd read books on the famous Big Burn of 1910, but it was our Slightly Less Bigger Burn that truly piqued her interest. A brothel had burned, but Betty was not satisfied with the casual mention, knew a better story existed between the lines. The record keeper of the city, Mr. Francine, never questioned her requests to dig through the mountains of filing cabinets, and our public librarian surrendered the microfiche machine, probably delighted it was not another complaint about the content of Danielle Steel. She dug through files and squinted at microfiches and harangued the newspaper office until they gave her free rein of their archives. Betty Gabrian dove head-first into that space between the lines, and swam around in the dust, most likely wearing her white gloves, until a story took shape.

"It was better than needlepoint," she said. "Retirement is boring, my dear. I could never stand to read Agatha Christie. It was much more exciting to solve a real-life mystery. So few mysteries exist in this life. Before I die in this tiny town, I'm going to crack every case."

I didn't doubt her. "If you need any muscle, let me know." I tipped my glass of soda at her, imagining our private investigation firm.

She shared clippings with me, her research on the brothel. The town of Gabardine had tried to erase them from history, and Betty told me that this was something that always happened to strong women. I admit that there was something about those women that reminded me of my mother, and of myself.

I returned to English class with 2,500 words. My paper unpacked the grisly deaths, but I cited the news articles Betty had photocopied, and my bibliography was perfect. I assumed my teacher would just stop reading after the first thousand, because that's how our teachers are. Instead, he gave me an A and scribbled a little note at the end—nothing about the subject matter, but a warning about writing in passive voice. This would be the first and last time I would ever be warned for doing anything passively.

Chapter Six

MY PROBATION OFFICER CAME TO Gabardine once a month, and they made room for her in city hall.

City hall was in the center of town. It was a low-slung, incredibly long building, and it took up most of Second Street. I would guess that it filled an entire block, but there were no side streets, let alone sidewalks. It's impossible to measure a town that was built by drunkards, destroyed by fire, and then rebuilt by the sons of the same drunkards.

Like everything in Gabardine, it served multiple functions. The left end was really a garage that contained the three rigs for the volunteer fire department and the one rig for the volunteer ambulance. We had one ambulance for nine hundred people—there was always talk of purchasing another, but my mother showed up at every city council meeting to yell about the tax base. If our one ambulance broke down, Gabardinians would most likely just throw the bodies in the back of their trucks and drive to the hospital in Fortune. The emergency crews in Fortune got a paycheck, and they were the ones who dealt with the big emergencies, speeding to Gabardine for any drunk-driving wrecks or pipe-bomb explosions.

A crude addition had been built onto the garage for our volunteer dispatch. It was supposedly staffed twenty-four hours a day, but the ladies were notoriously unreliable. I know of two chimney fires that ended up engulfing entire houses: once, the dispatcher got drunk and fell asleep in her car, and the second time, the dispatcher went to play in her pool league—but people understood, because it was the championships.

City hall was also where my father started the food bank. Gabardine needed one, and years of doing taxes had sparked an awakening in my father. It also angered my mother, which pleased him. For twenty-eight years, my father volunteered in the afternoons, Monday through Friday. On Saturdays, the food bank was closed, but it was the day we got all the donations, and I spent every Saturday afternoon stocking shelves and checking expiration dates. After my father died, our neighbor Lou Ann took over the food bank, but I stopped volunteering.

The only occupant of city hall who wasn't a volunteer was Mr. Francine, and his office was at the opposite end of the building. You could actually call it an office, because he had filing cabinets and windows. His space was tiny and crammed, even though the room next door was mostly empty and twice the size, but it was reserved for official city business. He was forced to act as a receptionist in addition to his official title. Being the City Clerk meant that he did everything from collecting utility bills and property taxes to issuing marriage licenses and hunting licenses—occasionally at the same time.

Mr. Francine waved a clipboard at me as soon as I entered. I knew he hated having the door in his office, the only entrance to the room that hosted city council meetings, occasional weddings, and juvenile probation. He would probably block it off with file cabinets if he had the chance, but he knew the fire codes. I signed my name with the pen he had attached to the clip, wound repeatedly with circles of twine, and then duct-taped. Another short leash.

Our town was named after a fabric, and Mr. Francine was proud of his curtains, made from the namesake gabardine. He brought it up at city council meetings, as an example of his civic pride. He wouldn't let anybody touch his curtains, of course, but I couldn't help but stare at them while I waited. They were dense things, and he pulled them over his window, blocking the natural light. Tough, tightly woven, uncomfortable, and durable. This was a perfect description of my hometown.

There were scented candles all over the desk. Mr. Francine had a thing about scented candles, probably because he was so close to the public bathroom. They were usually lit during normal business hours, but not today. He was probably worried about one of us committing arson. Too bad, because he needed the candles—the room reeked of teenage boys. But he didn't seem frightened of us, even though our crimes had made the newspaper, names redacted because of our age.

Five folding chairs jammed most of Mr. Francine's office, and I could tell that he blamed me.

Two Sweet brothers, Jimmy and Phil, related to Lorraine, perhaps even my brothers-in-law. Like me, they'd made the newspaper. Pipe bomb, not the first, and as usual, unsuccessful. They'd tried to blow up a forest service truck. Unfortunately, Ronnie was not inside it. In Gabardine, explosions no longer startled me. Pipe bombs were the recreation of boys without highspeed internet. Like most things in Gabardine, sometimes they worked, and sometimes they didn't. The Sweets had declared war upon government, local and federal, but my mother was adamant they were not real Libertarians, they just didn't want to pay property taxes.

Next to the Sweets, Rufus Baker, also on probation for pipe

bombs. Unlike the Sweets, he was adept at mixing gunpowder and ball bearings, blew up fifteen mailboxes. I wish I had thought of that. Mrs. Bitzche would have surrendered after a few explosions.

TJ McMackin was my neighbor, eternally on probation, a minor in possession who never made the newspapers, but was legendary enough. He was always drunk at school, and once, at a high school basketball game, he threw a full can of beer at Becky, nailed her at the three-point line during the national anthem.

When the frosted glass door cracked open, a woman's head poked out.

She was young and had an expensive haircut, cropped close to her head, shaped perfectly. It felt weird to acknowledge that she was the first black person I had ever seen in real life; after my father died, David's free month of HBO spotlighted all the Madea movies, and Tyler Perry transformed us both into social justice warriors.

From ten feet away, I could smell her perfume, and it reminded me of my father studding oranges with whole cloves at Christmas.

"Jimmy and Phil," she announced. She raised a hand and stopped them before they entered her office. I didn't see a wedding ring. "No explosive devices in your pockets?"

The Sweets shook their heads. As she swung open the door and ushered them in, I admired her heavy mascara, spotted a small stain on the collar of her crisply ironed white shirt, a smear of foundation. David would have gasped.

Across an empty folding chair, I could smell TJ's armpits, and the cheap beer seeping from his pores.

None of these boys had been sent away to an actual reformatory. I was the most hard-core juvenile delinquent in the room.

Twelve minutes later, the frosted door sprung open, and the Sweets escaped, slack-jawed and sleepy. The woman called for Rufus.

TJ reached into his jacket pocket. I glanced over at Mr. Francine, just in case it was a gun, but he didn't even look up from his desk. Out of the corner of my eye, I saw a flash of red and turned to watch TJ take a big swig from a bottle of cherry NyQuil.

I don't think he had a cold.

When Rufus was released, TJ wiped his mouth, walked toward the probation officer, cough syrup lost in the pockets of his giant winter coat.

I tried to hear their conversation, but Mr. Francine was a mouth breather.

Instead, I watched the clock, and thirteen minutes later, TJ swept past me, jacket making whisking sounds as his arms swung.

She stood in her doorway, and for the first time that day, I saw her smile. I followed but refused to look at her when she sat down in a wheeled office chair, parked behind the same folding table they used for city council meetings. I trained my eyes on the cheap gray carpet, my chair still warm from TJ.

"Tiffany," she said. "Is that how you'd like to be addressed?"

"That's my name," I said.

"Sorry," she said, as she opened up the light-brown folder on the table. "That's my training. I'm supposed to ask you that. Sometimes kids have nicknames or gang names, and I want to be respectful."

"I don't have a gang name," I said. "Yet."

She just stared at me, like I was serious. When I didn't respond, she clutched at her collar, attempting to hide the smear of foundation. I think I made her nervous. I liked that.

"My name is Kelly Plotz," she said. "You can call me Kelly, if you're comfortable with that." I liked her last name, an appropriate verb. The juvenile delinquent plots against the entire town of Gabardine. "Before we start, I need to tell you that I'm not a probation officer. I'm a practicum student."

"What does that mean?"

"I go to the University of Montana," she said. "I need six hundred hours of fieldwork to graduate. I just want to be up front with you."

"You're doing this for free?" I tried to do the math in my head. Her probation was almost as bad as mine.

"The experience is priceless," she said. "At least that's what my professors keep saying." She leaned toward me and whispered. "Honestly, I've been looking forward to meeting you," she said. "All those pipe bombs were starting to bore me."

"I could build a pipe bomb," I said. "Those boys are morons. It can't be that hard."

"All boys are morons," she said. "The sooner you figure that out, the better."

"Don't treat me any different," I said. "I know I'm a girl, but I don't think that should change things."

"I'm from Cleveland," she said. "You might feel like you're some kind of pioneer, but I can assure you that there are girls tougher and meaner than you. I think I was the only girl in my class who wasn't on some kind of probation." She leaned back in her chair. "Are you nervous?"

"No," I said. "I think I'm still feeling the Seroquel."

She read from my file and raised one eyebrow. "You're a writer," she said.

"Kind of," I said.

"What do you write?" When I didn't respond, she examined my leather jacket and black jeans. "Let me guess. Lyrics to death metal songs."

"I don't listen to death metal," I said. "We don't even get radio reception here." I zipped up my jacket. I looked up at the clock. "I guess I write about whatever I'm feeling."

"Your father died last year," she said. "I'm sorry."

"I don't write about that," I said.

She smiled at me in that sad way I'd gotten used to. At Dogwood, the social workers had the same expression of pity, but with a paycheck.

"I've got to ask you about your charges," she said. "It's my job."

"Okay," I said.

"Harassment and intimidation of a federal employee," she said, reading from her folder. "The charge of terrorist threats was dropped."

"Yep," I said. "It's all true."

"Larceny," she continued.

"Petty theft, really," I countered. "Under five dollars."

"Did you steal from the Ben Franklin on August 19, 2017?"

"Yes."

She paused. "You don't seem like the arts and crafts type." I saw her face cloud over, and she suddenly looked at me with alarm. "Please don't tell me you were going to huff model airplane glue."

"What? Is that a thing?"

"Cleveland," she said. "Forget I said it. I don't want to start a drug epidemic."

"I stole Thank You cards," I said. "I don't do drugs, and I'm not a threat."

She looked down at her file again. "Not a threat," she said. "I think Ronald Templeton Jr. might disagree with you."

"Jesus," I said.

"Domestic violence," she said. "Aggravated assault."

"Not domestic," I said. "We were in his truck. But definitely aggravated."

"Do you want to talk about it?"

"Fine. I stabbed him. If you met him, you'd understand."

"I'll take your word for it," she said. I didn't think she was satisfied, and she wanted to try to dig deeper, but something stopped her. Instead, she reached behind her chair and dropped a denim backpack on the table in front of me to riffle through it. The backpack surprised me, the first time she'd actually seemed like a college student. What kind of young woman got dressed up to come to Gabardine? After the first field visit, most girls would have returned in sweatpants.

"He wasn't seriously injured," I said. I felt it needed to be clarified.

"I'm sure you had your reasons," she said. "That's the difference between girls and boys. Those boys don't have a reason for what they did. They blow stuff up and get drunk because they have nothing better to do."

"They need to wear deodorant," I said.

"I'm legitimately interested in you," she said. "I want to know what makes you tick."

"That sounds like there's a bomb inside of me."

"You've got a story," she said. "I can tell." She finally found what she was looking for, and removed a brand-new yellow legal pad.

"Write it down," she said and pushed the pad across the table. "The truth. Tell your story. I can promise that nobody else will ever read it."

"I don't know," I said. "There's lots of stuff that nobody knows about."

"The small crimes of Tiffany Templeton," she said.

"Some of them weren't small," I protested. Tough Tiff's ego flared. "You promise that nobody else will read them? Isn't it your job to report back to the state?"

"Did you murder anybody?"

"No," I said.

"Then I will keep your secrets. I think you need somebody to listen to you. I think you're afraid of getting hurt. I want to hear your stories." I considered this. I could tell her the whole story. I don't want to die like my father, unknown.

"Fine," I said. "But if I die suddenly, you have to promise to burn them."

"Maybe I'll blow them up with a pipe bomb," she said. "I want you to have a safe space. Bring something to me every month." She paused. "Does your mother allow you to have pencils?"

I slid the yellow pad back across the table. "I don't need this."

Her face flashed with anger for a split second, until she caught herself. "I bet you have a computer," she said.

"No," I said, as I stood up to leave. "A typewriter. I do things the hard way."

FROM THE DESK OF TIFFANY TEMPLETON

You are probably going to laugh at the stationery, but it was a gift from my father. He ordered a whole case of it, all this paper with my name on top, even though I don't have a desk. I carry my typewriter to the Laundromat. It's thirty pounds, and it builds muscle. I've only got forty-eight pieces left, the case of paper another reminder of what I lost. I guess I could get more photocopied, but the only Xerox machines in Gabardine belong to Principal Beaudin and Mr. Francine.

I don't carry a purse. I carry this typewriter, a Remington Quiet-Riter. It's too loud to use in the house, but I don't mind lugging it to my office in the Laundromat. I can type as loud as I want, but sometimes I find a dryer sheet stuck between old pages, so some of my short stories smell like fabric softener. My dad told me that the color of my typewriter was seafoam, but I don't think the ocean looks like mint ice cream. Thankfully, the case is black, so David can't yell at me for not matching my accessories.

I'm going to start at the beginning. My earliest

memory involves an explosion, which seems appropriate. After my mother had enough of the meatloaf smell, she banished Ronnie to the back porch. The room had no natural light, perfect for a twelve-year-old boy. A man from the Bad Check List, determined to have his name removed from the public shaming, reinforced and insulated the room, covered the rough pine boards with the cheapest linoleum. The screens on the porch were covered in sheet rock, because my mother refused to spend the money on windows. Ronnie and his meatloaf smell were crammed into a tiny space, only big enough for his odor, a bed, a dresser, and his weight set.

Although he despised my parents, Ronnie was obsessed with his own heavy things. Pumping iron exhausted him, and sleeping in a windowless porch made him oblivious to natural light. When he slept, it was for great stretches of time, and he could not be roused unless he was shaken. We learned this the hard way.

I remember that it was October. I remember leaping from my own bed, startled by an enormous boom, and the walls continued to reverberate. Frightened, I found my mother and father in the living room. It was two o'clock in the morning, but my father already had a fire extinguisher in his arms, and my mother a baseball bat. The three of us stumbled out the front door and into the yard, stiff with frost.

Our next-door neighbor was an old man who lived there from the beginning, a trailer court pioneer.

I only remember him vaguely, watching him navigate the loop, dragging an oxygen tank on wheels, always smoking a Lucky Strike. That night, his luck ran out.

The trailer exploded, the side closest to our house still on fire, the middle a blackened cavern, smoldering. My father waddled closer, to inspect, but my mother remained on our property, clutching her baseball bat. The neighbors stumbled out into their own yards in shivering flocks. Five-year-old David was the only one with common sense, and he ran into his house to call 911.

It took twenty minutes for the volunteer fire department to arrive, sirens and lights. I believed there was some sort of magic to his brand of ciga-rettes, because the old man had been ejected from the living room and into the front yard. The ambu-lance arrived minutes after the fire department, and he had not broken a bone. They would have taken him to the hospital for smoke inhalation, but he was already an expert at it. The firemen and the ambulance crew watched the house burn, as the old man removed the cannula from his nose. He sat in his pajamas on the frosty lawn, and lit another.

When the trailer exploded, the cheap siding flew through the night, including a six-foot panel in our front yard. Small piles of pink fiberglass insula-tion scattered on the street, and hung on the barren trees, still smoking. After ten minutes, the vol-unteer ambulance decided to take the old man to a hotel in Fortune, after he promised not to smoke in the back of the rig.

The night was nearly quiet again, and the firemen rolled up their hoses and used wrenches to crank the hydrants shut. Assured by that stillness, our neighbors herded back toward their own homes, until a scream cut through the frosty air.

My brother, weighted with sleep, did not wake through the explosion. Unfortunately, the pack rats that lived underneath the old man's trailer house were light sleepers, and being pack rats, they were unstoppable. They were not incinerated, just confused. They sought cover and scurried to the closest shelter.

We burst into Ronnie's room. When my mother flipped on the light, he stood on his bed, clinging to the wall, and the rats were everywhere, blinking at the overhead light. They stared back at us, at least twenty, but if you ask Ronnie now, he would claim a hundred, and he would also claim that they hissed at him.

Pack rats on the bed, perched on his sheets and blankets. On the floor, squirming on the new linoleum. Even a pack rat on the bench of his weight set, probably attracted to the smell of his meatloaf sweat.

Ronnie kept screaming, but the pack rats would not budge. Most people in Gabardine would have reached for one of many guns, but my sensible mother ripped the fire extinguisher from the arms of my father and filled every inch of the room with foam. Ronnie leapt from the bed and ran toward safety, kicking up the white spray, maybe even kicking a confused pack rat.

I remember that we left all of the doors wide open and piled into my mother's car. We drove to Fortune, and that was the first night I ever spent in a hotel. Three doors down, the old man had a room of his own. Perhaps he slept. Perhaps he smoked and thought about the loss.

Chapter Seven

EVERY THIRD FRIDAY, I GAVE David a ride to the allergist in
Fortune. I had come back seven days early and nobody was
expecting me, but there was no grace period, no honeymoon, no
time to readjust. Things just picked up where they had left off.

After school, I walked to the gas station to borrow my mother's
car, the same routine for two years, ever since David developed
"allergies" that were as fickle as his friendship with me. Janelle
didn't have a car, which was enough for my mother to pronounce
David as a "disadvantaged youth." My mother hated charity, but
she loved David.

Outside, the reader board announced my mother had lost two
pounds. I also noticed that the price of unleaded and diesel had
increased by four cents. I don't think there was a correlation.

When the bell rang out, announcing my arrival, her neck
snapped toward me, but she sighed when she realized I wasn't a
customer.

"What happened to Mrs. Gabrian?"

My mother pushed a tube of quarters at me across the counter.
This was also the ritual, in case David wanted dinner. "She got
old," said my mother.

"Seriously."

"She's in the old folks' home in Fortune," said my mother.
"Trust me, she went against her will."

Outside, Waterbed Fred pulled the giant Frito-Lay truck up next to the gas pumps. Normally, I would rush to the popcorn machine, because he liked it fresh. Today, however, my mother stalked past me, to do it herself. There used to be a time my mother trusted me with a cauldron of boiling grease, but now she didn't trust me with a telephone.

The popcorn machine was twenty years old, and the health department looked the other way but warned of an electrical fire. When I was six, she trusted me with the machine, even though a slip could result in a skin graft, and I knew what that looked like. One of our customers was a former logger with half a face, a chain saw explosion. He was nice enough, but the sheen of his face, his cheeks like steaks wrapped in cellophane, gave me a healthy fear of the machine.

I watched my mother pull the tub of the buttery substance from the cupboard below the machine. The stuff didn't need to be refrigerated, which was suspect, dyed the spatula and the walls around the machine a yellow like the fingers of a chain-smoker.

Waterbed Fred pushed through the door with his back, wheeling a hand truck stacked to his chin with boxes. My hands clenched when I saw the new merchandise. I knew my mother would not allow me to use the price gun, a chore I loved, lining up the gun over the old sticker, and pulling the trigger.

"You're back," he said, as he spun around and wheeled past me.

"Pretend she's not," said my mother, as she flipped the cylinder at the top of the machine, and I could hear the wire arm stirring the bottom of the kettle. Inside, I knew it was glowing bright red.

Waterbed Fred unwedged the hand truck from the stack of boxes and winked at me. He had delivered for Frito-Lay for years, ever since the waterbed industry went bust. He still had a bill-board just outside of town, mostly of his face, features long faded in the sun, except for the dark commas of his famous mustache. Even though he was no longer flush with waterbed money, he was still the most eligible bachelor in town.

The wire arm whirred in circles as it coated the kettle. Waterbed Fred lugged the boxes to the back of the store, just as the cauldron hissed. As did my mother. "Don't even think about touching the box cutter."

David burst through the door, wearing the black overcoat my mother had bought him for his birthday. He ignored me, drawn like a magnet to my mother, as always.

"Hello, David," she said, standing on a milk crate, launching a handful of popcorn kernels into the vat. David took her hand as she stepped down.

"Did Tiffany tell you that we are working on a project?"

"Makeover!" My mother actually clapped her hands at this.

"Oh, Vy. You know I've tried. Some wars you just can't win."

My mother looked at my hair. "Agreed."

"Your daughter wrote a play. An entire play about the history of Gabardine." David announced this loud enough for Waterbed Fred to hear, but my mother didn't react. Instead, she slammed the stubborn plastic windows of the popcorn machine; years of sizzling grease had warped the edges.

From the back of the store, Waterbed Fred shouted at David, "Your mom still on the market?"

"He's coarse," said David, dismissing him. "When Tiffany applies herself, she is capable of greatness. I've always said so."

"You've never said that," I said.

David smoothed the lapel of his jacket, his other hand still grasping my mother.

"We can't use school property, because of your daughter."

"Oh, Tiffany," said my mother. I rolled my eyes, just as the first ping sounded in the cauldron.

"We have until November to find a theater," said David. "But we need to hold auditions soon. Theater waits for no one." The gas station began to smell like a carnival, and the pings rang out, as popcorn exploded. This was a war zone. David bowed down—actually bowed—and my mother was a short woman. Folded in half, he begged. "I want the fire station."

My mother immediately reached for her phone. I grabbed the keys from the shelf next to the cash register. I wanted to warm up the car, because David would complain about the cold, even in that stupid coat. She drove a 2003 PT Cruiser, and it slunk low to the ground, the shocks destroyed from so many years. The driver's seat was broken, and she had my brother disable the seat belt alarm. She could have afforded any car she wanted but had made a vow to buy a new car as soon as she hit her goal weight. I wasn't sure if that would ever happen. My mother was the type of person who enjoyed sitting in her shame and guilt but only if she was the driver.

When I reentered, my mother was still on the phone, and David was eating a hot dog. Waterbed Fred had abandoned his boxes, and leaned against the counter, munching on popcorn as my mother issued commandments.

"You only need to move the trucks for an afternoon, Joe. It's for the children. Yes, I'm speaking about my daughter. She's still a child in my eyes. It's a community service. You're called volunteer firemen for a reason. That means you volunteer. Do I need to tell you how many of your knuckleheads are on my Bad Check List? Those trucks need to be out of there next month. I don't care if you have to move them yourself. What? Don't take that tone with me. That garage will be empty. Don't put it past me to burn something down."

AS WE DROVE, DAVID TALKED about the play. He had pages of notes. His stack of notes was thicker than the actual script, but I didn't say anything. I was silent, and he chattered on and on.

In the waiting room of the allergist, the chairs were empty. I'd been driving David for two years, and this was always the case. No patients, but I knew he would still wait a half hour. I thought the doctor might be meditating or drinking, because David was a lot to handle.

David was still talking about scenes, and ignoring the receptionist as she pointed to the empty seats and returned to her computer monitor. The same moon-faced receptionist as always, and once again, I had expected things to have changed. I was getting used to the disappointment.

"It's gross," he said as we sat down in the chairs that faced the window. Outside, the parking lot was nearly obscured by snow berms that hadn't melted.

"I agree," I said, figuring he was talking about the waiting room. All the magazines were for golfers or expectant mothers, and I hoped I never became either.

"I'm so glad you feel that way," he said. "You'll have to find a different way to end the play."

I snapped to attention. "What did you say?"

"The deaths." He said this loudly, on purpose. The receptionist looked up from her computer, and David glared at her before he continued. "I don't want the audience to leave on that kind of note."

"It's a true story, David. It's got to be accurate. People want that."

"Not me," he said. "I don't want to direct something so devastating." He hissed the word.

"Devastating? You're just being a dick." I regretted the words as soon as I said them. He wanted this. He wanted to tangle. I swore I could feel the heat rise from his body. I closed my eyes like they taught me at Dogwood. Focused on the present. I honestly thought I'd never have to use any of these tricks. I'm here. Right here, right now. I touched the lump of quarters bulging in my pants pocket.

He cleared his throat. Here it came, the trap. "I'm going to ignore the name-calling, Tiffany." He paused, a trick that I was used to. He wanted me to admit that I was being unreasonable. He was waiting for me to apologize, but I wasn't going to give it to him. Eyes closed, I counted to fifteen. He couldn't help himself. "It's bad enough that I have to direct a play about prostitutes! You've got to make it a happy prostitute story, like *Pretty Woman*!"

I took a deep breath. When I opened my eyes, the receptionist stared at me, like she was afraid I was going to freak out and throw a chair. "It's a true story," I repeated as evenly and as calmly as I could. "Those women lived terrible lives. They died terrible deaths. It's not a damn musical."

His eyes lit up, but then he sighed. "You're right," he admitted. "I don't think anybody around here can sing or dance."

"This was a lot of work, David." My hands clenched, but there would be no punching. "I'm not going to let you destroy it."

"I have a reputation!" He leapt to his feet and pumped his fist, and the receptionist was transfixed. "I will not allow my name to be associated with a disaster!"

From another room, I could hear the doctor clear his throat.

This caused the receptionist to snap back to reality, and she addressed us curtly. "The doctor will be with you shortly, David."

David ignored her, remained standing. He wanted me to yell. He didn't know that I had practiced for this. I had done three months of role-playing exercises. I used the words they taught me: "I'm not comfortable with this."

Silence, until a delivery truck roared into the parking lot, squeezed between the banks of snow, narrowly missing my mother's car.

"Everybody loves a musical," said the receptionist, trying to be helpful.

"Thank you," said David. Satisfied, he finally sat down.

The receptionist lifted a lipstick-stained coffee mug to her mouth. "Just so you know, I used to do community theater."

"Fabulous," said David. He grabbed my forearm, but I looked away, stared at the glitter of salt, our trail across the carpet. "Get her phone number."

I nodded my head, and I knew the deaths would be rewritten. I could live with that, as long as my characters wouldn't be bursting into song.

Chapter Eight

AFTER THE ALLERGIST, I DIDN'T give David a choice. I drove us straight to the nursing home. He knew about Betty Gabrian, but of course, I had to find out from my mother.

"I'll wait in the car," he said.

"I figured," I said.

"I have issues with mortality," he said.

"Especially when it comes to prostitutes," I responded and left him sitting there.

I expected there to be a receptionist at the nursing home or a nurse at the front desk.

Instead, I walked past two open rooms filled with women peering at jigsaw puzzles and nurses reading tabloids. At the end of the hallway, through the windows of the doors, I could see Betty Gabrian sitting beneath a bulletin board decorated with crude attempts at decoupage.

"Thank god," she said. "Just the girl I've been waiting for. The only girl that can help me with a jailbreak."

"What happened?"

"My children are assholes," she said. "I had one small stroke, and all of a sudden they were in charge of me. Legal guardians. All three of those ingrates. I wouldn't trust them to decide on a pizza topping."

Unfortunately, I was the one who needed reassurance. I wanted Betty Gabrian to see what she had helped create, but I also needed her to check it for historical accuracy. Mr. Graff would not be interested in fact-checking a three-act play about prostitutes. For a social studies teacher, he was a terrible historian. Mr. Graff was on record as being a Holocaust denier, skimmed through those pages in our books, only telling us that it was "unseemly and inappropriate to discuss." If the man didn't believe in Hitler, the untold tales of the prostitutes of Gabardine would probably be a hard sell.

Eagerly, Betty Gabrian clutched my script. I could tell this place bored her.

"My next project is to make some friends," she said. "But there's only two Democrats in the entire building. I will need to recalibrate."

"I've got faith in you," I said. "You are a tough cookie."

"Please come back and tell me all the sordid details of your incarceration," she said. "Finally, someone in this town has done something interesting."

I explained about David, and his hostile takeover, and his latest demand. "He wants a happy ending."

"Gays are like that, my dear."

FROM THE DESK OF TIFFANY TEMPLETON

I was in seventh grade, and for six weeks, my mother got a prescription for diet pills. She did lose a lot of weight, but then she started to lose her hair. The worst side effect was her impulsive need to tell the truth, and the worst truths, the kinds she should have kept to herself.

She called us together for a grim family meeting, where she announced that neither of her children would inherit the gas station.

"It's painful to me," she said. "It was supposed to be a legacy."

"Grandpa only had it for six years," said Ronnie. "And he wanted to trade it for a llama farm. You told us that."

"Llamas were the next big thing," countered my mother. "He was an entrepreneur. The two of you do not have an entrepreneurial bone in your body. You are a religious fanatic," she said. She turned to me. "And you are on your way to being a serial killer."

"Not really," I said. "That's kind of a stretch." It was. At that point, I just wore all black and watched slasher movies. My crime spree had not even begun.

"I can't trust either of you," she said. "So don't count on an inheritance."

"Serial killers have their own kind of legacy," offered my father, trying to smooth things out, as always.

"This is bullshit," said Ronnie.

She crossed her arms, and stared at all three of us, dead-eyed. "You're welcome."

I was the one who broke the silence. "What if I want to go to college?" I expected my dad to respond to this, but my mother's eyes were fearsome things.

Instead, Ronnie decided that my dilemma was solid. "She should probably go to college. She would be the first, and that's like a super-big deal."

"She wouldn't be the first," said my dad out of nowhere. "My mom went to college."

At this, my mother snorted. "Hippies," she said. "Your mother helped ruin America."

"She wasn't a hippie," said my father. "She got a degree in civil engineering."

Ronnie and I swiveled our heads, shocked, desperate for my father to continue, admit a success for his side of the family. He said nothing.

"Secrets." My mother hissed the word. "You know I hate secrets."

"It's not a secret," said my dad. "She had the diploma on our wall. In a frame and everything."

This made my mother livid. For once, my dad was

actually making things worse. "Here's a secret, kids. I wanted your father to homeschool you. He refused."

"Thank god he didn't," said Ronnie. "Homeschool kids are freaks."

"They win all the spelling bees," said my mother.

Ronnie stood up and pointed a finger at my mother. "You are a terrible person," he said. "Selfish and mean. I hope you die before you retire."

I guess the idea of homeschooling struck a nerve in me, too. I jumped up from my chair, and it fell back on the linoleum, and the clatter echoed through our kitchen. My mother just stared at me, as I thought of something mean to say. My father put his head in his hands. Ronnie nodded encouragingly.

"I hope your stupid gas station blows up!" This was the best I could do.

Ronnie winced. I was just as embarrassed. In heated moments, I was much better with my fists. I couldn't come up with something hurtful, even though I could fill an entire notebook with hateful things. For now, they would remain unspoken, and I stomped to my bedroom and slammed the door.

I seethed in my room for a half hour, until there was a soft knock on the door. My dad put his finger to his lips, and we snuck from the house. He drove me straight to Fortune, and it was my first time at the pawn shop. I picked out my first leather jacket, and then he pulled me to the rear of the store, and we regarded a shelf of typewriters.

"If you're going to be a professional, you're going to need one of these." I was too excited to point out that a laptop computer would probably be more efficient. He let me choose the Remington. He also let me buy an empty case, gray tweed, with a working lock and key. He knew that I needed to keep some things from my mother. I didn't need diet pills to tell the truth.

The next week, things began to arrive in the mail. My mother said nothing. My father had won this war. Each box that arrived was another shot fired. Stationery, extra ribbon, Hoppe's No. 9 Lubricating Oil, six small bottles of correcting fluid. He left the bottles of Wite-Out on the kitchen table, the counter, made sure my mother would see.

Even then, my father knew that I would make mistakes.

Chapter Nine

I ARRIVED TEN MINUTES EARLY, but those stupid boys were already there, and I had to stand in Mr. Francine's doorway like an idiot.

Once again, Kelly called in the Sweets as a team. I didn't notice their T-shirts until they stood. It seemed weird that they would both wear matching red T-shirts, but then I saw the Confederate flag emblazoned across their chests. These were probably the first new clothes they had ever owned. As they approached Kelly, she rolled her eyes before ushering them inside her office.

I sat next to TJ, and the body odor seeped out of the neck of his jacket, zipped all the way, all those boy juices marinating.

As usual, Kelly could not break the Sweets. The door swung back open after four minutes, and they shuffled past, and Kelly was flustered. She called for Rufus with a sting in her voice.

"Aren't you hot?"

TJ swung his shaggy head toward my voice and stared at me, blurry-eyed.

I tried again. I was trying to be casual and friendly, but my words were straight out of a prison movie. "How much time do you got?"

"No fraternizing," said Mr. Francine without looking up. "This. Is. My. Workplace."

TJ spread his giant hands on his knees and folded one hand,

except for a thumb. Six months, I thought. But knowing the McMackins, it could very well be six years. His right hand disappeared in a flash, and TJ was so hard-core that he didn't carry around the little plastic cup. He was good at this. He took a swig and tucked it back in his massive coat just as Rufus pushed open the door.

With TJ gone, it was just me and Mr. Francine, in our ghost town. The file cabinets towered around us, and the tile was spotless, no chance of tumbleweeds.

Kelly had relaxed a little bit. I sat down in the folding chair, and she sprayed the air with a can of aerosol freshener, and the room smelled like fake laundry instead of real teenage boys.

"I would like to spray them directly," she admitted as she sat down. "But that would be unprofessional."

"I brought some stuff," I said. "I think I explained some things."

"Good," she said. I pushed my typewritten pages across the table, and she pressed them open with her hand, smoothed them into submission. "You have nice penmanship," she said and folded them closed. She waited for me to respond. "That was a joke," she said finally.

"Aren't you going to read them?"

"Of course," she said. "But I need to spend this time talking to you, not reading about your teenage crushes."

"Gross," I said. "I double-checked the spelling."

"Mysterious," she said and slipped the pages into her backpack. "I can't wait." Again, a cloud on her face, and she resettled herself in the chair, and I think she was trying to look professional. "I'm really easy to talk to, Tiffany. I'm not as old as you think. I'm sure we've got some things in common. Rufus and I talk about serial killers, and TJ and I talk about rap music. The Sweets don't talk. Ever. Maybe it's because I'm black."

"My mom says they're all heathens," I said. "That's the word she uses."

"Tell me about your parents," she said. "I've called your mom several times, but she always says she's busy and hangs up. She's supposed to be a part of this process."

"That's not going to happen," I said. "She works nonstop. She won't leave the gas station. She was born in that gas station, and she'll probably die there."

"She was born in the gas station?"

"Not literally."

"I'd like her to be included," she said. "I drove by the gas station, but I chickened out. The gas prices confused me, I guess. I couldn't figure out what that last number was. Is it for chainsaws or something?"

"No," I said. "My mom posts her current weight on the board, so everybody in town can see it. Her surgeon was concerned that she didn't have a team to support her at home."

"There are support groups on the internet," said Kelly. "Forums and groups for bariatric surgery."

Kelly didn't know about the internet in Gabardine. In addition to being a dead zone for cell phones, we had the slowest internet connection in America. This was an actual fact. My mom took me to the city council meeting where they passed around the report. We even saw a map of the world, red flares of communication hotspots, and I swear to you that Antarctica had more red dots. There were parts of Africa that were the same gray as Gabardine, so we were basically a third-world country, without the tsetse flies and cholera. We didn't have aid workers, either. Libertarians would probably shoot them. Supposedly we were waiting for a grant from the federal government to build the infrastructure. Until then, we had dial-up that worked occasionally, depending on the weather. "We get by without the internet," I said. "We get by without a lot of things."

"You said she didn't have a team to support her at home."

"She's been trying to lose weight since I was born," I said. "At some point, I just got tired of hearing about it. I think I felt bad for my dad."

"What about him? Was he born here?"

"Pocatello," I said. "That's in Idaho."

"I'm aware," she said. "Did he have family there?"

"We don't have a big family. All my grandparents are dead, and I don't think I have any cousins or anything like that. I mean, that's what I was told. They don't have a reason to lie. My mom got the gas station when her dad died, and he was a horrible bookkeeper. That's all I know. My dad never talked about his past. He just said Idaho was the worst place on earth, and he complained about the sales tax. He said that his life really began when he met my mother, but when I ask my mom about it, she always said he was a hobo that fell off a train. I don't know the real story. She burned all the wedding pictures when she started losing weight."

"Your mom sounds like a real character," she said.

"He got stuck here, and he got stuck with her. I guess he was an unlucky hobo."

"Don't you want to know the truth?"

"I'm sure it's boring," I said. "I always just figured that when two really fat people find each other, they figure out how to make it work." I stopped myself. I knew it sounded terrible and mean.

"It's okay if you cry," she said. Again, she ducked down to

her backpack, unzipped the front pocket, removed two shrink-wrapped packages of Kleenex, travel size. One pack was pink, and the other blue, and I thought it was really sexist when she chose the pink, and attempted to open the plastic wrapping. I was angry, so I let her struggle, and eventually she used her teeth to rip one end. I was glad that her lipstick smeared. Before she could remove a tissue, I waved it away. I knew I was just being passive-aggressive. At Dogwood, they taught us to say our emotions out loud, to name them, because it made things less scary. When you name something, that means you own it, like emotions are stray dogs or something. I didn't feel like telling Kelly I was being passive-aggressive. She had enough clinical hours to make that diagnosis.

"I'm not going to cry," I said.

She let go of the package reluctantly. "I bought these when they told me I was coming here. They've been sitting in my backpack for months. My professors told us to always carry Kleenex. And pepper spray."

"Pepper spray is better than a pipe bomb," I said. "More accurate. Can I go?" She nodded, and I got up from my chair. She probably spent her own money on all that stuff, and it never did any good. If she hung around the bars in Gabardine, she might use the pepper spray, though.

"I'm going to get through to you," she said. "The tough-girl thing is an act, Tiffany. It's okay to cry. I cry all the time. Heck, I cry every time I think about my student loans."

"Okay," I said.

Kelly stuffed the Kleenex back into her bag. "Nobody cries here. Not one of you."

"It's this town," I said and walked out the door.

Chapter Ten

I SPENT AN ENTIRE SATURDAY driving David all over the county to post flyers for the auditions. According to the sign, my mother had dropped down to 179, but the cost of fuel remained the same. I think the weight loss is why my mother gave us three rolls of change. Instead of food, David spent all our money in Fortune on a Rihanna CD. For once, I wish he would shoplift, because by the time we returned to the trailer court, I was starving. Despite posting flyers on every bulletin board, despite scotch-taping them in the windows of every business that was not terrified of us, we showed up at the fire station on the last Saturday of April and it was nearly empty aside from the lawn chairs we'd borrowed for seating. Maybe Principal Beaudin's professional secretary had gone door-to-door, warning of salacious content, convincing all 21,000 residents of the county. She was good at her job, so I wouldn't be surprised.

The only women that showed up for the audition were the senior citizens. The van from the senior center had pulled up fifteen minutes early, and it was crammed completely full, old people wedged in like the worst clown car ever, no way they had enough seat belts. Betty Gabrian had found an activity for her new friends. We stood in the open garage door and watched as the double doors of the white van sprung open. The occupants removed the winter coats and purses from their laps and gingerly dismounted onto the sidewalk. Thankfully, the driver had steered the van up onto the pavement, which made it tilt like it was at sea. The women all wore the same white pants and American flag T-shirts, but I knew there wasn't a uniform at the senior center. Peer pressure, apparently. The driver doubled as the nurse, which David deduced by her choice in footwear.

"Nobody wears shoes like that on purpose," he declared. "Now I know who buys all those clothes at Shopko. Why are old people so patriotic?"

"They fought in wars, David."

"It looks like it." He pointed his head at the trio of old men, who immediately distanced themselves from the eight women and gathered in the very back corner of the room, near the giant hoops of rolled-up fire hose. I knew those old men—they attended every city council meeting in Gabardine for as long as I could remember. I knew they were not going to audition. At least they were dressed normally. I didn't want to comment on anybody's fashion choices, as David was wearing a lemon-colored beret. I hoped that this would not be a permanent thing.

David hissed at me. "I'm afraid they are going to pee on the lawn chairs," he said. "We're going to have to put some pads down or something."

"I'm sure they have control of their bladders," I offered. "They have a nurse with them. I'm sure she will take care of it."

"Why do all old people smell like pee?" He was trying to whisper, but that was an impossible thing for him.

I smelled them as they filed past us, and I didn't smell pee. I smelled White Diamonds perfume and menthol rub. I studied the nurse. I didn't think she would be much help. Her nose was buried in a crossword puzzle, and even though she had a pen in her hand, I could see that the boxes were still blank.

Betty Gabrian had conquered the septuagenarian clique and probably sat at the head of the jigsaw table. Her new friends carefully lowered themselves into the lawn chairs at the front of the room, but Betty Gabrian stopped to address me. She waved my script in the gloomy light.

"Historically accurate," she said. "Minus the ending, of course."

"So you approve?"

"You don't need my permission, my dear. I'm sure it will be a smashing success."

"I don't know," I said. I pointed at David, who was pacing back and forth, wringing his hands. At least he had removed his beret. "All this is scary. I think it would just be easier to put on a puppet show."

"You have a tin ear when it comes to dialogue. Puppets might be a viable option."

I didn't know what a tin ear was, but I thanked her anyway.

"Please come back and visit me," she said. "I want to hear your jailhouse confessions. I'm quite looking forward to it."

The other women were listening, and they nodded. Entertainment was in short supply.

"I hope we can play some part." She looked around the garage, and it was empty, no hubbub of young women clamoring to audition for the roles. I had a hard time imagining the elderly ladies portraying teenage hookers. Teenage hookers didn't use walkers, so we would have to figure something out.

Waterbed Fred stepped through the open bay of the fire station and stood behind the row of old ladies, steadying himself on the metal rail of the lawn chair. I think he'd had a few, even though it was ten o'clock in the morning. At least it was a Saturday.

He looked up in the great expanse of the roof, like there were spotlights. When nothing happened, when he wasn't cast in dramatic lighting, he righted himself and launched into a full-throated version of "Abilene."

His voice was deep and strong, warbling and breaking in just the right spots. He had practiced this in his Frito-Lay truck, I was sure. I watched a row of American flags swoon; one woman grabbed her purse and brought it to her face, perhaps to keep from sobbing.

David exhaled beside me. "I wasn't expecting that," he confessed. "He's got star power. He should play the villain."

"There is no villain," I said.

He jabbed me with one finger, right next to the armpit. "Write one."

Waterbed Fred finished to great applause. He bowed and almost fell over.

David leapt to his feet. The old men in the corner watched this sudden explosion of energy, suspicious. Maybe they did have trauma from the war.

"Wonderful. Just wonderful!" David's face lit up. He turned to me and attempted another whisper. "This is just like a white trash version of *A Star Is Born*. I have discovered a great new talent." He stopped and clarified. "The Judy Garland version, of course."

"Well, he probably is an alcoholic," I said. "But the Kris Kristofferson kind."

"Thank you," said Waterbed Fred. "Can I sit down now?"

"No," said David.

"No!" shouted the old women.

"Your voice is glorious," said David. "Unfortunately, this isn't a musical." At that, there was a commotion among the ladies, as several grabbed their purses, ready to leave.

"Wait!" David turned to me. "You could write a few songs, right?"

"I don't think so," I said.

"I've got it," said David. "He could just sing 'Abilene' at the beginning, except we'll change it to Gabardine." He was very pleased with this.

"I don't think that's okay," I said. "I'm pretty sure there's copyright laws and stuff like that."

David turned to me, completely serious. "I would break the law for that man."

At this, the old women applauded. Waterbed Fred looked sheepish, his mustache twitched. I don't think he was used to this much attention. My mother barely looked up when she signed invoices. He probably hadn't been such a hot commodity since 1985, the year waterbeds peaked.

"You can come sit down," offered David.

"Or he can sit by me," catcalled Betty Gabrian.

Disgusted, the nurse grabbed her crossword book and walked outside to wait in the van.

Instead, Waterbed Fred's cowboy boots echoed through the fire station. The elderly women craned their necks to get a good view of his ass. He nodded as he passed us, and I swear David gasped. Waterbed Fred took the remaining lounge chair in the corner with the old men, seeking some sort of refuge.

DAVID STOOD IN THE OPEN bay of the fire station, and the sun poured through and lit up the dust like sparks. He always looked for the most dramatic lighting. To his credit, he always found it.

David addressed the row of women in lawn chairs. I sat behind the ladies, on a cold cinder block. Two of the old men had fallen asleep, but a pair had joined Waterbed Fred in examining a row of fire axes. "We are a troupe," announced David.

"Like Girl Scouts," declared Betty Gabrian, nudging another old woman, who was sleeping with her mouth open.

"Different spelling," said David. "Actors are a family, and we take care of each other. The stage is frightening, and we must trust each other. We must have an investment in the success of the group, and we are only as strong as our weakest link."

He stepped out of the circle of light, and crouched down in front of my cinder block. "Jesus Christ," he said. "This is impossible. All these old ladies are exactly the same. I don't know how we're going to do this. I don't feel right making them wear name tags." He turned back to the women and spoke loudly, slowly, as if they were deaf. "I am looking forward to getting to know each and every one of you."

I stared at the back of their heads, and every woman had the exact same wash-and-wear hairstyle, vaguely white, vaguely curly. Was this something that came with age? Did your hair give up, dissolve, and fade into the color of cornstarch, retreat, perch on your scalp like a starving barnacle? I shuddered. Maybe there was only one beautician that visited the nursing home, and she just lacked imagination. "We're going to need wigs," I said. "The Soiled Doves of Gabardine must have prostitute hair. There's no other way around it."

"We don't have a budget for wigs," said David, near tears. He turned away from them because he didn't care if I saw him fall apart.

"Cheerleader car wash," I said. "If they have different wigs, you might be able to tell them apart."

"True," he said. "But right now, I can't remember their names.

I can't just call them Colostomy Bag and Lady with the Eyebrows Painted in the Wrong Place."

"No," I said. "I don't think they'd like that."

OF COURSE, DAVID MADE ME do the most painful work. While he led the women through vocal warm-ups, I was dispatched out to the parking lot, David's clipboard under one arm.

Just like the beautician, the nurse in the parking lot was lazy. She left the van running, blaring a Celine Dion CD from her open window, and I could hear that hateful song from *Titanic*.

The nurse seemed annoyed when I opened the passenger door, but ignored me until I jabbed the power button on the CD player. She sighed and jammed a cigarette in her mouth but paused before lighting. She turned around in her seat and examined the rows behind her.

"Gotta check for an oxygen tank," she said, and seeing none, she inhaled, didn't even bother to blow the smoke out of her open window.

"I need to ask you some questions."

"No," said the nurse. "Every goddamn teenage girl sees my uniform and they think I work for free. I don't give a shit about your sex life. Go to Planned Parenthood."

I clicked the ballpoint pen and tapped the clipboard. "The old ladies. We don't know their names," I said. "We can't even tell them apart."

"I know the feeling," said the nurse. "It's not worth it, really."

"I need names and stuff like that. Probably food allergies, just in case."

"Don't feed them," she said. "Never, ever feed them." She was serious about this, like the old women were Gremlins or some-thing. "Look, I'm from an agency. They swap us out every month. Nobody wants this gig. We take turns. I don't get invested, and I don't learn their names. I come back in a year and most of them have died." This nurse had a terrible bedside manner. "Or maybe they didn't die. I don't know. I can't tell them apart, either."

The nurse tossed her cigarette out the open window. The dis-gruntled nurse couldn't see the irony in throwing a lit cigarette at a fire station, which should be a safe place for such things, but our town had a habit of burning down. She knew all the words to Celine Dion, but nothing about emergencies. She reached beneath the driver's seat and pulled out a stack of shiny purple folders, clasped together with a leopard-spotted alligator clip. This nurse did not believe in office supplies, only hair accessories. Mr. Francine would have had a heart attack.

"There," she said. "A file for each of them. Everything is in there. Copy what you want, but give it back. Don't write down any social security numbers. I'm pretty sure that's against the law. There's lots of big words, and we just ignore them. The thing you need to look out for is a DNR: do not resuscitate."

"I don't know CPR," I said. "I guess that won't be a problem."

"Even if they beg," she said. "Don't perform any extraordi-nary measures. Trust me, they all change their mind at the end. Don't fall for it. They may offer you money."

"Okay," I said.

INSIDE THE GARAGE, DAVID LED the women through stretches. When he saw my clipboard, he told them to rest, and the lawn chairs filled with stars and stripes.

"I know you haven't started casting yet," I said. "But I think this might help with your decisions."

"At this point, it's not about star power," he said. "Not a thespian in the bunch. I think most of them are in the middle of assisted suicide."

"My notes," I said, and shoved the clipboard into his hand. "I organized them in order of medical fragility."

"Thoughtful," said David.

The women did as they were told, even though David was sixty years younger and the stress had caused a rash of pimples across both of his cheeks. It was now two o'clock in the afternoon, and between the sun in the cloudless sky and all of the drama (not from my script, but from David's energy), it was hot in the fire station, and David mopped his glistening pustules with an embroidered handkerchief, purple, a cunning peacock. Another Christmas gift from my mother, but it didn't seem particularly hygienic.

He directed them to stand in a row, and for two whole minutes, he swapped them out and made them change places until he was satisfied. The end result reminded me of a police lineup, if the criminals were dwarfed with age and curled with osteoporosis. I felt sorry for them. They were willing, however, and after another minute of deliberation, David shuffled through a deck of index cards, and carefully chose one for each of his actresses.

Line readings. I guess this was the real audition. In a lawn chair, I propped the clipboard against my lap, referring to my notes, scribbling down any casting decisions.

"When I point to you, I would like you to state your name, and then read the line as if your life depends on it. Not your real life, of course!" The medical information suggested otherwise.

"I need you to practice your breathing, just like I taught you. Center yourself, and imagine the forest fire, feel the heat. Don't forget to state your name."

"You know our names," said Betty Gabrian, the leader. "We introduced ourselves almost three hours ago."

"Of course," said David. "We are a family! It's not for my benefit." He waved his handkerchief at me. "My assistant is sloppy. You can tell just by looking at her."

He pointed at Betty Gabrian, and she stepped forward, and when she took a deep breath and tried to center herself, I heard an old man laugh from the back of the room.

"Betty Gabrian," she said, even though I knew it, but I found her name on my list. No real medical issues, but occasionally suffered from dangerously low blood pressure, prone to fainting, just like one of those goats. Her stroke had been a singular occurrence, and despite what her terrible children thought, a neurologist confirmed it was a random event. Betty Gabrian pushed her hands toward an imagined wall of fire. "The flames! Oh my lord, the flames!"

"Fantastic," he said. "I could feel it. I could feel the heat!" Betty Gabrian stepped back into the line. I wrote her name under the character of Miss Julie. Madam of the brothel, maybe a lesbian. My character description was bare, but I didn't think these ladies were method actresses.

"Diana Whipple," and the plumpest of the ladies stepped forward. In my notes, Diana Whipple was allergic to penicillin and shellfish, and exhibiting the beginning of dementia. She seemed alert as she held the index card up to her face, squinting at the line. "We will not run! We do not have the appropriate footwear!"

"Delightful," declared David.

The most infirm of the women would play the three blonde sisters, who had been rescued by Miss Julie after being abducted by Indians. Each blonde suffered some sort of frostbite. Diana Whipple would portray Miss Joanna, who lost two fingers from frostbite, and her hand was off-putting to most of the patrons, so she only performed oral sex.

A solid, healthy woman cleared her throat, stepped forward without being asked. "Irene Vanek. I would like to address the young lady. I appreciate your artistic expression, and I realize that you have grown up in a sheltered environment. But I spent much of my life marching in the streets and fighting for women's rights. I know you only see us as old people, but we made this world better for you. I would be remiss if I didn't tell you that this script is sexist and racist. And trashy. Very, very trashy."

"Inga!" David ripped an index card from the clutches of a frightened lady, and just like that, the roles were swapped. "You're my Inga!"

"She doesn't have any lines," said Irene Vanek. "All she does is walk around and say *uff-da*."

"Exactly," said David, recoiling from her lecture. God bless David. "But Inga has spunk. Inga shoots guns. I'm pretty sure she's a feminist." The character of Inga Liszak was the prettiest whore in Gabardine but spoke no English. She was indispensable, however, shooting her rifle at anything that could be boiled on the cookstove.

"There is nothing feminist about a frightened immigrant forced into sex trafficking," said Irene.

"She has short hair," said David. "She was ahead of her time."

"Or maybe she had lice," offered Betty Gabrian.

Irene Vanek spoke the truth. Irene had no choice but to speak the truth. She was the client with the DNR. She meant what she said, and my feelings were a bit hurt, so I wouldn't feel compelled to break the law and perform any heroic measures if her heart burst open or she suddenly stroked out, especially since I was already on probation.

"Could you say the line, please?" David asked this timidly, as if Irene was a sharpshooter in real life.

"Uff-da," said Irene. She rolled her eyes and stepped back into the line. She didn't even bother with a Hungarian accent, but I wasn't about to point that out.

"Next," said David, and a woman with a walker, decorated with red, white, and blue tassels, eased forward.

"Eileen Lambert," she said. "I have Native American blood." She was as white as Styrofoam, really white, could have stood in David's bedroom undetected. "I would never get in the way of your artistic vision, but please stop referring to my people as Indians. My people do not worship Vishnu."

David turned to me and pointed at my clipboard. "Write it down. Get rid of anything culturally offensive. I have a reputation." I wrote it down, mostly to appease Eileen Lambert.

Eileen Lambert clutched the index card assuredly, and I shrunk down in my lawn chair, feeling like a white supremacist. Her stage voice was commanding. "No man shall save us from this cursed inferno! Only God shall save us, and you youngest whores better get to praying!"

"Holy shit," said David, and then apologized for his language. "You are absolutely perfect for Miss Connie. Perfect! Write that down!" Again, I scribbled on my clipboard. Miss Connie was the oldest prostitute in the brothel, but the most popular, because her lengthy career had taught her the dirtiest of sex acts. In addition to the walker, Eileen Lambert had a colostomy bag and eczema. I was sure we could hide the colostomy bag with a hoop skirt, and stage makeup could cover any skin flares. The walker would be another issue entirely. Maybe we could make it a pony, but it would seem weird for her to be riding a small horse around a brothel.

I could have sworn the next woman had always been a dwarf, but I was beginning to understand that old age was cruel and dehydrated bodies, shrunk them like beef jerky. "Loretta McQuilkin," she said. "Formerly Loretta Lang, formerly Loretta Lambert."

"My brother," announced Eileen Lambert. "No hard feelings. Trust me. My brother was a real turd." I could identify with that.

Loretta McQuilkin had the shortest line, but struggled. I think she was trying to sound dramatic, but instead it was stilted and disinterested. "Where is the whiskey?"

"This is *The Soiled Doves of Gabardine*," said David. "This is not *Guiding Light*. I'd like you to reread the line, but pretend your skirt is on fire. Right now, you're reading it like you just found out you have a secret twin sister and she stole your credit card."

"Got it," said Loretta. "WHERE IS THE WHISKEY?!?"

"Yes," said David. He nodded at me, and I consulted the clipboard. Loretta McQuilkin, formerly Lang and Lambert, was not only allergic to commitment, but apparently the entire environment. Pollen, peanuts, carpet, glue, animals with and without fur, cilantro. She really should be living in a bubble, not a nursing home. Miss Leslie was the drunk of the brothel, usually wasted and unusually limber. If she really committed to the character, stilted and disinterested could work, because the real drunks I saw at the gas station moved through life in a distant bubble, not the hypoallergenic kind.

Beatrice Smetanka (dementia, irregular heartbeat) and Ruby

Bardsley (dementia, renal failure in 2015, glaucoma) proved to be terrible actresses, shy and demure, maybe because their dementia was far along, and they thought David was an angry police officer due to his demeanor.

Beatrice Smetanka could barely be heard, but that was okay, because my dialogue was pretty lame: "Damn this town! Damn the flapdoodle men of Gabardine!"

Ruby Bardsley, nearly blind, delivered her line to Waterbed Fred at the back of the room. "Fill every bucket! Fill every bathtub! Even the bathtub with the drunkard! He has not paid his bill!"

I didn't need David to pencil in Beatrice and Ruby for the roles of Miss Neva and Miss Aimee, the other two blonde sisters. In my script, they had been saved from Indians, and there was no way I was going to change it to Native Americans. David got his happy ending, and that was enough. Frostbite claimed the tip of Miss Neva's nose, and it was gray from the frigid trauma. Miss Aimee's injuries had left her legs without any feeling, so she serviced the fattest of patrons.

"Erika Hickey," and the tallest of the elderly women stepped forward, and David was suddenly crouching down at her feet.

"Heels!" He pointed excitedly, like they were stilettos or something. Erika Hickey's black loafers had a kitten heel, but that was enough to send David into palpitations. Today, glamour was in short supply, the fire station's only pops of color belonged to snaking orange extension cords.

Betty Gabrian cackled. "Wait until you see her legs! We've got a saying at the nursing home. She's got two great legs and five terrible boyfriends!"

"Betty, please." Erika was embarrassed, but tugged at her

knee to slide up a pant leg, and sure enough, it was gorgeous and finely muscled. The nurse had said nothing about sex, but apparently the nursing home had at least one randy grandma and five men who didn't mind being part of a geriatric harem. She released the cuff and smoothed her slacks back into place. "Nature has cursed us, yet again! All this damnation! We have been cursed with beauty, and now we are cursed with impossible meteorological conditions!"

"Bravo," said David, but I was humiliated, hearing my words spoken out loud for the very first time. This was terrible. *Faces of Death* had better dialogue, and that was just a bunch of snuff scenes strung together.

Erika Hickey was relatively healthy and perfect to portray Judith, the scullery maid with the cleft lip. According to my notes, Erika exercised every day, but she was a brittle diabetic, and her blood sugar spiked and plummeted, without warning. I didn't think it would take much convincing to stack the front row with her five boyfriends, close to those incredible legs, ready to throw candy at their beloved in case of a diabetic reaction.

FROM THE DESK OF TIFFANY TEMPLETON

Even though Lou Ann Holland lived on the other side
of the trailer court, my mother blamed her for the
ants, convinced they crawled all the way from her
flower bed next to the Laundromat. It wasn't that
big of a deal, really. For a few weeks during the
summer, we had ants in our kitchen, but like most
things, my father took care of them. Lou Ann culti-
vated peonies, hid the cinder-block foundation of
her trailer house with giant bushes, some as high
as her windows. I always thought they were ridiculous flowers, so top-heavy, bowing to the ground,
the wilted petals flying around for months, rot-
ting in the potholes. They bloomed for two weeks in
June, and that was it. Not only did peonies bring
this litter, but my mother swore they were an ant
farm.

"She's an artist," my father always said. "She's
supposed to be a mess."

Lou Ann Holland was an artist, but I don't think
she ever sold anything. I always thought artists wore
black, but Lou Ann wore a men's V-neck T-shirt and
white canvas pants, her limbs sharp edges against

the draping fabric. It seemed odd to wear white when you worked with so much paint, but her clothes served another purpose: to clean her brushes. She worked with oil paints, and the tail of her T-shirt hung close to her knees, heavy with stains.

Lou Ann overdosed on Thanksgiving. She lived alone, so I was never really sure who found her. Maybe she called 911 on herself. She was pretty neurotic. We had already eaten, and Ronnie and his family had gone home for the evening, excused themselves as quickly as possible. It was a surprise when he came back, an hour later, bursting through the door.

"Ambulances at Lou Ann's," he said. "Sirens and everything."

"Figures," said my mother. "Artists are so dramatic. If she wanted to be invited over for Thanksgiving, all she had to do was ask. She didn't need to shoot herself in the head."

I don't know why my mother immediately jumped to that conclusion. Lou Ann didn't seem the type to have a gun, and I knew that most tortured artists drowned themselves or swallowed poison.

I was close. It was a different kind of poison.

"Overdose," reported Lorraine, who had also returned to our house, baby in tow, as we heard the sirens wail and fade as they sped away.

"Overdose," Lorraine repeated. "At my house, that usually happens on Christmas."

We watched silently as my father grabbed his coat

and keys. "I'm going to the hospital," he declared.

"Of course you are," said my mother. "I used the good dishes today, Ronald. If you leave our family celebration to dash off to be a Good Samaritan, I will throw all the leftovers in the trash. No midnight turkey sandwiches. I guess it takes a junkie to teach you how to practice portion control."

My father said nothing, which was not surprising. I was the one that had to clean up the kitchen anyway, and I would stash leftovers in the refrigerator. My mom never opened it—she was on a mission to qualify for her bariatric surgery.

As his car drove away, my mother shook her head. "That big weirdo is probably getting her stomach pumped." I could hear the jealousy in her voice.

My father returned just before midnight, and my mother had been asleep for hours. I made him the turkey sandwich and joined him at the kitchen table. He was pale, and nervous.

"Thank you," he said. "The cafeteria at the hospital is closed for the holiday."

"What kind of pills did she take?"

"Painkillers," he said, after swallowing. He considered his next words very carefully, paused with his half-eaten sandwich in the air. "It's not like her, really. Painkillers. She likes red wine and marijuana."

"She's an artist," I said. "Of course."

"She wouldn't tell the doctors or the cops where she got them. She wouldn't tell me, either."

"Why would she tell you? Is a drug overdose something you have to put on your taxes?"

"No," he said. "She's not a drug addict. She's an artist, and sometimes, artists have really bad days."

"Thanksgiving sucks," I said and took his empty plate to the sink.

"I just wish she picked up the phone," he said. "I'm only two minutes away."

"Dad, you're not the suicide hotline. I think you need training for something like that. If she was having a bad day, I guess you could have dressed up like a clown and brought her balloons or something."

"A clown," said my father. That word brought the color back to his cheeks, and I watched him push back his chair. My mom only focused on the surgery, and I think there was no place for my dad on that path. He knew he would be rerouted, just like her stomach.

I could tell he was angry. He shook his head and walked down the hallway to the master bedroom. I rinsed the dish, careful to get all the bread crumbs into the drain. My mother would look for evidence.

As I wiped the dish dry and reached to replace it in the cupboard, it began shaking in my hand. Truth is like that sometimes. It hits you like a tremor, and then before you know it, it splits you apart like a fault line.

My father was in love with Lou Ann.

I never said a word. I think I liked the fact that my father kept something from my mother. He gave everything else away, to anyone who asked. He kept this for himself.

When my father died, six months later, Lou Ann Holland finally painted the rusty and peeling metal siding of her rickety trailer house. My mother, of course, had something to say.

"Mauve." She slapped the dining table with her hand. "Who paints their house mauve? Jesus Christ."

I would have called it lavender and assumed it was supposed to match the pink peonies that only lasted two weeks. She knew colors, that was her passion.

"She's an artist," I said, the only response I could think of.

Chapter Eleven

I COULD HEAR THE KIDS playing on the sand hill as I dug my arm through the juniper bush. I made sure nobody was watching as I slid out the typewriter case. I crouched down and unlocked it, pulled back one corner of the lid, peered inside. Everything was still there. It was light outside, and I did not want to be spotted, so I pushed it back inside the bush as quickly as possible. These things inside the box would not destroy me, but in four nearby trailer houses, they could explode like homemade pipe bombs.

The sand hill rose up behind the north wall of the Laundromat, and a trail led through the rotten crab apple trees and under a chain-link fence that had never been repaired. Sand was a foreign thing in Gabardine, something they had in California, but here it was only used for the icy roads in our endless winters. The hill had been there for generations. This was where trailer park families had barbecues, where young couples got engaged. I guess it felt tropical, exotic.

In reality, it was useful. During the worst days of winter, the highway department would bring their trucks at four o'clock in the morning, load up, and spread the grains out of a tiny chute in the back of a dump truck with a massive bed. When I was a kid, the trucks used to park here, but then the county built them a new garage, on the outskirts of town, right next to an old billboard for Waterbed Fred's business.

I sat at the top of the sand hill, queen of the mountain. Tough Tiff would not wear a tiara, but I was royalty, nonetheless. I would not be challenged. I would whip any of the little kids in a fistfight, but it would never come to that. They did not know about the short leash I was on, and they were still scared of me.

From the top of the sand hill, you could see all of the trailer houses and most of the town. You could see all the way past the high school, all the way to the second-tallest thing in Gabardine, that billboard of Waterbed Fred's face, most of the paint chipped away or faded, except for his mustache.

Below me, I watched little boys build collapsing forts for their G.I. Joes and He-Men, and little girls built sets, a kitchen of sand, playing house, I guess. I hoped that they invented fathers. We had a lot of sand but a serious lack of fathers.

The McGurty girls did not play house. Even though they were hundreds of feet away, they were so loud, I could hear every word. The sand cave they inhabited was an office, and the oldest McGurty sat behind a pile of sand shaped into a bar, her version of a desk. One by one, her little sisters would stand in front of her desk and hold out empty hands.

The oldest McGurty was unimpressed by their humility. "I'm Mr. Francine! And your damn power bill is late!"

I leaned against a pole sunk into a clump of concrete as big as one of the McGurty girls. This pole contained the remnants of a metal sign: *No Trespassing*. All around me, the sand hill was smoothed and mounded, but this pole remained.

May had arrived with unseasonably warm days but still frosted overnight. The sand stopped clumping with ice crystals by the time the sun hit the zenith. The days remained foreshortened, the sun setting before dinnertime. In this county, winter usually lasted through the end of April and occasionally all the way to June. This sun was a rare thing. The grass in the lawns was still brown, the trees bare, no leaves. The power lines and the flat faint blue sky were empty of birds.

The dirty children tumbled down all around me, but I was left alone on the peak. I always kept a small notebook in the inside pocket of my jacket, and from another pocket I removed a pen. I cursed when I realized the ballpoint pen was filled with pink ink, barely legible. I did not own a pink ballpoint pen, I would never own a pink ballpoint pen, and I was pretty sure David had slipped it in my pocket just to annoy me.

The pine trees atop the ridge glowed more fiercely. Low gray clouds moved rapidly from the south, sagging and lumpy but still skittering toward the sand hill, toward the trailer park. Those were snow clouds, and the undersides were lit with the tangerine glow of the sunset.

I had nowhere to go. I was just as locked up in Gabardine as I had been in Dogwood. At least at Dogwood, the stories were interesting. I sat there for another twenty minutes, until I saw a figure crawling through the chain-link fence behind the Laundromat.

Bitsy sat down on the sand next to me, spit tobacco into the sand. "Tough Tiff," he said. "I've been waiting for you."

"I'm sorry about your mom," I said.

"I think it's funny," he said. "I know that weird, but it's true."

"I didn't mean to scare her."

"She needed it," he said. "She forgot about my dad for a while."

"That's good," I said. I would say nothing else.

We both watched as a trio of boys took turns sliding down the hill on the lid of a garbage can.

"Do you want to make out?"

"Fuck off," I said.

"I want to kiss you," he said.

"Okay. But spit that shit out."

He dug a finger into his bottom lip, hooked a wad of chew, flung it down toward the maintenance shed at the bottom of the hill. He grinned slyly and pulled me close. We kissed, and I could still taste the chew, wintergreen. I opened my eyes, and Bitsy's eyelashes were long like a girl's, jet black and fluttering as he concentrated. I wondered if he had ever kissed a girl before.

He leaned back and opened his eyes. "That's real nice," he said. He dug a hand into the pocket of his black jeans. "You're pretty rad." All of a sudden, he was coy, kicked the sand near his feet.

"Bye," I said, but then he was grabbing me again and pulling me down the hill. Normally, I would have punched any boy that did this. But I'd never kissed any of my combatants. This was weird.

At the bottom of the hill, the Quonset hut that once housed the sanding trucks still stood. The giant structure they had abandoned was covered in grime, decades of diesel exhaust. The windows were boarded up, even though they had long been shattered by my fellow trailer park delinquents.

Bitsy leapt up on a thick ledge, and grunted as he pulled a two-by-four from a windowsill, and the nails shrieked as they sprung free.

"Awesome," he said. He didn't offer to help me, just pushed himself through. I could hear his landing, as his feet took purchase on what sounded like a box of canning jars.

I hoisted myself through the gap and swung a leg around the sill. I eased myself down, and indeed, it was a box of jars, a case of empty baby food.

"You ever been in here?"

"No," I said. "It's been empty for years. My mom says it's a tax shelter for liberals."

"I don't know what that means," he said.

"I don't, either. Who ate all this baby food? Fucking weirdos."

Inside, the Quonset hut was an enormous cavern, reeking of diesel, the ghosts of snowplows. Bitsy yanked me to a torn green couch in one corner, the fabric stained from wet and dirty boots. I was not the type of girl to get yanked.

An idea sprung into my head. "This place is perfect."

"I know," he said. "Everybody does it here." He leaned in to kiss me again, but this time I pushed him away.

"No," I said. "This is where we need to have the play."

"I don't want to talk about the play," he said. He reached across the couch, and I wish I could say he was tender, but he touched my face like he thought it was a football. He kissed me again, and now I was sure he'd never kissed anybody before.

"It's probably cheap real estate," I said. "And lots of space for chairs. If David gets his way, he's going to want those velvet rows, like at a real theater."

"I don't know anything about real estate," he said and kissed me again.

I pulled away after a few moments. I wasn't sure if we were going too fast. I wasn't sure about any of this, really. "Maybe we could have a concession stand," I said. "My mother might let us use the popcorn machine for the night." He sighed and pulled me back toward him, and this time I felt his tongue. I couldn't help but recoil, not because it was disgusting, but because it was new. He stared at me, expectantly.

I didn't know what to say, so I let Tough Tiff do the talking. "Your mouth tastes like chew," I said. I sat there for a few seconds, expecting him to kiss me again, but he didn't. His mouth turned down, and he looked away from me. "It's not terrible or anything." I would have liked to kiss him, but I think he was traumatized by my description of how his mouth tasted.

When he didn't kiss me, I left him there, zipped up my leather jacket in a hurry, hoisted myself up and out of the window.

When I got to the Laundromat, I could hear him calling my name, but I just kept walking. It was almost dark, and my mother would be home soon.

FROM THE DESK OF TIFFANY TEMPLETON

My dad was the tax man of Gabardine, from January until the end of April, and sometimes during random months, for the frantic and delinquent. He prepared individual income tax returns and small business tax returns, and his office was our front porch. He had a favorite armchair, and balanced a piece of plywood on his knees to write on. He and his armchair guarded the trailer court. He had to be nagged by my mother to come inside. On days below zero, he sat uncomfortably at our kitchen table, and I know he hated every moment.

During fire season, my mother also begged him to leave his beloved chair; the sky was thick with smoke and the sun burned bright red. He refused, so she tried to convince him to wear a surgical mask like the weird cashier at the grocery store.

"It's not good for you," she always said. "You've already got breathing problems."

"I don't have breathing problems," my dad would respond. "I'm just fat."

He accepted his size. He was content in his armchair, carrying his own weight but always willing to lift more, taking the burden of income taxes away from an entire town. He was beloved. I know he must have been embarrassed by the things his size would not let him do, the things that he needed help with. When he got a flat tire, somebody from the garage had to come and remove the spare and change it in front of our house.

I know my father did a lot of the taxes for free because housewives and dirty loggers came into our house on some afternoons, after I was home from school, before my mother was home from work. It was always rushed because my mother would have freaked out on these people. It was bad enough hearing her freak out about the pies or jars of jelly that they left behind as the only payment they could afford. The loggers didn't bake or can, but when my father did their taxes, our freezers were always full of wild game, wrapped with white paper and scribbled on with black grease pencil. Even though our grocery bill was minuscule, it was not enough for my mother. My father's lack of income was like a splinter in my mother's pride, and she dug like a human needle. His kindness was yet another weakness, and she poked and poked, determined to not let it infect us.

Adults have that saying about death and taxes. I'm pretty sure they're not supposed to happen at the same time.

It was the eighth of May, and in Montana, that means the grass is green, but snow can fall any minute.

My father had never been one of those sleepy fat people. I know you've seen them, napping after a meal, like a bear.

As I approached the porch, I saw his chin sunk into his chest, so far down that the back of his neck was visible, and I knew right then and there. I bounded up the steps, and the porch barely shook, and that damn pile of mail slid from his knee.

I didn't call out his name. I didn't do the thing you see in movies, where they shake the person and repeat their name, louder and louder, frantic. I stood in front of him and considered things. I guess I had always been waiting for it to happen. In my mind, he was always dying, smothered by his own body, suffocating every day in our quiet house.

I considered things and stared at the back of his neck, so white and so unfamiliar to me. Envelopes and papers scattered around his feet, and I picked them up. I carried them inside and dropped them on the counter, and then I called my mother.

Chapter Twelve

THE QUONSET HUT WAS MY idea, but David was the one who thought of how to fund it. Of course, my mother was aware of the sand hill, knew about the Quonset hut, broken windows and baby food jars and all. I couldn't help but wonder if my mother had also made out with boys in that airless, dusty space. It was hard to imagine such a thing. But she had been a teenager once, and she had been a teenager in Gabardine, and it was a rite of passage, I think. In my imagination, she lined up five boys at gunpoint and forced them to kiss her until she picked the very best one. This was how she chose new products from the truck of Waterbed Fred, a taste test, and I finished all the samples that she threw aside. Those boys were lucky. They could have been devoured, or they could have been slapped with a tiny sticker from the price gun.

The reader board displayed 168. I didn't know who else knew the magic number, the goal weight. One hundred and fifty-six. I had heard that number for so many years that it meant nothing to me. I lived with two obese people, and I stopped paying attention after so many failed diets, even when the bathroom scale was kept in the kitchen, important like a microwave or something. The prices for unleaded, premium, and diesel were rising, as summer approached, and traffic from Canada picked up. All of these numbers were on our side.

My mother usually saw through every attempt to butter her up, unless it was David, and his brand of butter could have powered the menacing popcorn machine.

"Is that a new blouse?" David reached across the counter and touched my mother's shoulder. She would have punched anybody else.

"Yes," my mother said and blushed. "I actually ordered three, all the way from Spokane. I had to go to the goddamn post office to pick it up." She glared at me, and I grimaced. The post office was a quarter of a mile farther down the highway, not a real burden. "You know how hard it is to find decent clothes in this county."

"The bane of my existence," said David. "I want to burn Shopko to the ground. Big and tall shouldn't mean shapeless and unfashionable." They both laughed, and I was slightly sick to my stomach. David bought T-shirts in sizes too small. I guess this was his aesthetic. "Black is your color, Vy. It suits you."

"It hides stains," I offered.

"Not for you, Tiffany." David pointed at my jacket. "It washes you out. Only your mother can get away with black. You should be wearing warmer colors. Warmer colors would distract from the dark circles under your eyes. Everybody thinks so."

"Everybody?" They both looked at me, but did not respond. I took a deep breath, summoned my Dogwood training, reminded myself that I had a goal. And goals took work. Or bariatric surgery. "Maybe you and my mom could do my school shopping this year," I said, imagining a junior year spent in red sweaters and orange slacks.

"Oh, really?" My mother was suspicious, for good reason. "What exactly do you want?"

David made his pitch, and I stood back. He knew what he

was doing. He knew my mother would swing.

"Tiffany needs this," he claimed. "I think it is imperative for her rehabilitation."

"She already has a probation officer," said my mother. "And I've memorized the recidivism rates. You're wasting your time."

I was standing right there, but I was used to their only two topics: my mother's graces, and my lack thereof. Normally, I would have ignored it, busied myself with refilling the bun steamer, but I was still not allowed to touch anything.

"We don't have a place for the community to gather," said David. "Most small towns have potlucks, fund-raisers, quilting circles, and bar mitzvahs."

"Bar mitzvahs?"

"The world is evolving," said David.

"I am open-minded about faith," said my mother. "Even though my son was brainwashed by a cult."

"We don't have a town square," said David.

"We also don't have sidewalks or streetlights," said my mother. "Public safety should come first. There's always a Sweet getting hit by a car. And now that my daughter's back in town, we need to worry about a crime wave."

"You are the most powerful woman in Gabardine," said David. "Everybody knows that."

"Not the Canadians," said my mother. "Word hasn't gotten across the border yet."

Chapter Thirteen

NINE DAYS LATER, THE CITY council chambers were filled to capacity. David had choreographed yet another high drama. The four cheerleaders had been instructed to applaud. His mother had been instructed not to burn any sage to cleanse the tension in the air. Waterbed Fred and I sat together in the front row, along with the three old men from the play. There was not a van outside or a nurse lurking around, so I wasn't sure how they got there. Given the history of Gabardine, I wouldn't be surprised if there was a secret tunnel.

My mother didn't need a seat.

She didn't even wait for public comment, stood in front of the table during the roll call and the Pledge of Allegiance.

She launched into her speech and listed her demands. They were used to this. Mr. Francine grasped his gavel so hard that his gray knuckles were white.

"I've got a quote from a contractor," she said. "The garage is in decent shape. It has good bones. Good enough for a theater."

The other councilmen nodded, but Mr. Francine peppered my mother with questions about liability insurance, dust from the gravel pit, and most of all, money.

"I will pay for the materials," said my mother. "But I have my conditions."

"Here we go again," said one of the old men.

"Materials are one thing," said Mr. Francine, his voice slightly quivering. "But labor is the real expense."

At this, my mother squatted down and picked up her giant purse, plopped it on the table in front of the councilmen. She unclasped her purse, but didn't have to dig for the piece of folded paper that still had scotch tape on the corners. She waved it in the air. We all knew what it was, and I swear I heard Waterbed Fred gasp. The Bad Check List, ripped right off the door.

"Maybe you should stop taking personal checks," suggested one of the old men, genuinely trying to be helpful.

"Here's your labor," said my mother. "There's at least twenty able-bodied men on this list, and a couple on fake disability. I'm giving them four months to fix up the garage, which is more than enough time. After that, we'll call it even. A few months of hard labor and those knuckleheads will think twice about bouncing a check."

"Blackmail," called out an old man.

David leapt to his feet. "Out of order!" His mother reached for his sleeve and pulled him back down into the folding chair.

My mother's neck swiveled, and she stared the old man down. "I expect you to waive any of your bullshit zoning."

"You created the bullshit zoning," said Mr. Francine. Over the years, my mother had terrorized the city council over zoning regulations. She did not believe in handicapped parking spaces.

Kaitlynn raised her hand. She leaned forward, pulled at her blouse to expose the rim of her black lace bra.

Mr. Francine pointed at her. "Yes?"

"We need civic pride," said Kaitlynn, coached well as always.

The motion passed, four to zero.

* * *

IN THE QUONSET HUT, DAVID paced back and forth. Waterbed Fred and I watched him, but neither of us cared enough to stop him.

"I have one concern," said David, clearly nervous.

"You created a monster," I said. "You're worried that my mother is going to ruin everything."

"Yes," he said. "Now we have to call her a producer."

"I'll do the talking," said Waterbed Fred. I think he liked taking charge of this, a taste of his glory years. From what I've heard from my mother, nearly everybody who had owned a waterbed had also had a cocaine habit.

Five minutes after six, my mother arrived in her tilted car. Surprisingly, Waterbed Fred took her hand as she exited her car.

"I feel like I'm going to vomit," said David.

Inside the Quonset hut, the weight of a front-end loader and two sanders had worn paths, parked during their decades of use. The fluorescent light did no favors. David was always preaching about overhead lighting, but this unforgiving industrial brightness made me respect his aversion. Waterbed Fred's mustache stain was jarring, but even worse, I could see my mother had applied blush, and with a heavy hand.

"This will be a breeze," said Waterbed Fred. "We aren't going to have to do much building at all. Just a platform for the stage, really."

"I wanted a bathroom," said David.

"Dreams die hard," said my mother. "I double-checked with the health department. A Porta-Potty is all we need, and all I'm paying for."

"Of course," said David. "The office will be our dressing room and our backstage. We will have mirrors, which I will pay for of course. And we will have lamps. The last thing we need is for those old ladies to see themselves in fluorescent lights. Horrifying. I don't want that nurse back there with a defibrillator."

"Electric," said Waterbed Fred. "It's not just the lamps. This whole place needs to be wired, Vy. That's gonna be pricey."

"I've got three electricians on the Bad Check List," said my mother. "One is the slowest man I've ever met, and I still don't know how he got certified."

"Bill?" Waterbed Fred knew everyone. My mother nodded. "Head injury. Ex-wife threw a piece of firewood at him."

"I always liked her," said my mother.

"Whomever you get will rewire the place, and then we move into framing out the walls. The only place in this building with insulation is the office. The show is in November. We're going to need to put in a barrel stove and a chimney. And then we come in with a contractor. He's gonna blow spray foam insulation over the entire garage, even the roof. Four inches. It shoots out of a pack on his back just like *Ghostbusters*."

"Ghosts," said my mother. "I know what went on here. I don't have the money for an exorcism."

"Relax," said Waterbed Fred. "He sprays it all over, and then it hardens, and boom, you've got new walls."

David knew a lot of things, but general contracting was not in his arsenal. "It hardens? Is it smooth?"

"No," said Waterbed Fred. "He blows it all over, and it shoots out and does the trick. Once it's blasted all over, you walk away."

"What color is it? Can we pick a color?"

"No," said Waterbed Fred. "It's all the same color. He's gonna have to buy it in Fortune. They might not have enough, so he may need to go to Spokane."

"What color?" David, as always, had a vision, and uneven spray insulation was not part of it.

"Oh, kind of yellow-brown, I guess."

"Ochre?"

"I don't know what color that is," said Waterbed Fred. "It's kind of like the color of a head cold, I suppose. A bad one. Not green like a sinus infection, though."

"A snot cave," said David. "This whole place is going to look like a snot cave."

My mother touched David on the shoulder. "It's going to be fine," she said. "You'll make the most of it. I have no doubt." My mother would never have such kind words for me. Reassurance had always been my father's job.

"It's a steal," said Waterbed Fred. "You got a good price, Vy."

"I always do," she said. Waterbed Fred knew this to be the truth. He had delivered enough Cheetos and beef jerky to fear her business acumen.

ON MAY 16, THE SWEETS were already in Kelly's office when I arrived. I watched Rufus pick at the skin around his thumbnail until it started bleeding, and then watched as he wiped it on his pants.

The Sweets emerged, red Confederate flag shirts starting to show the wear and tear. Jimmy had a stain around his collar, and it looked like dried milk. I wondered if they only wore them for probation meetings, or if they had been clinging to their dirty backs for the last thirty days.

Rufus went in, and it was just me and TJ. I watched the clock, and I found comfort in the smell of the cough syrup.

"It's been a year," said Kelly. "The anniversary must be tough. How are you doing?"

"I miss him," I said. "I still expect him to be on the front porch, or in the kitchen."

"That's perfectly normal," said Kelly.

"He used to keep African violets," I said. "I know it sounds weird, but I miss watching him pull the dead blooms. He was a big man, but he was so careful. He could spend twenty minutes on one plant." He was a careful man, moved like a man who was used to breaking things. Furniture, car seats, and once an entire row at the movie theater in Fortune.

"He sounds like a tender soul," said Kelly.

"I don't know about souls," I said. "My brother ruined me on religion. But he was the kindest man I ever knew." I meant what I said. I forgot about it sometimes, but I think grief can change from hour to hour, minute to minute. Right then, it hit me like vertigo. My dad had been the part of my life that grounded me, and without him, I was left spinning.

"I visited the food bank," she said. "I didn't realize it was right next door."

"I used to help him on Saturdays," I said. "I guess I was doing my community service in advance."

"You aren't a bad kid," she said. "Maybe you take after your father, more than you realize." I said nothing, stared at her linen suit, and I couldn't figure out how she drove all the way to Gabardine without wrinkling. "TJ says they used to call you Tough Tiff."

"TJ drinks NyQuil right before he meets with you."

"But when is the last time you hit someone? Hurt somebody?"

"Besides my brother?"

"Yes."

"I don't know." I actually had to think about it. "Three years, I guess? Seventh grade? I think it was TJ, as a matter of fact."

"It's been three years since you physically assaulted some-body."

"Yes." This was true. "And I only gave Ronnie a flesh wound. He didn't even need stitches." I regretted that.

"The problem with nicknames is that they stick around for-ever," she said. "Even when they don't fit the person anymore."

I wished that weren't true. I wished that people could for-get things, especially my mother. She had always judged me, but she was even worse with my father. When she lost seventy-five pounds, the bariatric surgery caused her to vomit, and she could never control when it happened. Little pukes in the kitchen sink or beside the car door. She took out her frustration on my dad, and he never fought back. She was still pretty fat, but she lec-tured him about food. I think he took it because he knew she was scared. There would always be a fat person inside of her, no matter how much weight she lost.

Tough Tiff was still inside of me, and no amount of work with Kelly would kill her forever.

I stood up and slid my pages across the table, and Kelly didn't say a word, just let me go.

FROM THE DESK OF TIFFANY TEMPLETON

This is what I remember. My father's funeral seemed like it took place underwater. After his funeral, I tried to swim back up to the surface. Unfortunately, when I broke through and breathed again, I was determined to drown everyone around me.

I'd always taken Waterbed Fred's glorious mustache for granted until the funeral. In the church, the lighting was different, and after fourteen years, I finally realized it was dyed. I saw the stain around his mouth, a shadow, a bruise. He was drunk at the funeral, because it was on a Saturday and he wasn't responsible for ferrying thousands of bags of corn chips. He watched me grow up in the gas station, ripping his boxes open with an X-acto knife, and I guess the nostalgia and the beer made him extra emotional. When he leaned in close, I could only focus on his breath, the Pabst Blue Ribbon he had probably shotgunned in the parking lot.

"I'm really very sorry," he said, and put a hand on my shoulder, grasped on for support. That's when I saw it.

"Your mustache," I responded, because that's all

I could say. I was overwhelmed by grief, I was underwater.

"For fuck's sake, Tiffany!" My mother, who was standing next to me in the receiving line, slapped away Waterbed Fred's hand and pushed me out of the church and into the parking lot. She pointed at the first hopscotch box, spray-painted on the sidewalk. "You stand right here until you can behave your-self."

"He dyes it," I mumbled.

"People are shitty and they never tell the truth," she said. "The sooner you know that, the better."

"Dad told the truth," I responded, still swim-ming, still holding on to the secret, like it would keep me weighted, submerged.

"Your dad lived in a bubble," she said. "It was better that way."

I was the tough girl, so I stayed on that hop-scotch square just to prove a point. After the last mourner drove out of the parking lot, after my mother and Ronnie and the preacher came out of the church and locked the door, I stayed in that stupid box. I hoped my mother would notice. But she just brushed past me and sat in the car and smoked a cig-arette, like it was a normal thing for me to loiter in front of a church.

It wasn't just Waterbed Fred's mustache. That day, the world ripped open and revealed itself, and I couldn't look away. Instead, I looked deeper. That's when I started spying.

Monday, I returned to school. Now I was the girl with the dead father, but nobody said a word. It was okay to call him fat, but not okay to call him dead.

I didn't even make it through the first day.

We were still doing the Presidential Fitness Test in PE. David was sure that Coach Bitzche had added some requirements of his own, just to be sadistic. We had no choice. For the past three weeks, Coach Bitzche had counted our push-ups, forced us to keep going until we collapsed or vomited, or in the case of Kaitlynn, broke into fake tears. We ran the hundred-yard dash, the four-hundred, and the mile. We did sprints in the gym, dashing to the half-court line to pick up a chalkboard eraser, dashed back for another. We did the bench press, and although I had high hopes, Kaitlynn had beat me by ten pounds. I swear he saved the worst for that Monday.

A rope had always hung from the beams of the gymnasium, and until that day, I never gave it much thought. When he unmoored it, I watched the boys go first. At thirteen, the boys in my class were still basically monkeys. Almost all of them made it to the top. I was the first girl, and again, I think he did it on purpose. My class expected me to conquer the rope and maybe even climb up a second time, just for show. Unfortunately, all I could do was hang there, feet on the bottom knot. Red-faced, I tried everything to get hold and pull myself up with pure determination. No luck. When he told me to quit, I refused.

All I could think of was getting to the beams above, scrawled with initials, in Magic Marker. After I had dangled for a full minute, Coach Bitzche physically removed me from the rope, and I collapsed in his arms. I tried to break free, tried to go back to that rope, full of fury. He restrained me. My classmates were silent, and all I could think about was coming back to the gym that night and setting the rope on fire, watching the smoke snake up the rough knots, a line of flames climbing and climbing and finally devouring, and the rope would come crashing to the ground.

"Fuck you," I said.

I guess that's what started it all.

A conference was called, a rare night meeting, the only way my mother would agree to attend. She would not close the gas station, certainly not for a carpetbagger and a dumb jock.

At six thirty, she arrived, pissed off, and she let them know it.

"This," she hissed, waving her hand around the principal's office. "This is not important. None of this bullshit has anything to do with real life. Don't you dare try to tell me otherwise. My daughter does not need to know how to climb a rope. She should be learning algebra or whatever. Maybe you should offer a class on obscenity and how to be a decent person."

"I think that's the job of the church," suggested Principal Beaudin.

"Or her parents," offered Coach Bitzche, and caught himself. "I'm sorry."

"I will burn down your house," said my mother. "I have an unlimited supply of gasoline."

And with that, she exited, and I followed closely behind, navigating her wake.

When we got home, she threw her purse across the kitchen, and it flew and collided with the wall. Before she started carrying a phone around, her purse was still capable of an impressive trajectory.

She sat down at the dining room table, lit a cigarette.

"That Bitzche is at the top of my list," she said. "You watch him, Tiffany. You study every goddamn move he makes." Sometimes, my mother could read my mind. Just like with Waterbed Fred's mustache, I wanted everybody to know the truth.

That night, I pulled on black track pants in case I had to crouch, stuffed my pockets with gloves, gum, matches, a tiny flashlight that only worked if you stuck your finger inside and pushed on the battery. When I entered the kitchen, my mother was still awake, rare at ten o'clock. I was sure she would comment on my ensemble, but she remained silent as I walked past. She knew exactly where I was going, but I guess she didn't want to be an accomplice.

The Bitzches lived in a single-wide and defined their yard with cinder blocks, set a foot apart, spray-painted bright yellow. We had a problem with drunk drivers who thought the trailer park was a good place to cruise, sloppy laps with cases of beer on the dashboard, driving through people's yards and spinning out in mud season. In the winter, the plows ran over the Bitzches' cinder blocks, pushed them out of whack, and after spring thaw, it was amazing to see where they landed.

I crouched between the dumpster and a random pile of gravel, abandoned so long that trees grew from it. I felt a thrill in that darkness. All my life, I had wanted to disappear, and at night, in that dark trailer court, none of the neighbors could see me.

Most importantly, the Bitzches couldn't either. In the living room, Bitsy and his mom watched television, a dating show. My view was so clear that I could see the commercials.

When Coach Bitzche came home an hour later, I pushed myself against the dumpster, dodging the wake of his headlights. I watched him enter the house, and he passed his wife and son without a word.

The window at the far end of the trailer suddenly filled with light, and I could see it was the master bedroom. Dutifully, I watched as he stretched out on the perfectly made bed, still wearing his stupid whistle. For an hour, I crouched there, waiting for Coach Bitzche to expose some sort of weakness. Instead, he fell asleep. I didn't want to leave. I wanted to find his rope, but little did I know, it would end up entangling me forever.

I heard Ronnie's stupid diesel engine a full minute before he arrived, so I had plenty of time to creep around the corner of the dumpster. His red truck stopped in front of the Bitzches'. It was nearly midnight on a Monday, and I knew it was church night, so I stayed to watch. Lorraine and the baby waited in the truck, even though they lived four trailers away. The Meatloaf was no gentleman.

I saw the shape of Lorraine's giant hair when he opened his door, the interior light revealing a package he clutched to his chest, a flat cardboard box.

I watched as he knocked, and Bitsy and his mom never even got off the couch. It was late, but they just stared at the television. Now I knew why Bitsy looked so tired all the time. Ronnie walked right past them, all the way to the master bedroom. Coach Bitzche nodded when Ronnie handed him the package, and with his right hand, offered the Meatloaf a firm handshake. That was it. Ronnie left and drove Lorraine home. I waited another twenty minutes for Coach Bitzche to unwrap the package, but it remained untouched. When he finally left the room, another light flickered on. It must have been the bathroom, because he returned wearing pajamas.

I wanted to talk to Ronnie before I told my mother anything, so I went to his house the next day, an hour before my mother would arrive home from work.

He heard my footsteps on the porch and swung open

the door before I could even knock.

"Be quiet," he said. "Lorraine is taking a nap. She's exhausted."

"I saw you at the coach's last night," I said. "I didn't know you two were close."

"He's going to teach me a sleeper hold," he said. "He knows lots of things about hand-to-hand combat."

"I thought you were at church," I said. "You go to Idaho every Monday. You talk about it all the time." Which was true. On Monday nights, his church said special prayers for drunk drivers.

"Why do you care? You chose to be a dirty heathen, so it's none of your business." He tried to push the door shut, but I stuck my boot out.

"You're right," I said. "I was just walking past the coach's house, and I saw you give him a package. I thought it was weird, that's all. I know you've got issues with Mom, but the coach is her new archnemesis. I know how much you like revenge."

"I do," he said. "But if I wanted revenge on Mom, it would be spectacular. You would know. The whole world would know." This was true. "If you paid attention to anybody other than yourself, you would know I go to Brother Bitzche's house every Monday night."

"He's in your church?"

"Don't act so shocked," he said. "Our followers are everywhere. We look just like everybody else." I wasn't sure about that. Lorraine had to wear an ankle-length dress every time they crossed the state line, and in Gabardine, everybody wore jeans, except for the cheerleaders, and their dresses barely covered their thighs.

"Is he doing some sort of correspondence course or something? Why doesn't he go to Idaho?"

"He is a busy man," said Ronnie. "He does God's work every time a young man learns how to discipline his body."

"Gross," I said.

"I bring the church to him," said Ronnie. "And I'm proud of it. My pastor prepares his homework every Monday, and I deliver the good word."

I removed my boot. "Whatever," I said. "I just wanted to make sure you weren't messing with Mom."

"I could bring you homework," offered the Meatloaf, as I scurried off the porch and into the frozen yard. "You are my blood, and I would help you through the Rapture. We would go slow, I promise."

"The Rapture can't come quick enough," I said.

The next night, I waited until my mother got off work and made my report to her at the kitchen table. I made sure to mention Ronnie's offer to save my soul.

"Bible study?" She was incredulous. "That's the most disgusting thing I've ever heard."

Chapter Fourteen

ON THE LAST DAY OF school, I overheard the bonfire plans. David partnered with me in home ec because he had issues with food safety and he knew I washed my hands. Of course, I was doing most of the work because he was lecturing his four cheerleaders. While he crushed the potato chips for our tuna noodle casserole with a giant hand, he warned them about the party in the woods. In David's opinion, the forests did not contain trees, only alcohol and obscure venereal diseases.

He had good reason to worry, especially about Kaitlynn, always the most sexually adventurous. David was constantly trying to pump the brakes on her hormones. He sent her home to change clothes at least once per week. We didn't have a school dress code, but David enforced one of his own.

After his lecture, he returned his attention to the casserole dish, but continued to discuss his precious girls. "For the most part, I think we've got a successful team, which is rare for women. It's just like Destiny's Child," he said, washing the potato chip crumbs from his hands. "Except I've got four LaTavias."

"LaTavia got fired, David. You've got to have a Beyoncé."

"I'm the Beyoncé," he said. "Make no mistake about it."

"I wouldn't dare," I said and covered the baking pan with aluminum foil.

"You owe me," he said. "Don't forget that. You just left without a word."

"I was sent away by the court," I said. "I figured you read about it in the paper."

"You owe me," he repeated and slid the pan into the oven, twisted the dial to a number that could have been four hundred. Our ovens were ancient things. "I made arrangements. Bitsy is picking you up at seven o'clock."

"I'm not going to the bonfire," I said. "I'm not going to babysit your cheerleaders."

"I got you a date," he said. "Shut up and think about what you're going to wear." He leaned down to peer into the warped window of the oven. "Christ," he said. "I forgot who I'm dealing with. Just make sure you brush your hair."

FROM THE DESK OF TIFFANY TEMPLETON

You might have read in my file that I sat for a while with my father's body.

The counselors at Dogwood made a big deal out of this, but I know Mrs. Bitzche saw him first. I know she did nothing. Taxes are due on April 15. Everybody knows that. But Mrs. Bitzche was twenty-three days late, and I recognized the form right away: she had filed for an extension. I know for a fact she gently placed her tax forms on one knee of his dead body and our regular mail on his other knee, and just walked away, continued her route. I know he was already dead. The coroner told us he had a massive heart attack, and he would have twitched or flinched or something, and her tax forms and all that mail would have scattered on the porch.

I couldn't let it go. You can ask anybody, and they will tell you that my dad was the nicest man in town. Maybe he'd been dead for hours. I don't know. She could have called 911 and waited for the volunteer dispatch to contact the volunteer ambulance. Like a normal person in Gabardine.

I had spied on her husband, and it gave me no

satisfaction. I still wanted someone to drown.

A week after I spied on her husband, I left a knife in our mailbox for Mrs. Bitzche, covered in ketchup.

Two days later, I untied the mean dogs on First Street.

Mrs. Bitzche went to the gas station, not just to tell on me, but also to ask if she could get her tax form back. That made me hate her even more, but my mother was more concerned about an interruption in our delivery.

"You need to cool it with the Mail Lady," warned my mother.

The knife and the dogs didn't scare her away as I hoped. I honestly thought she would ask for a different route or something, but I didn't realize there was only one delivery person in Gabardine. I hated her even more for being so efficient.

I started writing notes. I didn't think they were that bad, considering. I never threatened to blow up any federal buildings, so the terrorist thing was just something the Mail Lady dreamed up. My threats were specific but vicious, but the only law I broke was leaving them in other people's mail-boxes, written on the back of their junk mail. Never real letters, but apparently, you're not allowed to open a mailbox that does not belong to you. And I wrote things that pushed her over the edge.

I hope you die in a fiery car crash.

Blue eye shadow is for whores.

I know you steal disability checks.

Someday, a dog is going to bite your tits off.

I've got an anger problem. Anybody will tell you that. I punch, I push, and before I became a B cup, I was known to throw boys down, known to wrestle. It's always been this way. I don't scream or say terrible things out loud; I write them down. But I guess you shouldn't write them down on the back of other people's mail, no matter how much you disguise your handwriting. I wish I'd been harder to catch. But in a town as small as Gabardine, you can only have one archnemesis.

At Dogwood, they controlled my anger with medication, because my mind can get hooked like a fish. I'm pulled. Anger reels me in, no matter how much I fight it, and someday I will figure it out. Maybe you can help me learn how to snap the line.

Chapter Fifteen

BITSY PICKED ME UP, EVEN though he lived less than a thousand feet away. I waited for him on our front porch, and I had brushed my hair. I made an effort. Bitsy, however, arrived in his battered truck. He opened the door for me, but it wasn't chivalry. He had to use a pair of pliers. His truck used to be red, but now it had a tan hood and blue doors. Salvaged from the junkyard, I guess. The day after his dad disappeared, Bitsy crashed his brand-new truck into the side of the Laundromat, but it wasn't a suicide attempt. He could only get it going thirty miles an hour because of the speed bumps. The cinder-block building chipped a little but didn't budge. I never understood teenage boys, but I assumed that when a ferocious tackle lost a football team and a father, he had to find something else to hit. Thankfully, he missed my juniper bush.

In May, it froze at night, and Bitsy navigated across unbreakable furrows of cemented mud, and in his headlights, the forest roads looked like the surface of the moon.

We rode in silence, save for the crash as he followed the tire tracks to veer off through a meadow, past a stand of tamarack trees, blonde since October. The trunks were the size of broomsticks, gray fingers of branches. I knew they would burst open in a few weeks. Bitsy dodged the trees, reflexes from the football, avoiding saplings that could lodge under his truck. My eyes caught the glow first, a lightening of the sky, and then glints of orange lights, the fire.

"You'll be fine," said Bitsy, as he parked his truck in an outer ring of vehicles, circled around the trampled clearing. Mostly high school kids, thirty or so, and I recognized a few dirtbags from the Bad Check List. I watched as one threw a car seat into the flames. I looked over at Bitsy for reassurance as the bonfire nearly disappeared in all the green smoke as the car seat caught flame. "Seriously," said Bitsy. I remained in my seat as he got out of the truck. I had no choice. Bitsy freed me with the pliers, and it wasn't how I had envisioned my grand entrance to my first high school party.

I didn't want to get too close to the fire. Or the kids. The green chemical cloud continued to rise from the pyre, so Bitsy and I took refuge among the trees.

Through the swirls and the fumes of melting plastic, Kaitlynn emerged from the acrid smoke, which was fitting. She laughed when she saw me, and I said nothing as she looked me up and down, a thorough inspection. I was used to it. Bitsy spit a plug of tobacco at her feet, but she didn't take the hint. Instead, she swayed on her feet, regarding us with slits for eyes, clearly wasted.

"Psycho and spaz," she said. "Sounds like a cop show."

"You're an asshole," said Bitsy. "You've always been an asshole."

"Whatever," she said. She slurred her words, but I watched as she threw her Diet Coke can at a group of freshman girls. She wasn't drunk. It became clear when she dug into her coat pocket, and removed a sandwich bag. The white bread had a glow of its own, not one speck of mold. We had learned about the danger of preservatives in home economics, and here was proof. She didn't care who watched. I knew this trick, another window from another house.

When she threw the bread into the woods, and I saw the flash of white against her dark tongue, I was certain. She flinched as she dry-swallowed the pills. She gave me a wry smile, daring me to comment. When I said nothing, she threw the empty plastic at me, ripped off her coat, and then her T-shirt. Still, I didn't react. Bitsy, however, looked away. Clad only in a bra and jeans with rhinestones on the back pockets, she glittered as she stomped past the fire, freshman girls leaping out of the way. She pushed Victoria against the trunk of a giant ponderosa pine and kissed her on the mouth. She must have been eating pills for hours, and I was sure there were more slices of white bread scattered through-out the forest. In fairy tales, there is a trail of bread crumbs, but Kaitlynn was a different kind of witch, and the green smoke swirled around her legs, as if she summoned it.

Now, Victoria removed her shirt, and boys I recognized from the football team hooted, wanting more. A few yards away, a freshman girl vomited loudly, but that did nothing to distract them. Victoria kicked her shirt into the fire, shook her boobs in our direction.

Bitsy had grown up here, and he had not experienced Dogwood, or David's free month of HBO. I felt the need to explain. "They're not real lesbians. Real lesbians are useful and dependable."

"Those boys are morons," he said. "I'm not like them."

"I know," I said. "I can't believe your mother is letting you hang out with me."

"She doesn't know," he said. He took risks, and that was attractive to me. I might give him more than friendship. If he kept spitting chew at Kaitlynn, definitely more.

"It's a small town," I said. "I threatened to kill her."

"True," he said. "But maybe it was worth it. They gave her a raise."

"What?" That familiar fury rushed back, and I took deep breaths, and instead of his mother, my mind flashed upon a girl with a blue mouth. The consequences of desperation. I would control my anger. I had been taught to reframe things at Dogwood, see things as they really were. I had been another mean dog in a yard. I exhaled. Bitsy's mother deserved the hazard pay. And I was on the first real date of my life.

"Sorry," he said. "I shouldn't have told you."

The boys threw a pile of winter coats onto the fire, and I recognized them, stolen from the teachers' lounge.

A burst and a whoosh as the sparks exploded toward the freshman girls, and they screamed and clung to each other. Typical. Except they kept screaming.

I looked closer, and they dashed away from bushes, a tree line suddenly lit with a blue glow. As the light brightened to glaring, I heard the motor, as the bushes burst open. My brother emerged, gunned his four-wheeler into the clearing.

He cut the engine and dismounted, stupid cowboy boots slipping in the muck. Nobody moved. We all knew who it was, but the freshman girls ran into the woods anyway.

Victoria threw a beer can at Ronnie, and it glanced off his helmet. He removed his leather gloves, flipped up his visor.

"You children are violating so many laws," he said, and the fire popped and swelled as if to prove his point, some teacher's blazer soaked with years of Lady Stetson. "This is an illegal burn, for starters."

When Ronnie saw me across the clearing, his eyes narrowed.

Kaitlynn stalked toward my brother, half a foot taller, and most likely stronger, years of being the base of every cheerleading pyramid.

"What are you going to do about it, Meatloaf?"

Ronnie tried to remove his helmet, too tight for a dramatic gesture. It took him several attempts to reveal that hateful face, forehead shellacked with a hunk of sweaty hair. He pointed at Victoria's bra. "Public indecency. Intoxicated minor."

"I should beat the crap out of you," said Kaitlynn. She crouched down into a boxing stance, wobbling slightly.

"Hopped up on diet pills," he said. "Felony possession."

Kaitlynn was outraged. She worked hard for her abs. She took a step forward and slapped her bare stomach. "Crunches, you pervert."

"Citizen's arrest," he said, and half of my peers groaned; they had heard this threat many times.

Victoria lunged toward me, grabbed my wrist. "Here! Right here, douchebag. She's breaking probation!"

"She's only been drinking Dr. Pepper," offered Bitsy.

Victoria dropped my wrist. "Don't you have a curfew or something?"

"It's only eight thirty," I said.

"You're so creepy," said Kaitlynn. "Stop pretending you're a cop."

"I never identified myself as a police officer," Ronnie responded.

Kaitlynn lunged for Ronnie's jacket, but he took a step backward. "Give me your stupid notebook," she demanded. We all knew about the notebook, his history of taking names at high school parties, even though most of them were fake. "Tonight, I'm going to burn it."

I was surprised when Ronnie reached into his pocket. I

actually thought he was going to give her his precious notebook, but instead he withdrew a can of bear spray. Kaitlynn shrieked when he sprayed her in the face.

"Self-defense," he said as she continued to scream.

The party was over.

FROM THE DESK OF TIFFANY TEMPLETON

I'm not a Peeping Tom, but our trailer court was perfect. I swear it gets darker in our trailer park than in the woods, or maybe we just swallow all the light like a black hole.

Mr. Francine was easy to watch. His windows were immaculately clean, and he kept a woodpile next to his house that was a perfect blind. He did not have a wood stove. I think he kept the wood because it looked appropriate. You don't know this, but he wears camouflage outfits all weekend. I think Mr. Francine really wanted to appear as if he belonged in Gabardine.

Unfortunately, he looked like a space alien. You've seen him. I watched him that first night, gray-skinned, large head, slight body, freakishly long fingers. His eyes are the only big thing about him, and they look weird set so deep in that gray skin. I figured if I spied long enough, I'd find out why his skin was that color. David likes to say that Mr. Francine looks like he just emerged from underground after a mining disaster. In the summer, we have stray dogs that roll around in the potholes, leap out of the dust with black, black eyes. That's what Mr. Francine reminded me of. But I spied on him and saw him in a bathrobe after a shower, and the dust never came off.

A year after I began to volunteer, we started noticing that things were disappearing. On Saturdays we did inventory, and restocked shelves, and there were always cans that showed up on our spreadsheet, but were nowhere to be found. My dad wasn't that concerned—he reminded me about charity and desperation.

One Friday night, I discovered where the cans had gone, and it was not out of desperation. Mr. Francine stole from the food bank after closing his office. He had a key, so it was easy.

I watched him drop a duffel bag on his kitchen counter, watched as he stacked twenty-one cans in a pyramid. I knew they weren't from the grocery store—at the food bank, most of our cans were dented or had peeling labels. He smiled and beheld that pyramid, seemed pleased with himself.

From the woodpile, I watched his front door open, flooding his yard with light. I scooted closer to the shadows, and he carefully navigated his front porch, his view blocked by the pile of cans in his arms. I watched as he disappeared into the stand of quaking aspens behind his house.

Besides my mom, Mr. Francine was the only person in the trailer park who owned his property. Of course, my mom found out what he paid, and she said she would never let it go. He also owned the half acre behind it, and that ring of aspen trees flooded every spring.

He returned fifteen minutes later, and as soon as his bedroom light was extinguished, I crept behind his house and stared into those trees. All I could see was a crooked storage shed, perched up on the rise of the mountains behind. Out of the flood zone.

The next Friday night, he had a stack of sixteen cans, and again, he lugged the perfectly shaped pile through his yard and disappeared into the darkness. I followed behind as quietly as possible.

Behind an aspen, in the full leaf of June, I watched a flashlight flicker to life inside the storage shed. Seconds later, the flashlight disappeared. Minutes passed, but I clung to that tree, determined, unmoving. When I saw the flashlight reappear, I snuggled as close to the trunk as I could.

When he passed by me, his arms were empty.

Three days later, I returned to his property. It was Monday, at ten o'clock in the morning, and I knew he was at work.

We had really old books in our public library, but I bet you had the girl detective books in Cleveland. I wrote down all sorts of titles in my notebook. *Nancy Drew and the Mystery of the Storage Shed. Nancy Drew and the Lair of the Town Clerk.*

It made me nervous to sneak around in the daylight. The sun flooded the inside of the storage shed when I opened the door. Tools, a lawnmower. On the floor, a blue tarp. When I pulled it back, I saw the trapdoor, new pinewood. I swear I could still smell the mill. I pulled the ring, and all I saw was darkness underneath.

Cursing, I ran the quarter mile to our trailer, returned with a flashlight.

A metal ladder had been screwed into the wooden frame. I shone the light and saw a dirt floor. I descended the ladder. Tough Tiff. The toughest girl in the trailer park.

Two hundred square feet, walls made of cinder blocks, turned on end. A chair, a cot, a carefully rolled sleeping bag. A stack of books, the flashlight glinting off the plastic jackets. Nicholas Sparks. Mr. Francine was a romantic, I guess, his little gray heart must have pumped out normal red blood. All along the walls, in perfectly arranged stacks, cans and cans of food. He had been stealing from the food bank for years. The stacks were taller than Mr. Francine, just like his filing cabinets at work. There must have been a thousand cans, each label perfectly centered, gleaming in the light. He must have dusted daily. A bunker. Mr. Francine was a survivalist. I would have pegged him as First to Die in an Apocalypse, but I was wrong. He was ready for a trailer park war.

That wasn't even the weirdest thing. He had scented candles there, too. Even in his bunker. I don't know what his obsession is. What kind of scent covers up the smell of the apocalypse?

All those cans enraged me. When I saw the brand-new can openers, I knew what I had to do. Three of them, the exact same model. He probably waited until they were on sale at Shopko.

It was cruel, I know.

I stole them.

The next time you see Mr. Francine, I hope you can see him for who he really is. You know something now, and that gives you power. Now you know why I did it.

He's not going to make it through the apocalypse, and I think that's a good thing, because I don't want him to repopulate the earth.

I know it sounds like a fortune cookie, but I don't care. Laugh at the man with a thousand cans but no can openers.

Chapter Sixteen

IN JUNE, ALL THE RIVERS were at their highest point. We were always warned about the undertow, but despite the cresting water, kids waded up to their thighs, watching weird things rocket past in all that rust, occasionally dodging an entire uprooted tree.

The high school students claimed the entire bridge, drank stolen booze and tethered inner tubes to the moorings, or yoked them to trees stripped bare before the end of the summer, skinned by clotheslines or twine. I never joined them.

The bravest boys jumped from the bridge. Three local kids had died, swept up by the undertow, but in Gabardine, death was part of our history, and drowning was better than incineration.

THAT MORNING, BITSY SHOWED UP at my front door, an inner tube hooked around each arm. At ten o'clock, it was barely fifty degrees, but there he was, shirtless. I'm not going to pretend that the sight made me swoon. Pale, and so skinny that his chest seemed caved in, and I don't think he'd brushed his teeth.

"Surf's up, dude." Crooked grin, charm attack.

"I just woke up," I said, peering out of the metal screen door. I didn't want him to see my pajamas, the enormous black T-shirt that had belonged to my dad, neck so stretched out that the collar scooped almost down to my boobs, the ancient black sweatpants dotted with light blue specks. I had forgotten to empty the lint trap on the dryer.

I let him in anyway.

I didn't know what was wrong with me. I was the toughest girl in Gabardine, but within ten minutes, we were sitting at opposite ends of the couch, eating yogurt with plastic spoons, watching my DVD of *Faces of Death*.

I sat there thinking that I should have been writing it all down. It was weird to finally be with a boy worth writing about.

"I don't have any summer clothes," I said. "I don't even own shorts."

"You got a pair of jeans you don't like?"

I nodded, and headed straight to my mother's closet, where she had hung her future skinny clothes. I pulled a pair of black jeans, twice my size, and dropped them in Bitsy's lap.

"We don't have scissors," I said. They'd gone the same way as the silverware.

"Jesus," he said, and slid a pocketknife from his own shorts, and began to hack away.

Suddenly, he sprung backward over the couch. He had a knife in his hand, so at first I was scared, and the less rational part of my brain convinced me that this all had been a setup and he had always planned on murdering me to get revenge for his mother. It was a relief when I turned around and saw that he had flattened himself on the carpet.

At first I was confused, but then I heard it. I had studied Bitsy's mother for an entire month, and I immediately recognized the jingle of her keys on a belt loop, the creak of a metal mailbox pried open, and the metal protesting again as it was wedged shut.

"Is she gone?" His voice was muffled by the carpet, and I didn't even want to think about how long it had been since somebody had vacuumed. Likely, it had been my dad, and he died quite a while ago.

"Hang on." From the couch, I watched Mrs. Bitzche take a wide berth around our mailbox, like it was poisonous, like she knew I was watching. She didn't even glance at our house. I guess I was expecting her to stare longingly at my father's empty chair. Instead, she powered past, and those athletic strides were familiar to me. Even at fifty degrees, she wore shorts, the official ones, the summer uniform. After she passed from view, I peered over the couch, at Bitsy's scrawny back, legs that would never be as finely developed as his mother's.

"All clear," I reported.

An hour later, we had eaten three Lean Cuisines. We each had a Chicken Alfredo and shared a Chicken Kiev, leaned across the vast distance between us as we passed it back and forth. He made me replay the electrocution scene three times.

I didn't have remote controls, for the television or the DVD player. I felt like a moron standing next to the entertainment center and pushing the rewind button with my finger. Ronnie stole the remote controls in 2012, after he caught me dumping piles of his protein powder around the dumpster to fatten up the pack rats.

Bitsy said nothing about the remote controls, and he said nothing about the plastic forks. I think I fell in love with him a little bit.

ON JUNE 20, THE SWEETS still wore their dumb T-shirts, but Rufus had fresh powder burns on his hands. Despite the heat, TJ still wore his enormous jacket, and the smell was terrible. But today, TJ did not drink NyQuil. I waited for him to reach into his pocket and remove the bottle, but nothing happened. He went in to see Kelly without his usual medication. Maybe we were all being rehabilitated. Maybe Kelly knew what she was doing.

Something had been bugging me, and I wanted an answer. "How come you don't ask me about my pages?"

"The stuff you write? Do you want me to ask you about it?"

"I don't know," I said. "I figured you'd be shocked or something. I figured you'd want to talk about why I did the things I did."

"No," she said. "I understand. I don't approve of breaking and entering, and I don't approve of spying on people, but I understand."

"Thanks for not ratting me out."

"I met your mother. I got gas yesterday, and she asked for two different kinds of identification. I paid with cash."

"I don't think she's racist," I said. "She's just a Libertarian."

"I think I caught her at a bad time," she said. "She was sticking a giant stick into a hole. At least that's what it looked like." I knew exactly what she was talking about, had seen it all of my life. I can imagine it, Kelly walking through the shimmer of fuel in the air of a hot summer day, the islands of pumps a mirage as the chemicals reacted to the sunshine. My mother and her pole, longer than the entire gas station, brought down from hooks that paralleled the gutter. My mother prying open the cistern, monkeying her hands as she dipped it down, until it arced into the sky. She read the numbers of the underground tanks, wrote them on the back of her hand, the diesel already dissolving the ink. But she remembered them. She always remembered them.

"Your mom is prickly," admitted Kelly. "I think she just wants to make sure everything is contained in its right place. Even if she has to use barbed wire."

"Bloody," I said.

"Yes," said Kelly. "But you're the same. You need things to be in order. You look through windows, and you think you see everything that's wrong. You write it all down. You shine a flashlight on it."

"I crawl around in the dark," I said. "I learned from the best. My mom is always waiting, just waiting. She knows that people are terrible. She's paranoid and suspicious. She always has been."

"Why do you think your mother is like that?"

"She was born mean," I said. "Everybody says so."

"Why do you think your mother is mean to you?"

"I'm a disappointment," I said. "Especially lately."

"You are not a disappointment," she said. "Maybe she thinks that you are exactly like her, and it scares her to death. She wants more for you."

"No," I said. "My mom cares more about disadvantaged youth. She buys them cashmere coats."

"Your mom is just a person, Tiffany. She's got the same problems as everybody else."

"That's not true," I said. "She controls the universe. Things wouldn't just happen to my mother. She wouldn't let them."

"She couldn't stop what happened to your dad," said Kelly. "She couldn't control the universe that day."

"No," I said. I felt a tinge of sympathy for my mom, and then I wanted to punch myself in the face. "She made him miserable. She made all of us miserable. She still does."

"You couldn't stop what happened to your dad, either."

"I know," I said. I was really starting to hate this appointment.

"But you spent the next four months trying to control the universe."

"I'm not my mother," I said. I nearly spit those words at her.

"No," said Kelly. "She's one of a kind. That's for sure."

"I wasn't trying to control the universe," I said. "I just wanted people to get what they deserved."

"You were in pain, Tiffany. And sometimes when you're in pain, the only thing that makes you feel better is to give it to somebody else."

I gave Kelly my pages. She could have some of my pain.

FROM THE DESK OF TIFFANY TEMPLETON

It's a good thing you only come to town once a month. If David ever met you, he'd probably hand-cuff himself to you. Not in a dangerous way. He likes pretty things and always has. His mother is the most beautiful woman in Gabardine, and David protects her like a museum exhibit.

Janelle was the cool mom, the youngest in the trailer court. She was the first person I ever saw use a hair dryer, and the last person I've seen that used actual hair spray from a can. She was stuck in the heavy metal years of her youth, and then she got stuck in a bad relationship. More than one. The biggest bad relationship was with David's dad, who just left in the middle of the night when David was nine. Normally, this would be a tragedy, but Janelle and David were the kind of people who thought the mystery was romantic. After they were abandoned, my mother began referring to David as a "disadvantaged youth."

Janelle was New Age, and she never stopped talking about it. She had powers, she had discovered them when a homeless person in Billings touched her forehead and said she was blessed. I'd never seen a homeless person, but I'd heard stories, so I was suspicious. Janelle's first big spiritual project was selfish.

"I can heal myself," she said. "I just know it."

"Sure," I said.

"I can heal myself," she repeated. "And then I can heal you."

"I'm not sick," I said.

"Everybody's sick," replied Janelle. "They just can't see it."

At this, I nodded my head and wondered if Janelle knew about X-rays and CAT scans. She wasn't very bright. I had figured this out on my own, though god knows my mother provided a nudge.

"Dingbat," my mother pronounced. "Harmless enough. But don't believe that hippie shit."

"She's not a hippie," I pointed out. "She's more like a witch."

"What's the difference? I mean, really?"

Janelle had dream catchers and crystals in every window, but we never got sun on that side of the trailer court, so the strings caught dirt and spiderwebs. Janelle had a giant piece of quartz that she rubbed on her forehead. Janelle had dried herbs she stirred into tiny pots of Vaseline and anointed herself. Janelle had a burgundy book that she wrote wishes in, and burgundy candles she found in Spokane that she lit to give the wishes some muscle.

Janelle also had an answering machine, unconnected to their phone, saved from 2011. She saved the answering machine, but more importantly, she saved the cassette inside, and every night at eight o'clock, she drank a glass of white wine and pushed play. It didn't matter who was in the living room. She wanted us to participate in her romance, I think.

"It's me. I'm not coming back. Don't forget to change the furnace filter."

Every single time we heard that message, Janelle clutched at her throat, as if this was the most heartbreaking thing in the world. I didn't see it.

I admitted this to David. "I don't get it. Is it some kind of code?"

"He cares. It's proof," he said huffily. "You don't understand."

When we were in junior high, David told me that he was sure of the reason that Dan had run off. Even as a child, David had been an obviously effeminate boy. David blamed it on himself. I think this was the first and last thing David ever blamed on himself, but it was sad, nonetheless.

Last June, their power was shut off. This wasn't shocking, since most everybody in Gabardine lived poor. Two weeks later, I caught Janelle in the Laundromat, the answering machine plugged into the wall. Listening to the message. Like most everybody else, she had not come to do laundry.

"I need it," she said, and I expected her to sound guilty. Dan's voice echoed above the whine of the fluorescent lights, the end cycle of someone else's clothes.

When I spied on Janelle, I wasn't expecting any secrets to be revealed, but I wanted to see how David was functioning without electricity. He was the definition of high-maintenance. When most people live in a brightly lit house, they cannot see anybody in the darkness. Since they had no power, the living room window was dim, lit with a single candle. I crouched down beside their porch to hide, close enough to see Janelle twirling around the living room, the useless answering machine clutched in her arms, held like a baby.

The next day, I snuck in when I knew Janelle would be out. The impotent machine was carefully laid on a piece of purple velvet cloth, surrounded by pieces of quartz and all the cassette mix tapes that Dan had made for her while they were courting. Janelle hoped she could use magical things, create a shrine to make the machine whir to life.

I stole it.

Just so you don't think I'm a complete monster, I made a point to sniff their furnace this winter. I don't know if she changed the filter, but I know what scorching smells like, all too well. I would have warned them.

Chapter Seventeen

ON SATURDAY, DAVID POUNDED ON the front door at eight o'clock in the morning. He'd read *Our Town* in the wee hours of the night, and according to him, it was a masterpiece. *The Soiled Doves of Gabardine* was destined for failure.

Between his tears and gasping breaths, I agreed with him, even though I wrote the damn thing. I knew he was mostly concerned with the actresses, whom he still could not tell apart.

"I will fix it," I said. "But you need to go away." I watched him walk across my mother's perfect yard, wet with the summer morning. I hoped my mother would give the phone back soon.

The reader board at the gas station displayed 161. Maybe my mom was on diet pills again, so desperate to hit the magic number. I didn't like it when my mom took diet pills, because she chain-smoked and wanted to have conversations.

I steeled myself and entered.

"I need money for wigs," I said.

"Wigs," said my mother thoughtfully. "I don't know about that. The people in this town already think you're a weirdo. And your hair isn't bad, Tiffany. It's just thin. You got that from your father. The only thin thing about him."

"My hair isn't thin," I said. "I like my hair."

"Wigs," my mother repeated, and she chewed on the word, thinking. Within seconds, she spat out yet another suspicion.

"Your spy games are over, young lady. No more lurking around. You can wear wigs and you can wear a fake mustache, but you will be caught. You will be prosecuted. This town is too small for disguises."

"It's for the play," I said. I really should have sent David to be the wig ambassador. If he asked, my mother would have collected real hair from the women on the Bad Check List. "It's for David, really. He's hysterical."

"I've only got a fifty-dollar bill," said my mother, and I was shocked, assuming I would be given the usual rolls of change. "I want receipts, and I want the change. Don't get any ideas. Don't think that I'm just handing out cash willy-nilly. I can write this off on my taxes."

"Charity," I said, vaguely familiar with tax laws, thanks to my father.

"I despise that word," said my mother. The purse sprung open, things glittered inside, contents a mystery. I was never the type of juvenile delinquent that swiped money from my mother's purse. I grew up frightened of the thing, battered black leather double-stitched and stitched again, the seams thick and dangling with unraveling white thread. It wouldn't surprise me to see her stirring the contents of her purse like a cauldron, using a giant spoon, green smoke collecting around her head. In a flash, she pulled out a fifty-dollar bill, crisp and folded exactly in half.

"I'm also going to need the car," I said, pressing my luck. "There are no wigs in Gabardine."

"Pay attention to things, Tiffany. There are wigs everywhere," said my mother. "Go lurk outside of a church potluck. Fake hair everywhere. And that cashier at the grocery store has alopecia. She doesn't even have hair on her arms, for god's sake. Like a lizard person." She stopped herself. "Sorry," she said. "Someday your thin hair may all fall out. Maybe your father's people in Pocatello are all bald-headed. There's really no way of knowing."

"You could hire a private investigator," I suggested.

"Let's wait until you lose your eyebrows," said my mother. "I don't think I can claim detectives on my taxes."

I'D FORGOTTEN ABOUT THE CONSEQUENCES. My crimes had changed the air around me, a swarm of bees I didn't see, but people prepared for the sting nonetheless. I just marched into the Ben Franklin, oblivious. Even though it was June, I knew the manager, knew he had already prepared for October, boxes of Halloween merchandise in the warehouse. I buzzed down the aisles, looking for an employee.

Consequences. I didn't recognize the first salesperson I encountered. He crouched down, hanging insulated socket sealers on a low-hanging peg. He stood as soon as he recognized me. Like I said, I knew the manager. Not in a good way.

"Out," Lionel said. "Get out of my store." Fussy as always, he grabbed my shoulder and marched me to the exit doors. Maybe a fake mustache would have worked on another employee, but Lionel never forgot a former shoplifter.

I stumbled out into the parking lot as he continued to berate me. I walked to the car, but he followed, waving an insulated socket sealer. To Lionel, I was a spark in a bad outlet. "I will call the cops! I will call the newspaper! I will call the corporate office!"

"Why?" I spun around and found Waterbed Fred. His Frito-Lay truck was parked thirty feet away. Parked poorly, but that was not unusual. "Why would you call the corporate office?"

Lionel collected himself and tucked the insulated socket sealer into his apron. "She's a thieving little bitch," he said finally. "I'm going to make a citizen's arrest." Lionel and the Meatloaf should become friends.

"She's just a girl," said Waterbed Fred. "Apologize right now."

"No," said Lionel. "I speak the truth. I communicate honestly and clearly. I was trained, you know."

"You manage a Ben Franklin," said Waterbed Fred. "I dated two of your cashiers. I know for a fact that you only make a dollar more an hour."

Lionel got huffy. "I am a professional, and I will be respected."

"I have a truck full of snack foods," said Waterbed Fred. "And today, Ben Franklin isn't going to get so much as a Ding Dong."

Lionel realized the depths of this threat. In a blue-collar county, snack cakes were packed in every lunch box. "I'm sorry," said Lionel. "I'm sorry I used that language. I would like to avoid this embargo."

I didn't know what that word meant, but I accepted his apology.

"I understand that she can't go into the store. I'm not about to run afoul of the law," said Waterbed Fred. "Tell me what you need, Tiffany. I'll run inside and grab it."

I unfolded the fifty-dollar bill, and he palmed it. "Wigs," I said. "All the wigs you can buy." Lionel's face lit up. I knew he was prepared. He was the type who waited to buy everything on clearance the day after a holiday, store it in the warehouse.

"Jesus," Waterbed Fred said. "Wigs?" He pushed Lionel toward the entrance, and I admired Waterbed Fred's stern demand. "You'd better give me wholesale prices," he said, and I watched them disappear into the store, the automatic doors swinging shut behind them.

* * *

EIGHT HOURS AFTER HE APPEARED on my front porch, I carried my box into the trailer park. David was still despondent. I knew this, because he was outside. In the sun. I'd heard enough of his skin care lectures to the cheerleaders to know it was a cry for help.

He brightened when he saw the box, probably thought it was another gift from my mother. He ushered me into his immaculate bedroom, still blindingly white on white. Even the handkerchief he clutched in his hand was white, but his eyes weren't puffy from crying, so I think he held it for dramatic effect.

The bed was perfectly made, and I purposely sat down on the white comforter, because I knew he hated the wrinkles, knew he smoothed out the quilted panels with his hands every time he passed.

I loved making David wait. He lunged for the box on my lap, but I slapped his hand away.

"Close your eyes," I said.

"I don't trust you," he said. "You have a history of violence. I will go wait in the hallway, and you can call me when you're ready."

"Whatever." The bedroom door closed behind him, and I could hear him pacing, the same creaking floor of every cheap trailer house. It took longer than I thought. All that cellophane, each wig individually wrapped, looking like small furry animals in colors so synthetic they would have been laughed out of the forest.

I arranged all eight wigs in a precise row, along the length of the bed, and spaced them apart carefully, an exact spread of my palm. David was already despondent, and the wigs were tacky things, so I hoped that my careful presentation would ease the blow.

"Now," I called out and stepped back against the wall.

He entered his bedroom, and gasped, not his theatrical gasp, but a real one. He threw the handkerchief to the floor.

In Gabardine, we have birds that suddenly appear in the dead of winter, in hues and shades that burst out of all that whiteness. The wigs were just like that. In a room that was meticulously monochromatic, the wigs actually glowed, the shades incredibly vivid, the colors impossible and strange.

Lou Ann Holland could have painted this. I shuddered to think of her, probably painting at that very moment, in her trailer house next to the Laundromat. I could almost smell the turpentine.

FROM THE DESK OF TIFFANY TEMPLETON

The problem with spying on Lou Ann Holland was that she didn't care if anybody was watching. She lived her whole life like that.

I started watching her in July, late at night, because the days were still so long. I leaned up against a concrete birdbath in her yard, hidden by hedges. Through her grimy living room window, I watched those canvases burst open like the damn peonies. I was mesmerized, and I hated that.

Lou Ann painted people, but I never saw her working from a photo, and there was never somebody reclining on her couch, trying to hold a pose. Maybe they were people she had known in her past, but made unrecognizable. Monstrous, skin improbable colors, lime green or tomato red. A woman talking on the phone, her face a nectarine. A child staring at a goldfish in a bowl, but the kid was orange and scaled, the fish painted with pale flesh. An elderly man painted like a zebra, cleaning his eyeglasses with a dirty cloth.

Lou Ann was fast, determined, occasionally frenzied. She could finish a painting in one night, and sometimes, I watched from start to finish. I'd climb back in through my bedroom window at three in the morning, exhausted, emptied, as if I'd been the one creating things. The colors swam behind my eyes when I tried to go to sleep.

For a month, I watched. One night in August, I sat down next to the birdbath, settled in with a box of raisins and a liter of Mountain Dew, ready for the show.

Dark blue, at the end of a brush, whisked across the canvas and left behind a box. Curved lines, the box became foreshortened, became an armchair. A note rang out in my heart, calling me. This was something familiar.

She continued with baby blue, and I watched her draw circles inside that chair, watched as she connected tiny circles to larger ones, until it was the shape of a man, made of marshmallows, the largest man you ever saw. I stopped breathing when the pose took shape, when the man leaned forward, chin in his hands, elbows propped up on the giant meat of his thighs. A man waiting in his beloved chair, waiting for his daughter to come home from school, waiting for the mail.

I went completely rigid, but I stopped myself from bursting through her door and slapping her face.

I jumped up and left my raisins and soda in her yard. Screw her, screw her, screw her. I ran home and crawled into bed. Shuddering breaths, eyes watering, I refused to acknowledge them as tears. I was tough, too tough for that.

The next day, I knew that Lou Ann volunteered at the food bank. I waited in the Laundromat until I saw her pass by, her purse under her arm, her shirt covered in brushstrokes that faded at the end, like tails of comets. Lou Ann cleaned her brushes, but as far as I was concerned, the rest of her was filthy.

I needed to see that finished painting.

Her house smelled like cigarettes and turpentine. Empty cans of solvent were piled on nearly every surface, and it would have been so easy just to burn the whole place down. Instead, I carefully lifted the painting, propped up, drying in the corner of the room.

My eyes stuck on his face, because the rest of him was unbearable. Grotesque, really. Shame lit up my face, hot, and I felt it swelling. I had watched her paint people, regular people doing regular things in regular clothes. For a month, I had spied on her, and this was the first time I saw a nude. The first time she painted somebody I knew. It was bad enough that she painted my father blue, but I couldn't forgive her for painting him naked.

I stole it.

Chapter Eighteen

THE BIGGEST NEWS SINCE MY arrest came to Gabardine: the National Christmas Tree.

I was totally okay with being replaced by a tree. This is what it's like to grow up in a small town. I made terrorist threats and stabbed somebody, but now the talk of the town was an Engelmann spruce.

At rehearsal, even the old ladies couldn't stop talking about it—something from our hometown would share a stage with Kathie Lee Gifford.

"Maybe Carrie Underwood," said Eileen. "Last year, they had the entire United States Marine Band, and one hundred foster children dressed like angels."

"Disgusting," said Irene Vanek. "Those poor kids."

"Maybe they got adopted afterward," offered Eileen. "They were onstage. Right next to our president. People could get a good look."

"You just described a slave auction," said Irene.

At last, we could block out the scenes in the Quonset hut. There was still work to be done, but Waterbed Fred assured us that we could rehearse without hard hats. The birds perched near the framework of the stage. At this point, it consisted of corners propped up two-by-fours, yellow string tied between them to mark the perimeter. Having those women so close to trip wire made me nervous. They continued clucking as David conferred with an electrician in the corner. That also made me nervous.

I hoped these women would channel this much energy on opening night. I made a mental note to check on medications and side effects, and if any of them were prescribed something that made them lethargic at night. Our show was at seven o'clock, and I had only seen them in the mornings or early afternoon. If necessary, I knew I could bribe the crappy nurse into holding the dose. I also wanted to double-check on incontinence, or the Soiled Doves of Gabardine would take on a whole new meaning.

"I heard they'd narrowed it down to eight," said Betty Gabrian. "No offense, Tiffany, but I'm glad your brother didn't get to choose." Ronnie took his job far too seriously and was unhealthily invested in the selection of the tree.

"He doesn't need any more glory," I said.

"Litigious," called out one of the old men, who had drifted to the corner, monitoring David as he supervised the electrician. Stunned at the outburst, we all turned to stare at him.

"Nurse!" David yelled, but as usual, the nurse was out in the van.

"Litigious," repeated the old man, and his two friends nodded. I knew they had dementia, and I think they thought they were at another city council meeting.

"You are getting a subpar education," one of his friends said when David looked visibly confused. "It means that dipshit likes to sue people."

Nobody argued that point. The women picked up the chatter again.

"I'd have liked to be on that jury," said Erika Hickey. "All those years I drove around with my husband, looking for just the right tree. One year I had diverticulitis, and I let him go on his own. That was a mistake. I sent him back to the woods twice, until he got it right."

"Typical," said Diana Whipple.

Erika was offended by this. "You didn't even know him," she said.

"All men are the same," said Betty Gabrian. "Furthermore, all trees are the same."

"Some trees bear fruit," countered Erika. "You are the most dismissive person I have ever met."

"Engelmann spruce," said Loretta McQuilkin. "They were hell-bent on an Engelmann spruce."

Diana Whipple harrumphed. "Those politicians know nothing. A real Christmas tree is a Douglas fir. It's been that way for centuries. Spruce shower the floor with needles."

"I broke a vacuum cleaner," said Loretta. "Needles everywhere, no matter how much you water."

"I believe in tree skirts," declared Erika Hickey.

Finally, something all the women could agree on.

TEN MINUTES LATER, DAVID CLAPPED his hands together to restore order and began to distribute fake hair to the ladies, pinching each wig disdainfully. He knew they were cheap.

Waterbed Fred crossed his arms as he stood beside me. We both knew that this would be entertaining.

David gingerly passed the three blonde wigs to Diana Whipple, Beatrice Smetanka, and Ruby Bardsley. The wigs were identical, the shade of hay and just as straight and thick. They were shoulder length, and as the women tugged them on, they really did look like prostitutes. But the kind that hang out at truck stops. "The Frostbite Sisters," pronounced David. Betty knew cheap when she saw it, and I watched as she bit her lip.

We had one red wig. Truthfully, it was purple in the fluorescent lights and nearly three feet long. Unfortunately, David had chosen it for the madam of the brothel. Betty took it from his hand but did not put it on, just draped it over her shoulder like a scarf. "I'm afraid I might be allergic. Let me try it on tonight, where we have a defibrillator."

"Smart lady," said Waterbed Fred.

Irene Vanek, the feminist, proudly yanked on the small brown pelt that looked like a piece of porcupine taxidermy. I think it was meant to be a wig for a punk rocker, but Irene was pleased to be given something short and spiky. It fit her personality, or at least the way she spoke to David.

Eileen Lambert was given a jet-black wig, parted down the middle. I shuddered, remembering her Native American roots, and hoped David wasn't being unconsciously racist. Her character, Miss Connie, was the oldest prostitute, and we could paint chunks of the wig silver, as long as it didn't match the metal of her walker.

Loretta McQuilkin and Erika Hickey were given the pair of curly brown wigs, and the curls were coarse brown clumps that sprung out randomly, even from the forehead. Loretta was supposed to be the drunk prostitute, and Erika the scullery maid, so I could destroy the curls by ratting them out until each woman was left with a halo of hair-sprayed frizz.

His task completed, David clasped his hands together and studied his actresses. With wigs, he could tell them apart.

"Perfection," he declared. "Time for vocal exercises!"

As the women made dolphin sounds, Waterbed Fred leaned close to me, concerned.

"Your brother came by my house last night," he said. "I let him borrow a bunch of stuff. Binoculars, subzero sleeping bag, collapsible hunting blind. Is there something I should know?"

"I have no idea."

"Is he hearing some chatter on the border? Is there going to be some sort of invasion?"

"My brother is an idiot, Fred. If there was going to be a war, I bet my mom would know before anybody else."

"True," he said. "But I'm going to fill up with gas, just in case."

RONNIE AND HIS FAMILY WAITED in the kitchen. He had to share his news with somebody, and he had no friends. Lorraine smiled at me, but her son was oblivious. I kind of liked him for that. He never reminded me of a toddler, more like a nectarine balanced on chopsticks. Ronnie preached about Jesus going out into nature, as little grim-faced Joseph clutched an old magazine, but never opened it. Like an old man, it seemed like he was just waiting for something bad to happen.

"Save your preaching for Mom," I finally said. "Let's go back to the days when you weren't talking to me."

"You tried to kill me," he pointed out.

"Not hard enough," I said.

He turned to Lorraine. "My sister sucks at everything. She can't even hit internal organs." He elbowed his wife, and she laughed like a dummy, like she should be sitting on Ronnie's lap, hinged jaw and strings. "My church is without a leader," said

Ronnie. "I got my orders directly from God."

I knew his pastor was gone, but unlike Ronnie, I knew the reason why. I said nothing as Joseph sat down at my feet, peering up at me, expectant. I don't know what he wanted. Maybe he wanted confirmation, wanted me to tell him that something bad always happened, and that he should run away as soon as possible.

"I don't care about Christmas trees," I said. "Seriously. You're wasting your time."

"I swear this is the best day of my life," said Ronnie. He dropped a ring of keys on the counter. Joseph rose from the floor when he heard the sound. He knew that they meant escape. When he grabbed for the keys, Ronnie pushed them out of his reach.

"I thought a wedding was supposed to be the best day of your life." I knew why he brought the keys, and I didn't want to take care of Lorraine. "Is this your only set?"

"Yes," said Ronnie.

"How is she supposed to unlock the door?"

"She doesn't need to," said Ronnie. "Jesus. She's going to be inside, you weirdo."

"What if she needs to go to the grocery store or something?"

He considered this. He shoved the keys back in his pocket. "I'm going to be gone for months," he said. "This is a special assignment."

"You're not getting paid for this, Ronnie."

"I'm a warrior for God," he said. "A true patriot. I've received my calling, and I must serve."

"Obviously," I said. "I don't understand what God has to do with a Christmas tree. I'm pretty sure he has bigger things to worry about."

His eyes narrowed. "Don't mock me," he said. "You of all people. I suffered because you were a heathen. I almost lost a kidney when you stabbed me." This was not true. It only required two Band-Aids.

I took a deep breath. "I've already apologized," I said.

Lorraine looked at me, dead in the eye. "Clear the way for the Lord in the wilderness. Then the glory of the Lord will be revealed. And all flesh will see it together; for the mouth of the Lord has spoken." She touched the crown of Joseph's head and smoothed his hair with a steady hand. "It's from Isaiah."

"Good job, babe." The Meatloaf reached across the kitchen table and touched her hand, and in that moment, I saw the truth. Lorraine wasn't an idiot. She suffered the church and she suffered the Meatloaf, all for a free ride.

He kissed Joseph on the forehead and Lorraine on the cheek, and then he fled.

We watched his truck through the kitchen window, back windows completely blocked with survival supplies. The sound of his engine blasted through the trailer court. As he drove away, Lorraine and I studied each other, and Joseph smacked his lips together.

"Goodbye," said Joseph.

"Good riddance," I said.

Lorraine laughed, and I think it was authentic.

FROM THE DESK OF TIFFANY TEMPLETON

David sent Thank You cards for everything, and over the years, I listened as he called people for their mailing address to tell them he was sending a Thank You card, which seemed ridiculous to me. If you were going to bother to call somebody, why not just say thank you and be done with it? He believed in niceties, even though he didn't mean them. He sent a Thank You card to every single teacher at the end of the school year, he sent Thank You cards to the sheriff after his yearly speech, and a Thank You card to the volunteer fire department during December, right in the middle of Christmas card season. His house had never caught fire, but he sent a card during the holidays just the same. Never a Christmas card, always a Thank You.

"Thank You is secular, and I respect religious diversity," he proclaimed, as if our fire department had Jews or atheists.

I've received two Thank You cards from David in my lifetime, both through the mail. The first was a painting on thick stock, when I wrote his paper on Harriet Tubman. The second card came last year, and when it opened, played a tinny version of "Send in the Clowns," his expression of gratitude for perming Janelle's hair, because he was allergic to the fumes. His Thank You card collection was impressive, and his mother didn't mind spending all that money on stamps, even though they couldn't always pay their power bill. Many of his cards could have been literally walked across the street. I coveted his collection, perfectly organized by color and pattern, in a Lucite box that had once held rocks from his ill-fated Rocks and Fossils high school club. I never collected anything. Now, I guess you could say I collect felonies.

At my father's funeral, I didn't hear a word, didn't even know what denomination it was or why my mother had picked that church or the preacher. I know that the Meatloaf had requested the funeral be held at his church in Idaho, but was flatly denied. As the preacher spoke about a man he never knew, I looked around the church. I couldn't believe it was full and not packed with people from the Bad Check List. These were people who were mourning, who knew my gentle father, who came to honor his kind soul. Waterbed Fred, and all of the residents of the trailer court, except for the Mail Lady and Bitsy. The McGurtys were there, without any of their children. Even TJ McMackin and his brother were there, and it didn't bother me that they were wearing giant winter jackets. Betty Gabrian and Lou Ann, who both cried; I saw it with my own eyes. The two guys from the garage in town, who rescued him when he got the flat tire. I counted at least twenty people who depended upon my dad to do their taxes, and another twenty from the food bank. Even Lorraine's family showed up, a whole row of Sweets on their best behavior.

It was an urge that built up inside me, took over until it was released. I needed to send them Thank You cards, even though I was three months late. Normal people would call it a conscience, but my mother has convinced me that I don't possess such a thing.

I knew I would never wear the dress from the funeral again, and I also knew my mother kept the receipt. I asked to borrow the car, to return the dress to Shopko, and I don't know if it was grief, but she agreed, as long as I brought her the money, the exact total.

After returning the dress to Shopko, I drove to the Ben Franklin. David had taught me only to strike on weekday afternoons, when the store was at a lull, the cashiers watching the clock like zombies, waiting to lock the doors, but it was a Saturday. The Ben Franklin had two extra cashiers on Saturdays, just to deal with the masses of ladies who needed scalloped paper for their scrapbooking projects or dried eucalyptus for ever-expanding wreaths, new inventory hot-glue-gunned until the wreaths were bigger than their children.

In the greeting card aisle, I made sure I was alone, and I grabbed the first clear plastic box of Thank You cards. Holding my head up high, trying to look like I belonged amongst the arts-and-crafters,

I stepped out into the main aisle. David tried to teach me how to appear inconspicuous, ironic for someone so flamboyant he could probably be seen from space. As I walked back toward the dressing room, I passed a flock of women fingering lengths of bugle beads, a herd at the fabric-cutting station, clutching at their numbers. The noise of the cloth guillotine made me remember that I had forgotten my scissors, usually tucked into the inner pocket of my jacket.

I veered left into the sporting goods aisle, and my eye caught on a pearl-handled penknife. It hooked me, and after what I'd witnessed in the windows of the trailer park, I decided that I could use the protection.

At Ben Franklin, the bathroom doubled as the dressing room, and I sat on the upholstered bench and realized my conundrum. The knife was encased in plastic, and I needed the knife itself to open its own packaging.

The Thank You cards were easy enough. I used my fingernail to pry open the bottom of the package, and they slid into my hand. I stood and stuffed them down the front of my jeans, and turned around in front of the mirror. The bulge was barely visible. As I studied the knife inside its plastic prison, I broke out in a sweat. I tried to pry it open with my fingernails, but it was impossible. I felt around in my pockets, looking for some sort of tool, but only found loose change and a cigarette lighter.

I didn't even think twice about melting the

plastic. I watched it brown and bubble and warp, and within seconds, the knife was in my jeans pocket. I stuffed the plastic into the wastebasket, covered it in a giant wad of toilet paper.

I should have walked right out of the store, but against the far wall, I noticed the seasonal items had changed, among them a stack of furnace filters. I thought of Janelle, and I stood in front of the display, but realized I didn't have a clue what size they needed, and that there was no way I could stuff a furnace filter down the front of my jeans.

I was startled when I felt the hand on my shoulder. Honestly, I nearly screamed.

A middle-aged woman had smelled the melting plastic, and alerted the manager. Where I live, we are always sniffing the air, because of the forest fires, and because we don't trust the volunteer fire department to get there in time. The Soiled Doves of Gabardine were proof of that.

When streams and creeks flow into rivers, it's called a confluence. All those things coming together, all those currents creating the undertow we were always warned about. This moment was my confluence.

Fortune had three cops, and apparently, my shoplifting was so heinous that it required all of them. I did not hear any sirens in the parking lot, and I was thankful for that. I could have given them a Thank You card. They were identical—deeply tanned, blond mustaches, square jaws. Two remained in the doorway, watching nonchalantly. This was not a hostage situation.

I surrendered the Thank You cards to the third cop, but I said nothing about the knife.

The grand total was three dollars and one cent, so the third officer wrote me a ticket, didn't cuff me or take me to jail. In the back pocket of my jeans, I had twenty-nine dollars and seventy-four cents, the money from returning the dress. In a box in the trailer court, I had over twenty thousand dollars. When I did the math, I could have afforded exactly 6,689 packs of Thank You cards. We don't have a sales tax in Montana, so the math was easy.

"Show up in court on Monday," said the cop. "First offense, easy judge, less than ten dollars. You're lucky. It's petty theft."

"There's nothing petty about this," said the store manager.

"Jesus, Lionel. She's just a kid. And she was stealing Thank You cards."

"I want her prosecuted to the fullest extent," said Lionel. "She could have burned down the entire store."

"Get over it," said the cop. He had obviously dealt with Lionel before. "Call your parents," he instructed, and before I could dial, all three left, leaving me alone with Lionel.

Lionel didn't know me, didn't know who my mother was. I took advantage of this. I called Ronnie. I still don't know why. He was the last person on earth who would be cavalier about thievery.

"Hi, Dad."

"What the hell? You're sick in the head, Tiffany. He's only been dead for three months."

"I know, Dad."

"Knock it off!" Ronnie shouted through the telephone. "You can't prank call me. I know your voice. I hate your voice."

As Lionel listened and tapped the Thank You cards with his index finger, I explained things to Ronnie. As soon as I mentioned shoplifting, Ronnie hung up.

He made the drive in less than twenty minutes, and for once, I was thankful that he was so rigid and strange. Lionel didn't think twice about letting me leave with a man who tucked in his shirt and wore a belt.

I expected a speech, but Ronnie was cold as ice, drove back to Gabardine without a word. Thankfully, he passed the gas station. Out of habit, I looked for my mother's car, but then I remembered it was still in the parking lot of the Ben Franklin. I started to hyperventilate, just as Ronnie turned off the highway to the trailer park, and eased into our driveway.

"Please don't tell Mom," I said. "I'll figure out how to get the car back. I can hitchhike."

"You aren't breaking any more laws today," he said.

"That's not even a law," I said. "It's like an ordinance or something."

"I don't know what to do with you," he said.

"Nothing," I said. "Just forget this even happened."

I reached for the door handle, and he snapped. He reached across and grabbed my hand. "You're not getting out until I have a plan."

"What the hell, Ronnie? I'm really sorry, and I won't do it again."

"Give me your hand," he said, and I obeyed. He reached below his seat and removed a fanny pack, always prepared for any kind of emergency. "I can't just let this go," he said. "I made an oath." His face had transformed, I swear to god. He was monstrous. More than anything, he hated being made a fool.

"It was just petty theft," I said as calmly and softly as I could. "There was a cop there. He didn't think it was that big of a deal. And he was a real cop."

That was the wrong choice of words. "Real cop?" He slammed his fist against the windshield, and I watched the safety glass crack and ripple outward, like water, another confluence. "I'm sick and tired of you disrespecting me. Disrespecting what I do!"

He yanked out a handful of zip ties from the fanny pack, and I just stared at him. When I realized he was going to zip-tie my hands together, I reached for the door handle and heard it lock automatically. My brother and his lightning reflexes, my brother the crime fighter. I had reflexes of my own. A fire lit inside of me, one that I knew could quickly blaze out of control.

I glared at him, felt the blaze rise into my chest. "Remember how your pastor disappeared?"

"Kidnapped," said Ronnie. "We think he was kidnapped."

"He was a criminal," I said and relished every word that came from my tongue.

"You are full of sin," he said. He looped a zip tie, and he dangled the circle in front of me. "You are a liar, and you will burn in hell for your disrespect."

"He fled town, Ronnie." I knew more, I knew so much more.

"You are an evil person," he said. "You are going to atone for your words."

"You broke worse laws than me, Ronnie. You're just too much of an idiot to realize it."

I winced when he screamed, the truck filled with his primal noise, and he slammed his hands on the steering wheel. For the first time, I was genuinely afraid of him.

"Put your hands through," he said. "Let's do this the easy way."

"Unlock the door," I said, but I knew things were in motion.

When he grabbed me, I didn't react in my usual way. I didn't punch him.

I dug into the pocket of my jeans. When I flicked open the pearl-handled knife, he stared at me strangely, like he had always expected this to happen.

I stabbed him once, but that was enough.

Chapter Nineteen

ON JULY 18, I ENTERED city hall, and Mr. Francine's office was jammed with people. I paused in the doorway and wondered if I had the wrong day, but then I saw they were Sweets, too many to count.

A middle-aged man pounded on Kelly's door with his fist, wearing the same stupid Confederate flag T-shirt as Jimmy and Phil. Probably their dad. I think Kelly had locked the door from the inside.

Mr. Francine clutched the phone to his ear with white knuckles. I'm sure he was calling 911, even though it was in the same building. A woman next to me was also wearing the T-shirt, but she was old and seemed sober. She looked me up and down, and I was repulsed.

"I know who you are," she said. I tried to move away from her, but the crowd made it impossible. "You're that spoiled rich girl."

"Yes," I said. It was better just to take it. The Sweets loved explosives, and I didn't want this siege to end in a mass casualty. I did my best to stay calm and seem friendly. "How's Lorraine?"

"Fine," she said. "Fine as can be. We're keeping that kid, so don't get any ideas."

"Ronnie isn't the father," I said.

"We're keeping the kid, and we're keeping the flat screen. Consider it a dowry."

Now the man kicked at the door, and demanded that Kelly come out. The room swelled with noise as other Sweets began to shout. The crowd pushed forward, and I was shoved into the old woman.

"You need to respect your elders," she snarled, spitting out the words. I recoiled when I felt the moisture on my face.

"You are a shriveled little racist," I said. "And you smell like cat pee."

I planted my feet in as wide a stance as possible, ready for a brawl.

Thankfully, Sheriff Schrader burst past, rushing into the room in a bulletproof vest that was too small, but carrying an extra-large megaphone. I jumped back and watched as Mr. Francine hung up the phone, and picked up a scented candle, waving it around his desk like a blessing.

The megaphone was raised, right next to my head.

"SWEETS. DISPERSE. I REPEAT. SWEETS. DISPERSE IMMEDIATELY."

My ears rang. This was not the first time the sheriff had used the megaphone for the Sweets, or uttered those words.

The Sweets pushed me as they swarmed the exits. Sheriff Schrader held up his nightstick, and stopped Jimmy and Phil, and their father.

"You need to apologize," he said.

"We need riot gear," said Mr. Francine.

"You never told us she was black," said the father.

"I've also got my gun," said Sheriff Schrader. He dropped the megaphone on Mr. Francine's desk and touched his sidearm. He pointed his nightstick at the father: "None of you are allowed on these premises ever again. Tomorrow, you are going to mail a letter of apology." He pointed at Jimmy and Phil: "And the two of you are going to mail written confessions."

Before the Sweets could bolt for freedom, Sheriff Schrader dug into his pants pocket and removed a crumpled dollar bill. He tossed it at Jimmy, but it fell limply to the floor. "For stamps," said Sheriff Schrader.

TEN MINUTES LATER, THE DOOR opened and Kelly summoned me into her office. I knew where she kept her Kleenex. She dabbed at her makeup, but her eyes had barely welled.

"I'm sorry," I said.

"Don't worry about me," she said. "This isn't the first time I've had to deal with people like that. We're here to talk about you."

"I know this town can be cruel," I said. "Anything different freaks them out."

"People have that same fear everywhere you go," she said. "It's not just Gabardine."

"I beat the hell out of any kid who made fun of my dad. I made sure they got to know what real fear felt like. I made sure to leave a mark to remind them."

"Did it change anything, Tiffany? Did acting like a bully make your dad skinny?"

"No," I said.

"Maybe your dad liked being heavy. Maybe he had his reasons."

"Why would anybody want to be fat?"

"Protection," she said. "Comfort. We all want those things."

I thought about it. I grew up with parents who were obsessed with food. In good ways and bad. Sometimes, I think my dad just went along with my mom's crazy schemes.

They tried diets. They clung to the rituals, held on with all four hands, all the spells and potions of weight loss. With every diet, there was magic in the first week, but then it stalled out, and then they shouted at the sky and shook their fists. Nothing stuck, except the fat.

My dad was supportive when my mom decided to have the surgery. It was her money. He was the one who kept the calendar, the countdown until she would get the knife, he was the secretary of the fat.

The last month before the surgery, she got crazy, like she was having a baby or something. But the opposite. She shopped for skinny clothes, hung them in her closet.

I sat on her bed and watched her put these things on hangers, and my dad questioned her. It was one of the only times he questioned her.

"How do you know what size you're going to end up?"

"Don't be an asshole, Ronald."

"I'm serious," he said. "Even skinny women are different sizes."

"I'm not going to stop until I'm a six." And then she started crying, and I think she was waiting for my dad to say something corny, like you'll always be a perfect ten in my eyes. Instead he left the bedroom, and I remained on the bed, surrounded by all the cardboard tags from her new clothes, and the tiny strings of plastic they had been yanked from.

I slid my pages across the table. Kelly had had a hard day, and I would leave her be. I'm sure she wanted to find some protection and comfort of her own.

Chapter Twenty

TWO MONTHS HAD PASSED SINCE we started work on the Quonset Hut, but David and I were still cleaning. The garage floor had been scrubbed, and the insulation had been blown into the framing. However, the office, the place where Bitsy and I shared our first kiss, had been neglected. For a reason.

In November, this would be our backstage and our dressing room. Today, it was still a hoard of moldering newspapers, cans of cigarette butts, and animal feces.

David knew better than to make me do it on my own, but I might as well have been by myself. David chose to wear tennis whites to conduct the deep cleaning, and was scared to touch a thing.

I wore my ragged jean shorts, a bandana tied around my head to keep the sweat from dripping into my eyes. The Quonset hut was boiling hot.

David watched as I poured bleach into a bucket. "You have a boyfriend now," he said. "You really need to try harder with your personal appearance."

"I'm cleaning, David." For once, I wished for his terrible cabal. "Why aren't your girls helping us?"

"Becky and Caitlyn are supposedly learning how to sew," he said. "The learning curve is going to kill me."

"Are they taking a class?"

"No. They went to the public library for the first time in their lives and checked out a book."

"I'm glad you are supporting literacy, David. But we really need help." I pointed at a portion of the office wall where, at eye level, five holes cratered the sheetrock. Some teenager had punched completely through. I admired the strength and the accuracy, but I didn't know if we had enough spackle. I wouldn't be surprised if it had been my teenage mother, freakishly strong from her manual labor at the gas station. Her aim was still lethal, and she proved it whenever she launched her purse at things.

"Kaitlynn is still recovering," said David. "Your brother could have done permanent damage to her eyes. I keep telling her to sue. It's been two months, but every time I see her, she still weeps."

I wasn't sure if her tears were from the bear spray, but I didn't want to say anything. I knew why Kaitlynn was the most powerful of the cheerleaders. I'd witnessed it many times. Her fake tears were weapons and as useful as her boobs.

"They are drifting away," said David sadly. "I can feel it. It's been happening since we lost the football team." I said nothing, scooped a pile of phone books into a black garbage bag. David watched me work, leaned against the wall, and sighed. "There is nothing sadder than cheerleaders without a sport to cheer for."

"Then they shouldn't exist," I said. "Disband them. Release them into the wild."

"That's ridiculous," said David. "You can't have a high school without cheerleaders." He reached for the broom, and I thought he was going to sweep up rat poop, but instead he held it like a prop. "They don't see the point in practicing, and I actually have empathy for them. Can you imagine? Empathy. Except for Becky. She needs to lose like ten more pounds, and cheerleading practice is much easier than following her around all day, counting her calories."

"I don't care about your cheerleaders, David. Go take over a Girl Scout troop or a beauty pageant or something."

"That's homophobic," he said.

"Really?" I was tired of this conversation. "It's not homophobic to say that all gay men are clean freaks. It's a fact." I knew what his bedroom looked like. "Obviously, you are okay with filth. You haven't helped at all. I can't wait to tell my mother you are a confirmed heterosexual."

This broke him out of his reverie, and he began to push the broom; the rat poop became a pyramid in the corner of the room. He liked getting presents from my mother.

"If I started a new sport, would that be really heterosexual?"

"The most," I said.

"Damn," he said. To his credit, he swept for another five minutes before he dropped the broom, and the clatter as it hit the concrete floor startled me. "I've got a plan," he said. He rubbed his hands together, the evil mastermind, and he was method acting as always.

"We don't need any plans, David. We need to clean this room."

"This is top secret," he said.

"It always is."

"I've got a sport, and I think you're going to like it."

"I doubt it."

"Revenge," he said.

"Okay," I said. "I like revenge, but I don't think your cheerleaders can find library books about it."

"They don't need books," he said. "Our target is Ronnie."

I was in. "Do I need a helmet?"

* * *

I TURNED SIXTEEN THAT TUESDAY. I wasn't the type of girl to have a sweet sixteen party, and after Dogwood, I expected nothing.

I woke up late on another summer day, already warm as I dragged myself to the gas station to check in, kind of hoping that my mother had done something special this year. The reader board revealed that fuel had climbed another two cents, but my mother had dropped down to 160, and maybe my mother was giddy, so close to the magic number.

Nope.

"There," she said, and pointed to the shelf underneath the cash register. "I know that's what you're looking for."

A universal remote, still in the box, straight from Shopko, on sale, the price tag halfheartedly removed. "Since your brother has gone on a mission from God, I figured we were never getting the remotes back from him."

"Thank you," I said. "I honestly wasn't expecting anything this year."

"I know it absolutely kills you to walk across the living room and push the play button," she said. "Now you know I care." The universal remote would control the DVD player and our elderly television set, only two things. I wish life were that simple.

"If your brother gets hung on a cross, you're the only kid I've got left."

"That's true," I said. "I'm sorry I've been so terrible to you."

Before she could respond, Kaitlynn's Geo Metro pulled up in front of the window, and we both could hear a terrible noise emanating from the hood. Inside the car, a bunch of hands waved, but it was Bitsy who emerged. This was bizarre.

He clearly thought so, too. He entered the gas station and nearly tripped on the rubber mat, his eyes looking everywhere but my mother. I clutched the universal remote to my chest. I had this fear that David had sent Bitsy to break up with me on my birthday, just because he felt like it.

Bitsy opened his mouth, and although it was David's script, it wasn't a breakup.

"Mrs. Templeton," he said.

"Tell that girl she needs to change her fan belt," said my mother, tapping on the window with her finger. "She'd better move it out of the damn parking lot before it dies here."

"Mrs. Templeton," he said, another attempt. "I'm here to ask your permission to take Tiffany for the afternoon."

"In that car? I don't think that car is going to make it around the block."

"It's a surprise party," he said.

"That's not how surprise parties work, young man. You're supposed to hide in somebody's house and jump out when they walk through the door. Unless they are morbidly obese. Don't surprise them. I know what can happen."

"Dad wasn't surprised," I pointed out.

"You don't know that, Tiffany. Maybe *his* mother"—she glared at Bitsy—"itemized too much."

He bit his lip. "I don't know about my mother's taxes," he said. He stood straighter and looked her directly in the eye. "I'm here to ask your permission to take Tiffany for the afternoon. I respect your rules and I respect her probation, and that's why I want to ask you first."

"Fine," said my mother. "Just get that girl to move her car."

"It's a tea party," said Bitsy. I guess he thought that would be helpful, but he looked like he was going to vomit.

"Oh, that David. He's a darling." She nodded at me, but as I circled around the counter, she stopped me.

"Oh, Tiffany. I almost forgot!" She fished beneath the cash register and threw a pack of AAA batteries at me. When I caught them, I wasn't sure if she had really bought them for the remote control, or just hadn't put them out as inventory. It was most likely to impress David, even though Bitsy was the boy I wanted her to notice.

KAITLYNN'S CAR DID MAKE IT around the block and deposited the seven of us and a giant wicker picnic basket in front of the gloomy garage at the sand hill. It felt like the beginning of a horror movie.

David had stuffed the basket full, but oh so carefully. First, he removed a plastic tarp, rolled tightly with at least ten rubber bands. We all watched in silence until the tarp was unfurled and smoothed onto the concrete floor.

"Sit," he said, and we did, and the next items in the basket emerged, two bottles of Mad Dog. Begrudgingly, he gave them to Victoria. "It's supposed to be a party," he said, explaining the bottles, caps twisted off and passed between the girls. "I don't like them to drink, but it's not like it was easy to get them to come to your party." He pointed at Becky. "Where's your notebook? You just consumed a hundred calories. Write it down."

Bitsy refused the bottle when it was passed to him, scooted backward on the slippery tarp until his leg was touching mine. David's next magic trick was to pull out a tea set, plastic, with settings for four little girls. The cheerleaders drank cheap booze, and Bitsy and I touched legs, and we all watched David unpack the entire set, arrange the saucers and cups and fake sugar and cream bowls, across the plywood counter. He jammed two fat candlesticks into the mouths of empty bottles of Mad Dog. I was glad the girls had contributed something.

"Lighter," he said, and Bitsy tossed it. At the far corner of the tarp, the girls had managed to finish an entire bottle. They were varsity, without question.

Bitsy leaned toward me, and whispered. "Happy birthday."

"This is completely fucked up," I said. "But thank you."

As he leaned back, a package tumbled out of his cargo shorts. Wrapped, leftover Christmas paper, silver trees on red paper, but still wrapped, and for a fifteen-year-old boy, that was amazing.

"What's this?"

"I kept the receipt. But I don't think you can return it. No offense, but I think they might arrest you."

I opened it, and it was true, I would need the receipt. Bitsy bought me the exact same universal remote as the one my mother had presented that morning, still floating around somewhere inside Kaitlynn's car.

David stood back, and inspected his display. He was satisfied, thank god. I'd known him for too long and could easily imagine him adjusting and readjusting for an hour. The flames flickered in the gloom, and in the weird light, the second bottle of Mad Dog shone in Kaitlynn's hand.

"Perfect," declared David. He returned to the basket, and I guess a part of me was hoping there was a cake in there somehow, but David would never have packed a cake at the bottom of the basket. He was better than that. He removed the last item, and it was definitely not a cake, nor was it something normally seen at a sweet sixteen party, even in the snowbelt.

He lugged the gallon of blue antifreeze to the plywood counter and carefully unscrewed the cap. The cheerleaders were finally drunk, and pointing out all the spots Becky had missed when she had shaved her legs, but Bitsy and I were transfixed.

I watched David carefully pour antifreeze into each tea cup, and he didn't spill a drop. The plastic saucers remained immaculate.

"This tea party isn't for you," he said.

"I figured that."

"We're going to kill some pack rats." With that, he screwed the lid back onto the jug of antifreeze and grabbed his picnic basket, and the cheerleaders hoisted themselves from the tarp and followed him, staggering. Apparently, the party was over.

"I know way too much about the Meatloaf," said David. "Unfortunately. I know how he feels about pack rats. I'm not going to let him get away with pepper spraying one of my girls."

"I'm not touching any dead animals," said Victoria. "This is like peer pressure."

David glared at her. "I don't consider any of you my peers."

"Wow," I said. I knew it was the truth, but always thought it would remain unspoken. He turned on a heel and exited, and as he opened the door, the room filled with the glare of the sun. His troupe rose and followed sluggishly behind. When the door shut, Bitsy and I sat in silence, as the gloom collected, and the candles flickered and reflected in the filthy window.

Bitsy stared at the tea set. "That's some dark shit," he said. "I think David might be a psychopath."

"I don't think he has an outfit for that," I said. Bitsy leaned back on the tarp, and I thought he was going to smoke a cigarette, but instead he kissed me.

It was my sweet sixteen. Candles and a tea party. Bitsy reached around my shoulder to pull me closer, a move he had never tried before.

Our bodies touched, and we forgot about the poison.

FROM THE DESK OF TIFFANY TEMPLETON

The court date was finally scheduled three months after I was caught. I thought it was a good sign that my crimes did not require urgency. Once again, I was wrong. Everything I had imagined was wrong. There was no jury. In juvenile court, the courtroom was closed. I remember meeting my court-appointed attorney for the first time an hour before my hearing. She told me I was probably just going to get community service. I had no reason to doubt her, but I was still scared. Honestly, it was the first time I remember wanting my father, needing him to be in court, to assure me that the damage meant nothing to him. He had predicted I would make mistakes.

I wish I could have used a bottle of Wite-Out to fix that day, but being a girl hurt my chances. Being the infamous daughter of Vy Templeton probably made things even worse.

As soon as the judge took the stand, I could tell he had been looking forward to this. He had prepared carefully, and my court-appointed attorney suddenly looked nervous. It only got worse when he began to read the written statement, smirking as he filled the chambers with a lordly baritone.

Lionel's account was two pages long, every single detail of that day, even the temperature. It was bad enough to listen to two pages of Lionel's witness statement, and I assumed we were done. But then the judge launched into the account of Ronald Templeton Jr. David would have been impressed with the judge's dramatic reading, unspooling the attack slowly, his volume rising to match the terror that Ronnie described.

Again, I was sure we were done and looked at my court-appointed attorney, who was stone-faced. She knew the judge was not finished. My mother's letter was the real surprise. It wasn't full of terror, just the tale of an exhausted woman. The judge switched his tone, and read it in a melodramatic way. To the court, it sounded like a woman who had been beaten down by years of a belligerent daughter. To me, it sounded like she just wanted a vacation.

I was sentenced to three months. When the judgment was announced, the court-appointed attorney was shocked. Not me. Bad luck for bad girls, that's how it goes.

The night I left, my mother stood in the doorway of my bedroom in her new skinny clothes. Yoga pants, tank top, like she had lost the weight from exercise. That look on her face, those deflated cheeks, sunken and grim. I was familiar with how my mother displayed disappointment.

"I just need a break," she said.

"Then maybe you should be the one going away," I said.

She had no response to this, crossed her arms, the extra skin moving like wings. "I bought you a new suitcase," she said, and that was the last time I spoke to her for three months.

Chapter Twenty-One

ON AUGUST 15, ONLY THREE chairs remained in Mr. Francine's office.

The Sweets were gone, having confessed, but I'm sure they were off somewhere shoving gunpowder into empty beer cans. While Rufus was in Kelly's office, I noticed that TJ was calm, clear-eyed.

"It's my last day," he said. "Being sober for two months was enough, I guess."

"Congratulations," I said. "I hope I see you around."

"We live in Gabardine," he pointed out.

"Right," I said.

"Silence," commanded Mr. Francine, a sheen of sweat on his forehead.

"WHAT DO YOU DO FOR fun?" Kelly leaned across the table. I think maybe she had run out of things to talk about. I wanted to bring up the Sweets, but I knew better.

"Right now? Killing pack rats, I guess."

"For sport? Is that a thing around here?" She leaned back, and I could see the horror on her face.

"No," I said. "There's not much sport involved, I guess. Don't you have rats in Cleveland?"

"Yes. But we also have museums and high-speed internet. There's better things to do."

"I know what you're thinking," I said. "I read a lot of true crime books. All psychopaths kill animals when they're younger. It's true. Every single one."

"I don't think you're a psychopath, Tiffany. Honestly, I don't even think you're that tough."

"I got sent away," I said. "The court would disagree with you."

"You never talk about Dogwood," she said. I had my reasons. The worst story wasn't mine to tell. It belonged to another girl, who was afraid of the dark.

"Nothing exciting happened there," I said. For eighty-two of the days, that was the truth. "I wanted to come back with some hard-core stories and maybe a scar or something." Kelly stared at me. "Not disfiguring or anything. I didn't want a scar on my face."

"Not all scars are on the outside," said Kelly.

I didn't respond, just pushed my pages at her. She surprised me by suddenly producing papers of her own, removed a folded *Chronicle* from her backpack. "The newspaper came out today," she said. She held it up for me to see, and unfortunately it was Ronnie's face.

"Keep it," I said. "I don't want to know."

"It's hilarious," she said. "No offense. But I wanted you to know that your reign as the most notorious Templeton is over."

"It was only a matter of time," I said. Begrudgingly, I unfolded the newspaper.

LOCAL MAN DEFENDS CHRISTMAS FROM UNKNOWN THREATS

Gloria Giefer, Staff Reporter

A local man has taken up an armed vigil to protect the National Christmas Tree, and many Carney County residents are wondering why.

Ronald Templeton Jr., 24, a resident of Gabardine, began his tactical operation last month, even though the National Christmas Tree is not scheduled to be harvested until Nov. 30 of this year.

Templeton, a longtime employee of the U.S. Forest Service, does not have any direct connection to the National Christmas Tree program.

A tree has been chosen every year since 1923, and this year's 79-foot Engelmann spruce was selected after a nationwide search and will travel to Washington, D.C., for the annual lighting and ceremony. The tree will be felled on Nov. 30, and transported by a locally owned 16-wheeler stretch trailer. Templeton's vigil is not supported by local law enforcement or the USFS, but the *Chronicle* confirmed that his AR-15 is legally registered and his carry permit is valid through 2019.

The tree, located in the Kamura Forest District, has attracted many sightseers and civic leaders. "I've sworn to protect it," said Templeton, in an interview on Friday. When asked for clarification, Templeton said that his oath was administered by a higher power and not through judicial channels. "I was called, and I answered, and I've got ammunition." In addition to ammunition, Templeton has a stockpile of granola bars, bottled water and energy drinks.

When reached for comment, Allison Shelly, USFS spokesperson, declined to make a statement and deferred to Jake Morton, chief of the Kamura Forest District. Morton, reached by phone, confirmed Templeton's employment, but explained Templeton's official duties as restroom maintenance and on occasion extinguishing campfires.

Morton, who has supervised the district since 1998, offered little explanation for Templeton's activity. "He's doing this on his own time. We appreciate his devotion, but we don't think there is any real threat at this time."

Templeton, via satellite phone, was asked for a response. All requests for clarification were met with silence, although Templeton did offer one word, just before unplugging his satellite connection.

"Terrorists."

Attempts to reach Templeton for further details have been unsuccessful. In an email, Shelly and officials from the U.S. Department of the Interior referred any additional media requests to the office of the state attorney general. Controversy erupted across some segments of Carney County on June 29, after Shelly issued a press release announcing that an Engelmann spruce had been chosen, instead of the traditional Douglas fir. As reported in the *Chronicle* last week, the FBI is investigating a series of death threats against Shelly, as the state attorney general continues to work in conjunction with cybersecurity experts from Homeland Security to investigate local social media accounts falsely accusing Shelly of being a member of ISIS, the Jewish Defense League, and Atheist Women in Media.

In his initial interview, Templeton confirmed that he would continue his armed vigil until the moment the sawyer arrives with the chainsaw on Nov. 26. "I'm not going anywhere," he said. "This is my duty. I'm not just defending Christmas. I'm defending America. I know he's got my address, but you can tell the president he doesn't need to send me a thank-you card."

Chapter Twenty-Two

BY THE LAST WEEK OF August, members of the Bad Check List had finished the stage. Twenty feet wide, ten feet deep, raised a foot from the floor. Twelve inches was good, I thought. If any of the actresses fell, or if any actresses were pushed by their imperious director, twelve inches didn't seem deadly. Bones broken, maybe, but not death. I wondered if we could surround the stage with pillows.

David scheduled rehearsal for ten, but called me that morning and asked me to keep the actresses occupied until ten thirty. He gave me a list of ways to do so, but I wasn't going to make them do the breathing exercises, and I was not going to play any improvisation games, because with dementia, I thought it could go to really bizarre places.

Instead, the women lined up on the new stage, sat in their stars and stripes. I had spent enough time with them to know they were used to waiting around, usually for the activities director or the nurse, but sometimes for death. They gossiped and argued, and I sat in the front row, script in hand, flipped through pages, trying to look busy.

One woman was not wearing stars and stripes. Irene Vanek wore a bright green T-shirt, with black letters: THIS IS WHAT A FEMINIST LOOKS LIKE.

I knew Irene had a DNR, and it seemed strange to believe in something so much, but yet be so willing to surrender to death. I had the notes. I knew she was healthy.

"I like your shirt," I said, and although she smiled broadly, a few of the women rolled their eyes.

"My daughter sent it to me," said Irene. "I used to have one just like it. It got lost along the way, I guess. As things do."

"It's awesome," I said.

"Are you a feminist?"

"I don't know," I admitted. "I've never met one before."

"Your mother," said Betty Gabrian. "Your mother might have questionable politics, but she is a feminist, through and through. Even if she doesn't realize it."

Irene's eyes sparkled. "I've watched you," she said. "I've known lots of girls just like you. Leather jackets, tough little faces. You don't need any of that. Writing this play was a feminist act."

"What does that mean? I thought you hated the play."

"Just the clichés," said Betty Gabrian, trying to be helpful as always.

"Being a feminist means being awake," said Irene. "Being a feminist means being true to yourself, no matter the consequences. You created art, and you put it out into the world. That's revolutionary."

Betty Gabrian nodded. "A feminist is fearless and she fights for her place in the world. And a feminist accepts that there will be consequences." She winked at me. "I know a girl just like that," she said.

Behind me, I heard David and his squad enter the garage, the clack of heels on concrete, most likely Becky. David made her

wear heels everywhere, until she figured out how to stop wobbling.

I thought about consequences, and I thought about Irene's
DNR. She lived her life without fear. She wasn't afraid of any-
thing, even death. "I've never belonged to a club before," I said.
"I guess I just joined the feminists."

"You'd better wear deodorant," said David, as he arrived with
a thick pile of sketches in his hand. "Don't be that kind of feminist." Behind him, all four cheerleaders, measuring tapes draped
around their necks, carrying pincushions and freezer bags filled
with spools of thread. He had done a good job making them look
like seamstresses, but I knew the girls had just taken these things
from drawers or cupboards their own mothers rarely opened.
We'd learned to sew a button in home economics, and that was
the extent of our education, and David, of course, was the only
one with any flair. He sewed his buttons, and then got frustrated,
and finished the buttons of the rest of the class. The teacher was
used to this.

"Good morning, ladies!" David didn't even comment on the
new stage, just rushed the row of stars and stripes, and stuffed
sketches in their hands. From the front row, I could see the detail,
the color. I know he'd spent days on this. Behind me, the varsity
squad took a row of seats. I could smell last night's booze, probably Becky, who seemed to be on some kind of bender, carbs be
damned.

"I've got costume designs!" The stars and stripes studied the
pages, some holding the paper a foot away from their face, to get
a good look. "And I've got the costume department!" He swept
his hand to gesture at the cheerleaders behind me. Immediately,
Betty Gabrian raised an eyebrow.

"You can't put an elderly woman in a corset," she said. "If you even try to cinch us in, you'll break ribs. And if you do manage to cinch us in, it takes fifteen minutes to unlace, and I don't think the paramedics would appreciate that."

"Okay," said David. "No corsets! We don't need them, really. All of you have gorgeous figures!"

"We've got two months to go," said Betty Gabrian. "I think it might take half a year just to find a crinoline in this town, let alone eight crinolines, and I hate to sound so negative, but I've sewn plenty of ruffles in my time. They are a pain in the ass." Betty Gabrian stood, and took the sketches from the other women, flipped through them quickly. "You've got ruffles on everything."

"That's my vision," said David. "You will be resplendent!"

"We will look like bed skirts, young man." Betty Gabrian cast a glance at the varsity squad. "Four seamstresses, working full-time, cannot accomplish this." She pointed at the sketch at the top of the pile. "You have Miss Julie in a three-tiered headpiece. She's not a showgirl in Las Vegas."

"Okay," said David, and I swear he shrunk, withered. Betty Gabrian had sucked all the lofty juice right out of him, and now he was just a raisin. "I went too big. It's a bad habit of mine." He never would have admitted such a thing, and Betty Gabrian continued to dehydrate him.

"Those are your seamstresses," said Diana Whipple, emboldened, pointing behind me. "I don't see a lot of fashion there. I don't see any personal style." Unfortunately, the cheerleaders had arrived in their normal outfits, strappy tank tops, sparkly butt jeans, flip-flops.

Kaitlynn, always the diplomat of the group, called out from behind me. "Don't talk to me about style, old lady. All I see is the Shopko clearance rack. The Fourth of July was over a month ago. Jesus. I'm not going to be insulted by some lady who wears stupid black sneakers with white socks." David turned, probably to admonish her, but it was too late, and we all watched Kaitlynn stomp toward the door. She threw a pincushion shaped like a tomato at the wall just above the nurse's head before she left.

"These are orthopedic," said Diana. Four of her fellow Soiled Doves wore the same exact shoes, and they nodded. "And the three of you can sew?"

David didn't give them a chance to respond. "I bought them a book. They've been studying." I knew the study habits of the varsity squad, and this was not a comfort.

"If we can execute a herkie jump from a pyramid of four people, we can do anything!"

"Thanks, Becky. See? They are willing to take on any challenge."

"It's a matter of supplies," said Betty Gabrian. "And budget, really. No matter how quick they sew, they aren't going to be able to find that many yards of lace."

"Nightgowns," said Loretta McQuilkin. "Easy to find, easy to alter. That's your solution."

"This play takes place at high noon," said David. "I don't think prostitutes slept in. There were roosters and stuff, and porridge to make."

"I can change it," I said. "Early morning. Judith goes outside to kill a pig for breakfast. Or whatever. She sees the fire had grown during the night, and she rushes inside to wake the ladies."

"I worked for days on those sketches," said David. "I did research! I had to watch *Gunsmoke*, and that was the worst!"

"These will be the most glamorous nightgowns in the county," said Betty Gabrian. She yelled to the back of the room. "Nurse! Bring me my purse!"

"Not my job," said the nurse, and returned to her crossword puzzle.

"Good lord," said Betty Gabrian. I rose from my chair, and at the back of the room, pointed at the row of purses, one by one, until Betty Gabrian nodded. It was not nearly as impressive as my mother's, but what it lacked in girth, it made up for in gold appliques. Betty Gabrian did not have to fish around like my mother, removed a black leather billfold, and called out for the costume department. "You!"

Becky, Caitlyn, and Victoria were terrified, I think, and leapt to the front of the stage, useless measuring tapes still dangling from their necks. From where I sat, all I saw were sparkly butt jeans, cowering before a wall of red, white, and blue. This was America.

Betty Gabrian removed a crisp stack of money, fanned it out to double-check. "There is four hundred and fifty-two dollars here. I want receipts. For everything. No chewing gum or trashy magazines. Got it?"

She slammed her billfold shut, stuffed it back in her purse. "Make a list, my dear." I realized she was pointing to me—I was the writer, after all, and the only person in the room with a clipboard and paper. "Shopko has them on clearance. The rack closest to the drinking fountain. Yesterday, they were fourteen dollars. Do not, I repeat do not, pay a nickel more. Eight nightgowns. Medium or large. Anything else won't work. Peach, black, or pink. Absolutely no white. We do not want to look like ghosts."

"No," said David. "Not ghosts."

"Do you have a glue gun, young man?"

"Of course," said David. I knew he had two, at the very least.

Betty Gabrian continued her dictation, and I dutifully transcribed. "At Ben Franklin, twenty yards of lace trim. If Shelly is working, make her do the cutting. The other girl can barely count to ten. Three bags of craft feathers, any color will do. I take that back. They have a bag that looks like murdered parrots. Don't buy those. Four bottles of fabric glue. One bottle of Liquid Stitch. Ten bags of rickrack. Go through that hateful tub next to the shoes, and buy every single bag of crystal beads they've got. Six packages of glue sticks."

"Sequins?" David's voice was meek, and Betty Gabrian was silent. Her icy glare said it all.

"Receipts, ladies. I mean it."

Becky handled the cash like it was radioactive.

David gave orders to Victoria. "If she eats anything and doesn't write it down, you'd better tell me," and the remainder of the varsity squad left for their mission, Becky's heels clicking like a metronome.

Outside, we heard the Geo squeal as it sprang to life.

"That idiot girl needs to change her belts," said Erika Hickey. "I have little hope for your generation."

FROM THE DESK OF TIFFANY TEMPLETON

I've only got two secrets about Dogwood. The first is that I didn't mind being there. Being a girl was actually a good thing. The detention center for boys has over three hundred juvenile delinquents, and they have to run it like a prison.

I finally belonged somewhere. Literally, those were the exact words from the court: this girl belongs in the detention center. Being put in a box gave me comfort. Maybe it was the drugs.

I was sentenced to three months, but only served eighty-three days, and for once, it was not my fault. There were sixteen girls when I arrived at the school, and by the time I left, three had graduated, and one had found another way out.

We were told to call it a school, and not a juvenile treatment program, but we knew the truth. They don't give you medications at regular school. At regular school, you have to get your drugs in the parking lot.

Once you've been shipped away by the state, you no longer need a permission slip from your parents. They can do whatever they want to do with you.

The doctor came from some town thirty miles away, and he had real patients to attend to. The girls' school was a side job, I guess. The nurse's office was tiny, held three metal folding chairs, and a cot folded in half and tucked into the corner.

"Do you have any allergies to any medications?"

"No."

"Do you have a history of addiction or mental illness in your family?"

"Of course," I said. He didn't even look up from his clipboard. My parents had been addicted to food, and Ronnie was delusional. I guess those things didn't matter.

"Have you ever taken Seroquel?"

"I only take multivitamins," I said.

"Being institutionalized is traumatic," he said. "We like to make things easier for the girls and for the staff. I'm going to start you on a low dose."

"I think I'd better ask my mom."

"Young lady, it's too late for that." He stood up, and I followed him out of the room. He gave the clipboard to the nurse on duty, and I never saw him again.

The Seroquel was prescribed for "behavior modification." I saw what it did that first night, as the girls slowed and moved like they were underwater. The nurse rolled out a cart after dinner, a tablecloth draped over top, but this was not a fancy restaurant. It did not contain desserts. On the metal trays, a row of tiny paper cups, each stuck with a Post-it note, all the names of all the girls.

I shared a room with three other girls, and by six o'clock, they slurred their words, wobbled down the hallway, weaving their way to the bathroom or the lounge or the yard. There was a name for it: the Seroquel Shuffle. Some of them liked it, that feeling of being heavy in the body and light in the mind. Every single one of us took Seroquel, and I was already numb from the arrest and the court hearing.

At Dogwood, I didn't have to be the toughest, because it wasn't a contest. We didn't have fights, even though some of the girls had been sentenced for assault. When I met the girls from the oil fields or the reservations, I saw what a real tough girl was like. We didn't have any murderers, however. Those girls were sent to regular prison, or shipped out of state. To the girls at Dogwood, I was a nerd from a small town, and I didn't have any sex stories or high-speed chases to recount after the lights went out. Most fell asleep after telling stories, but a girl down the hall was afraid of the dark, and it took me a week to get used to her crying.

At Dogwood, I was needed. Especially when it came to math and science. My public school in Gabardine was apparently like Harvard, and I tested out of everything, but I still had to go to classes during the day. When I wasn't helping the teacher help the girls, I wrote in my notebook.

We had a library, and I spent a lot of time

there, looking out the windows at the flat desert, a part of Montana foreign to me. I came from mountains and trees, and this was dry prairie.

I looked out at that flat horizon and read crappy romances, and the Seroquel hangover lasted all day, made my thoughts loop like a drunk you can't talk out of a bad idea. For me, I couldn't stop thinking about destroying my hometown. I wanted to burn it down again. Outside the windows, I knew the prairie wouldn't satisfy my desire for fire. At Dogwood, the flames would have to leap thirty yards and leapfrog from scrub bush to scrub bush.

After my first week, we were encouraged to write our families. I had nothing to say to anybody in my hometown, but I wanted to know about fire, so I wrote Betty Gabrian. She responded right away, in beautiful cursive on thick sheets of paper. When she asked if I wanted a care package, I only requested her material about the Slightly Less Bigger Burn. A package arrived within five days. I know they checked our mail at Dogwood, but I wasn't there for arson, so nobody was concerned. The packages kept coming, and I sent her a handmade Thank You card every single time, and I know there is irony in that.

I read about the giant forest fire of 1911, but I imagined present-day Gabardine, the gas station exploding, the trailer park disintegrating into melted plastic and blackened cinder blocks. I imagined my classmates seeking refuge in the grocery store, the flames visible and creeping closer to the parking lot, as the cheerleaders screamed.

Betty Gabrian thought I was writing another paper, and she was the only person I cared about pleasing. I don't know why it took the shape it did, but I started to write for Betty, and the scribbling became a stage play. Maybe I thought it would be easier to just write dialogue and stage directions, and not focus on building an entire universe of women who had all been forgotten. I lost myself in the writing, and my obsession with fire was abated; the inferno took place offstage. Instead, I chased the skinny myth of the Soiled Doves of Gabardine, and didn't stop until I had fed them fictional lives, fattened them with a history I could control.

I started writing, and it consumed me. I no longer heard the girl crying down the hallway, even ignored a whole week of erotic Harry Potter fan fiction that my roommates read aloud. I was eaten up by another story, and to me, the Soiled Doves became real. My story was just like life in Gabardine, too miserable not to be true.

I saw myself in those stubborn women. Like me, they had been warned repeatedly, had been given chances. They ignored the confluence, even as things burned down all around them. When the firefighters came to town, they only saw customers. All eight perished, and none were mourned.

At Dogwood, one of the therapists took the most-damaged girl out into the snowy yard and pushed and pushed until she elicited a scream. The therapist pushed harder, until the scream became an unholy thing, the sound of a natural disaster, so shocking and so overwhelming that it seemed it could only come from underground. The sound startled us, and we dropped things, ran to the windows to watch the girl exorcise her intimacy issues in zero-degree weather. At that temperature, breath is visible, but I think her primal scream had an even greater heat. As she pushed the rage out of her belly and into her lungs, it escaped her mouth in an enormous cloud, thicker than fog, darker than smoke.

In a quiet way, the play was my scream to the universe. I wanted to control the story.

The day I was finally satisfied, I had written ninety-one pages, single-spaced, spit out of the ancient mimeograph machine in the nurse's office.

That night, I held the script in my hands, an actual stack of paper. In the dark, I drew on the smooth pages with one finger, listening to the girls tell stories, trailing off as the Seroquel finally swallowed them, one by one.

Chapter Twenty-Three

ON THE LAST DAY OF August, I almost forgot about David's allergy appointment. School was starting next week, and for the first time ever, I was preoccupied with the first day back. I was worried about my clothes, about Bitsy, about my new allegiance with the cheerleaders. I knew I was going to be treated differently. Maybe this time for the right reasons.

As I neared the reader board, the first thing I noticed was the solitary balloon, dangling from the numbers of my mother's weight. In the heat, and without helium, the orange balloon hung like a testicle. I rounded the sign, and saw the new car, dark gray like cigarette smoke, sparkling in the sunlight. I did not think of testicles. I saw the dealer plates, and I knew my mother had finally hit her goal weight. The balloon was from David, obviously, but the car was my mother's gift to herself. I examined it closely—Buick Regal. I did not know if this was a nice kind of car, but it looked expensive and sporty, and these days, my mother believed she was both of those things.

Behind the counter, she dangled the keys in her hand, held them out in the air, jangling noises. I was sure she had done this exact same thing to every customer that day.

This had all been planned. My mother had no time to drive to the dealer in Fortune, so it had been pre-ordered, all paid, just waiting for that final tile to flip on the reader board.

"Drove it right off the lot," she said. "Still made it back here in time to open the store."

"Wow," I said. "So, it's fast."

"Fully loaded," she said. "I earned every single bell and whistle."

"Yes, you did," I said. "I'm proud of you."

"If I let you ride in it, you will be sitting on a garbage bag. No arguments. David insisted upon white leather."

"David?"

"He helped me pick it out."

"Where is he? I'm supposed to take him to the allergist." I looked out in the parking lot, but it was completely empty. I hadn't noticed that the PT Cruiser was missing. "Wow," I said. "You traded it in."

"What? Of course not. Getting their offer would have been embarrassing. I'm not that woman anymore, Tiffany. I am a woman who knows her own worth."

"Sure," I said. "Did you leave it at the dealer? How am I going to pick it up? You don't get off work for five more hours, and I've got David's appointment." I looked up at the clock for the first time. "Crap. He's supposed to be there in twenty minutes."

"Selfish," she said. "Selfish as always." She said this, still dangling her keys, which wasn't selfish, I guess. She lost the weight, and I'm sure she paid in cash, just like most Libertarians. Actually, most Libertarians switch their cash to gold coins, like trolls under a bridge, keep them in lockboxes, preparing for the failure of the banking system.

"I'm giving him a ride," I said. "I've been doing it for two years. That's not selfish. I'm like helping a disadvantaged youth."

"I gave the car to Janelle," she said. "Now you can stop pretending to be a martyr."

"Janelle doesn't know how to drive," I said. "Janelle doesn't even know how to use a can opener." This was true. She was frightened of the sharp edges of the lids, always had been. She only bought the cans with pull tabs, or she left the unopened cans on the counter for David and me.

"You were never very good at spying," she said. "Nearsighted. You only see what you want to see. David has been busting his ass, and you haven't even noticed."

I thought my mom might be taking diet pills again. It would explain hitting the goal weight, and would explain why she was talking nonsense. I knew how to talk to her on diet pills. I spent seventh grade talking to my mother like a baby. "Okay," I said. "You're right. David works very hard. That balloon was very thoughtful."

"He's in Fortune right now," she said. "Taking his driver's exam. Waterbed Fred is his responsible adult. They've been practicing. It's actually very adorable."

"I'm glad he has a ride to the allergist," I said. "But I still don't understand why you gave them the car. Go ahead and call me selfish, but I kind of thought you would give the car to me."

"Fat chance," she said. "The last thing you need is a getaway vehicle."

"You let me drive David all the time."

"David is responsible. David would not let you abscond to Washington or Idaho or Oregon. I know how your mind works."

"Jesus. If I was going to abscond, I would get the hell out of the northwest. Give me some credit. I'd probably go to Detroit or something." I wanted to tell my mother that I had over twenty thousand dollars in drug money. Leaving would not be a problem.

"That sounds about right," she said. "David needed the car. You did not. For him, it's a matter of life and death."

"He's allergic to pollen," I said. "Most people can just take a Benadryl. And if you haven't noticed, we only have pollen for five months. He doesn't need shots during the winter. That's like seven months of pointless injections. His allergist just wants the money."

"It's charity," she said. "But I wouldn't expect you to understand something like that."

"I thought charity began at home," I said. "That's the saying."

"Save the Bible-thumping for your idiot brother," she said. "I'm going to be charitable tonight, so save your high horse. I'm getting pizza, and Waterbed Fred is going to bring some forks. Real forks. There you go."

"You're going to eat pizza?"

"Of course not. But it's a date, and I'm not going to make him eat a Lean Cuisine."

"You have a date with Waterbed Fred?"

"I believe he's courting me. Unfortunately, you'll be there, too."

AS PROMISED, THE COURTSHIP INVOLVED real silverware, and it was pointless. Not the courtship, but the silverware, because Waterbed Fred and I used our hands to hold our slices. My mother wore a new outfit, black of course, but the neckline dipped lower than usual, and I could see the edge of a black lace bra, which was also new. I did the laundry, so I knew these things.

My mother ate nothing, watched us devour the pizza, and chattered on and on about her new car, and then property taxes, and finally, launched into the familiar speech in which she pontificated on campaign finance reform. She was absolutely terrible at flirting.

I picked up Waterbed Fred's plate, and the two forks, and walked to the kitchen sink. I was planning on washing the dishes, but my mother stopped me.

"Give me those forks," she said. I returned to the kitchen table, and deposited them into her waiting hand. When she tried to hand them to Waterbed Fred, he finally spoke.

"Vy, I think she's been punished enough."

"Oh, really?"

"I know it's not my place, but I don't think she's a menace anymore."

"It's not your place. You can take your forks, and you can leave."

Waterbed Fred looked at me, and I shook my head. I didn't want to be the reason this date went badly, because I knew I would be blamed for it for the rest of my life. I hoped Waterbed Fred would turn this around, maybe stand up from the table and launch into "Abilene."

Instead, he reached across the table and touched my mother's hand. "I should've brought flowers," he said.

"Yes," said my mother.

"David passed his test," he said. This was a good way to redirect. "It was the craziest thing. The written part, no problem. But then he went out for the driving test. They couldn't find more than one car on any street in Fortune. Maybe there's a quilt show or something. So the teacher told him to imaginary parallel park.

He told David, pretend there's a car right there."

"That boy has an impressive imagination," said my mother.

"I'll say. The whole way down to Fortune, he was freaking out about the parallel parking, but then he did it perfectly."

"I'm glad it worked out for him," I said, and of course I didn't mean it, but I was trying to calm the room. I carefully washed the plates, and put them in the drying rack, and exited the kitchen as soon as I could. I wasn't afraid that they would start kissing—that was not my mother's style. I knew Waterbed Fred would have to work up to that. My mother made people earn things, so it hurt even more when she took them away.

Chapter Twenty-Four

SCHOOL STARTED, AND I WAS now a junior, but nothing had changed. My summer with Bitsy and the cheerleaders did not make me popular. To most kids, I was still just a juvenile delinquent.

On September 19, I walked into Mr. Francine's office and stared at the empty chairs. TJ's plan had worked, apparently. At least Rufus was still on probation. He was in with Kelly, and I was sure of that, because of the smell he left behind.

Kelly listened to me complain about the car. I have to admit, she was good at her job. Her face was completely passive as I unleashed my tale of woe. I told her about Christmas, how I had to deliver a present to him every year, immaculately wrapped, ordered from Spokane. Ronnie and I got presents from Shopko. Not David. Every November, my mom made sure I was around when she ordered his gifts on the phone, read her credit card number extra loud.

"She gives David everything," I said.

"I don't know your mother," said Kelly. "I only know what you've told me."

"I told you the truth," I said. To prove it, I removed my pages from my backpack, and arranged them carefully in front of her. "You don't know what it's like. My father was the only one who thought about me. I never got attention from anybody else. David gets presents. Even Ronnie got picked for something special, even though it was by God."

"Your mom is a difficult person," admitted Kelly. "But you're going to run into difficult people for the rest of your life."

"I used to have my dad," I said. "I didn't mind being at home."

"And what do you think your dad would want?"

I really didn't know the answer. My dad helped people. When I volunteered at the food bank, I didn't mind the work, because it made him so happy. "My dad would want me to leave people alone," I said. "Unless they asked for help."

"So why do you think you started spying? Why did you take notes?"

"Somebody had to," I said. Kelly waited for me to continue. She was in no hurry. She took a sip of water. I couldn't stand the silence. "I wanted to keep track of people, I guess."

"You care about people," she said. I didn't want to correct her. "That's a good thing. After the Sweet boys, I don't want to work with any more psychopaths. There's too much paperwork."

"I'm not a psychopath. I'm not even a sociopath," I said. "I guess I'm just afraid some people will get lost, and nobody will notice."

"There's nine hundred people in this town, Tiffany. I don't think getting lost is a possibility."

"You'd be surprised," I said. I thought of my dad. It seemed strange that a man so big could get lost.

"Let me ask you again. If your dad were still alive, what would he want you to do?"

"He would want me to apologize. Probably not to my mother, though."

"Fine," said Kelly. "Maybe you can work on that."

"I'm trying," I said. "But then my mother gives David a car. Some people aren't worth it."

"Some people are," she said. "Especially the people you aren't related to. You're stuck with your mom, and you're going to be doing the sorry dance for the rest of your life."

"Gross," I said.

"There is a difference between saying sorry and making things right," she said. "When you make amends, you promise you won't continue the behavior. And you prove it. You take action."

I swallowed hard, thinking about the consequences. "I might end up in jail," I said. "And there are still a few things I'm afraid to tell you."

"Tough Tiff," said Kelly. "Bring her back if you need to."

"Okay," I said.

"But no punching," said Kelly. "And call me from jail."

She thought this was hilarious. I left her office, and I could still hear her laughing.

BITSY PARKED HIS BATTERED TRUCK in the parking lot of Ben Franklin. It was the third week of September, but after the wigs, we knew they had a jump on Halloween.

"I'll leave the truck running," he said. It was seventy degrees outside, and the sun blasted all of the Saturday shoppers in the parking lot.

"That's not necessary," I said, rolling down my window, the handle loose, threatening to break off in my hand. "I'm not going to get cold or anything."

"In case you need to make an escape," he said. I wondered why he had parked so far away, but I realized he was afraid I would be spotted by Lionel. It seemed so long ago. That seemed like a different girl.

"I appreciate it," I said.

"Remember it's a clutch," he said. "I feel weird buying makeup."

"It's Halloween," I said.

"Most of the stuff I need is real makeup. In the women's section."

"Take it from me," I said. "Just act like you belong there, and nobody will give you a second glance."

"That didn't work out so well for you," he said.

IN THE BATHROOM OF MY house, Bitsy went to work. I was so glad the bathroom was clean. It was just me and my mom who lived there now, and the days of the Meatloaf peeing everywhere but in the toilet were long past us.

He removed his items from the Ben Franklin bag, and stacked them up along the sink.

"Don't worry," he said. "I kept the receipt."

"I don't think you can bring back used makeup," I said. "I'm sure Lionel has some sort of policy. Flesh-eating bacteria or whatever."

"I know David doesn't want me to touch the faces of the other ladies. It's embarrassing, but I asked my mom to teach me. It doesn't matter. David doesn't trust me. He said that when straight men put makeup on ladies, they always end up looking like clowns."

"They're supposed to be prostitutes," I said. "They were called 'painted ladies' for a reason."

"He warned me," he repeated. "Specifically about blue eye shadow." Bitsy's mom wore blue eye shadow, and sometimes a dark blue mascara, but I didn't want to say anything.

"Hold still," he said. "Actually, close your eyes." I was scared.

I saw the bottle of Elmer's glue in his hand, and it was coming toward my face. "I'm not going to hurt you. I'm your boyfriend."

He unscrewed the orange tip, and dutifully, I closed my eyes. I flinched when he smeared it around my nose. It was cold, and slimy, and he wiped it all around my nostrils. He left the tip of my nose untouched. "Okay. We've got to wait for it to dry."

"Beatrice has dementia," I said. "Let's just pray she doesn't forget why you're squirting glue all over her face. She might think she's getting embalmed or something."

"Pull up your pant leg," he said. "Miss Aimee has dead legs, but David doesn't want them to look black."

"I don't think her customers would like that, either." I eased my jeans up over my knee. Bitsy crouched down, and I almost laughed when I saw the plastic package of blue eye shadow. Carefully, he used the tiny wand, and traced lines up and down my shin. "I figure we aren't going to see her skin unless she crosses her legs, but I want to be thorough."

I stared down at the lines on my shin. They were too regular, too perfect. It looked like the pin-striping inside David's favorite blazer, another gift from my mother. "I think the whole shin needs to be blue," I said. "I'm pretty sure Ruby already has varicose veins."

"Okay," he said. "I'm going to have to buy more eye shadow." He stared at my face, touched my chin, raised my face to the light. I couldn't help but shiver at his touch. "It's dry now." It was true—the glue had hardened. My mother had applied a clay mask to my face last year, because she had spotted a pimple. It felt like that. He reached for a bottle of foundation and struggled with the wrapping.

"I don't doubt you at all," I said. "But that shade isn't even close to my skin color. That's nearly ivory."

"It's the same shade as old ladies. My mother said so."

He was really taking this seriously. He successfully removed the cap, and began to dab the foundation on the dried glue. On the tip of my nose, more blue eye shadow, and at the very end, he used actual Halloween makeup, a tube of black lipstick. I rose from the toilet and studied myself in the mirror.

"You're a genius," I said. My nose was a mess of thickened, scarred skin, ending in a nose that looked completely dead.

"Now for the hard part," he said. "David doubts me, and wants Miss Joanna just to wear gloves during the whole play."

"To be fair, women in those days did wear gloves."

"I like a challenge," he said.

"Okay," I said.

"I'm dating you," he said. "I'm not scared of anything." He grabbed my hand and began to wrap it in a roll of beige bandage. "Bend your pointer finger and tuck your thumb underneath it." I watched him wrap my hand and then the remaining three fingers separately. He dabbed more of the blue eye shadow and black lipstick at the end of the stubs. We both stared at his work, and I didn't need to tell him that it looked like a Civil War wound. My hand was enormous and wrinkled with bandage lines. This would not work for Miss Joanna, unless Miss Julie had plucked her from a circus sideshow.

"Pantyhose," said Bitsy. I hoped this would be the first and last time I would ever hear that word come out of his mouth. "I'm going to have to go back to Ben Franklin."

"I hope people start whispering about you. Dating a cross-dresser would be exciting."

Chapter Twenty-Five

PLAY PRACTICE WAS AT TEN o'clock in the morning. Bitsy walked me from my house, but David ignored him. He was too fixated on the arrival of the woodstove. We left him inside the Quonset hut, pacing back and forth.

Before I knew it, we were making out by the front door. Another thing I never thought I would do, another type of girl I hated. But there we were, in public, which was bad enough, but I was so wrapped up in it that I didn't stop when the van pulled up.

As soon as Bitsy saw elderly women, his passion was extinguished. He bolted over the sand hill, leaving me standing there, watching the actresses dismount from the white van. This process usually took five minutes, but today they were brisk and moved with purpose. The horn on the van beeped, and through the fogged windows I stared into the driver's seat.

Not the nurse. Erika Hickey, with the great legs.

"It's not theft," explained Betty Gabrian. "And Erika still has a valid license."

"It's theft," insisted Diana Whipple. "When you take something that doesn't belong to you, that's theft."

"I private pay, my dear." Betty Gabrian smoothed her hair down around her ears. "The rest of you may use Medicare, but

I give them cash. Therefore, I own this van."

"An eighth of it," said Diana. "A valid license is one thing, but insurance is another."

"I got us here just fine," said Erika.

"The nurse called in sick," said Betty Gabrian. "Third time in two weeks. I keep track of such things." I had no doubt about that.

"We think she takes methamphetamines," announced Diana Whipple. I didn't know how to respond to that.

"The sub refused to take us," said Betty Gabrian. "We told her that it was an important rehearsal, but that meant nothing to her."

"She steals painkillers," said Erika. "I wouldn't have trusted her to drive us anyway."

"I left a note," said Betty Gabrian. "She probably won't even notice we're gone."

"That's a side effect of painkillers," said Diana.

"I forgot how much I loved driving," said Erika.

"You also forgot how to use a blinker," said Diana.

"Enough," declared Betty Gabrian. "Save all this bickering for the stage. It's rehearsal time, ladies. This is important." The women walked inside the theater, but Betty Gabrian waited outside. "We made an oath in the car. None of us are going to die before opening night. We will resuscitate each other, if necessary. No DNR will keep us from our theatrical debut."

"I have no doubts," I said.

"I'm glad you have faith," she said. "Now we need to work on your taste. That young man needs to comb his hair."

* * *

I KNEW EXACTLY HOW MUCH my mother paid for the Quonset hut, but she chose to show up at play practice, just in case we needed a reminder.

The actresses were running through a scene in which Inga had just shot a possum, and they were debating the best way in which to prepare it.

David seemed startled to see my mother, but it was Sunday, and quality control was inevitable. Up against the wall, our tea party was still laid out, even though I had warned David to get rid of it, had to remind him that several of our actresses had dementia.

My mother zeroed in on it immediately.

"Don't mind me," she said. "I'm not here to interrupt your artistic vision." She moved toward the tea set, as if she had paid for it, too. My mother, as usual, weaponized her money. She had no idea that I had $20,137 in a typewriter case behind the Laundromat. I would never have offered her one red cent. David blocked her immediately, and as the actresses continued to run their lines, he grabbed her hand and dragged her to the darkest corner. I could hear him chattering about the woodstove, as the actress portraying Inga brandished a fake knife in the air. Someone was going to have to teach Irene Vanek what it looked like to skin a possum. I didn't think David would be the right candidate.

Onstage, Irene Vanek stirred an imaginary cauldron. Possum stew. My mother and David had moved on to other things. When he removed the red velvet curtains from the garbage bag, my mother whistled lowly. She was impressed, but had no idea that they came from the receptionist at the allergist's office, who had offered them to us like they were no big deal. Maybe she was some kind of theater hoarder. Once again, Fortune had earned the name. The sight of red velvet was enough of a distraction for the actresses. They stopped the scene and broke character, and now everybody was admiring the curtains.

I watched my mother in the corner, and an image flashed through my head. Her gasoline hands. After every shift, she washed her hands in a special industrial soap that smelled like oranges, the water impossibly hot, knuckles and nail beds bright red. My mother was the original tough girl. I guess I was inspired, because I walked to the front of the stage and yelled at the actresses.

"Back to work!" I startled everybody in the Quonset hut.

"I'm the director," said David. "You don't get to boss them around."

"Back to work," repeated my mother. David's jaw dropped, as my mother admonished them further. "It's not like you ladies have never seen curtains before."

Chapter Twenty-Six

OCTOBER WAS A WICKED MONTH in northwestern Montana. Gales of bitterly cold wind, frost in the mornings, a scrawny sun during the day that set much, much too soon.

Bitsy waited for me in the parking lot, leaning against his battered red truck. This was where he usually was after school, in a group of dumb boys and girls who never dressed for the weather. But today, he was alone. I pulled my jacket tight around me as the leaves in the parking lot whipped in circles. I knew he was waiting for me, because he pointed. This was teenage romance.

"Templeton," he said. "Get in the truck." In another world, maybe he would have held a bouquet of flowers.

The passenger door creaked and protested as I slammed it shut into the frame. Bitsy's truck had lost every demolition derby, but he was the only contestant.

"It's not that cold," I said. "I can walk."

"Not today," he said. "Caitlyn and Becky slammed me into a locker."

"Jesus," I said. "They will bully anybody."

"It didn't hurt," he said. "They told me I was a bad boyfriend."

I was confused. I guess my mind was hung up on the visual image of two girls shoving Bitsy, overpowering him. I knew him well enough to know that he wasn't the type to hit girls, but

Caitlyn and Becky were probably taking caffeine pills from the gas station, so self-defense would have been justified.

"That's random," I said. "I'm sure they were high. Talking nonsense. You're lucky they didn't shake you down for money. That's what people on drugs do."

"Nonsense?" He looked over at me, and turned the key in the ignition. Of course, Bitsy's battered truck did not have a functional heater. "I think they might be right."

"Okay," I said. "I'm sorry that they messed with your head. I'm freezing. Can we please go?"

"I'm your boyfriend," he said.

My cheeks burned, and even though I was embarrassed, I welcomed the heat. "I guess," I stammered.

"And I'm apparently bad at it." I knew immediately David had sent his emissaries. Sometimes, David does nice things. Sometimes, he just wants to create gossip. It can be hard to tell the difference.

"You're not bad at it," I said. "I think you do okay."

"Thanks," he said. "I'm taking you out on a date."

"Right now?"

"I know it's not romantic, but you have a curfew and stuff."

"Romantic? We're in the wrong town for that. Even when it's dark. I guess we could rent a movie or something. I could pretend to get scared and grab you on the couch."

"Ever heard of the Rocky Mountain Roller?"

He yanked down on the gearshift, and we were backing out of the school parking lot, and suddenly I was terrified that my new boyfriend, my new bad boyfriend, was kinky. "I don't think we're ready for something like that. I mean, no offense, but we haven't even gone all the way."

"Death trap for pack rats," he said. "We're going to build one."

"Very romantic," I said. "You're full of surprises."

As he popped the gearshift into first gear, he leaned over and kissed me on the cheek, which was chaste, but he had to keep his eyes on the road.

IN THE THEATER, DAVID AND Betty Gabrian sat on the stage, scripts in hand, space heater connected to ropes of extension cords. I knew Betty's hands got cold—I don't think she always wore gloves for propriety.

They didn't seem surprised to see us, nor did they flinch at the bucket Bitsy held, loaded with supplies.

"We're running lines," offered David. "Without the distraction of the other actresses."

"If you can call them that," said Mrs. Gabrian.

"There's a reason you are the star of the show," said David. "I told you the car would come in handy," he said. I was still bitter, so I just stared back at him.

"We're honing my craft," declared Mrs. Gabrian. "I'm just happy to be sprung from that place. It's worth the gas money."

"They're on a date," David told her.

"I've been on many dates," said Mrs. Gabrian. "None that involved a bucket."

Bitsy was proud of his plans. "It's the Rocky Mountain Roller," he said.

"Sounds like the nickname of one of your cheerleaders," said Mrs. Gabrian. "Most likely the mouthy one with the terrible fan belt."

Bitsy ignored this, and I followed him into the darkest corner of the garage. This was not very romantic, but I didn't have much to compare it to. Onstage, Mrs. Gabrian recited her lines from the script.

"Forty-seven days and forty-seven nights," declared Mrs. Gabrian. "Not one drop of rain. God has cursed the town of Gabardine."

"You've been counting?" David didn't bother pitching his voice to the heights of Diana Whipple.

"I'm a thorough bookkeeper," said Mrs. Gabrian. "I write everything down, my darling girl. Daily temperatures, expenditures, and the strange proclivities of our callers from Idaho."

"Where's the whiskey?"

"And now we face a bigger threat than buggerers from Boise."

"Uff-da," said David.

"Heat lightning," said Mrs. Gabrian. "Surely, it is a wrath from God. No rain, only fingers of fire."

"I am known for my fingers of fire," said David.

"I apologize," said Mrs. Gabrian. "You are correct."

"It's a real moneymaker," said David.

In the dark corner, Bitsy ignored the high drama, concentrating on his contraption. It was simple, really. With a pocketknife, he dug out holes near the top of the bucket. He slid an empty, bottomless can onto a dowel, and then mounted the dowel through the holes. He spun the can, and was satisfied.

I followed him past the stage, as he lugged the bucket and nearly tripped over the extension cord. Mrs. Gabrian stared at us as she pointed to her chest. "We have something stronger than President Roosevelt, my sweet girls. We don't need his communist firefighting crew. We have good Christian hearts, and our faith has survived many a calamity."

"Mostly those men from Boise," said David.

Outside, Bitsy cranked the handle on the water spigot, and the bucket was filled three-quarters full. It was heavy, but he still had his football muscles.

Inside the garage, the thespian and the director had taken a break from my ill-wrought melodramatics.

"I hope he brought you flowers," said Mrs. Gabrian.

"There's no place to get flowers around here," said Bitsy.

"If I had known, I would have brought some from Fortune," she said. "Young love is a precious thing."

"Bitsy is a bad boyfriend," said David. "I'm doing my best to change that."

"I have no doubt," said Mrs. Gabrian.

The three of us followed Bitsy outside, and around to the back of the Quonset hut. As he lugged the bucket to the corner, the can clattered against the dowel. I doubt he expected a crowd, but he said nothing, a good boyfriend. We watched as he leaned a two-by-four against the lip of the bucket, rested the other end of the board in the gravel, a gangplank. Bitsy unscrewed the lid of a jar of peanut butter, fingered a giant gob, smeared it across the can, obscuring the fact it had ever contained green beans. Mrs. Gabrian flinched as Bitsy licked the remaining peanut butter from his fingers.

"Done," he said, and stood back to admire his work.

"I never want to see that contraption in my theater," said David. "Whatever it is, I think it's disgusting. And I'm pretty sure we've got two actresses with nut allergies."

"It's the Rocky Mountain Roller," said Bitsy. "Made famous right here in Gabardine."

"Famous?" David was incredulous. "We are only famous for incinerated prostitutes."

"Jesus," said Bitsy. "You wanted dead pack rats."

"That sounds out of character," said Mrs. Gabrian. "I've only known you for a few months, and I trusted that you had a gentle soul."

"Revenge," said David.

"I approve," said Mrs. Gabrian. "Just make sure you wear gloves."

Bitsy explained how it worked. The rats walked up the plank, and leapt for the peanut butter on the spinning can, only to miss and drown in the bucket. If peanut butter was enough bait for the people of Gabardine, I would build a giant Rocky Mountain Roller in the center of town. Maybe I could scotch-tape lottery tickets to a can. "Every day, that bucket is going to be full of dead pack rats."

"Flowers would have been better," said Mrs. Gabrian.

Chapter Twenty-Seven

ON SATURDAY, I SHOWED UP at the Laundromat, another production meeting demanded by David. I was ten minutes early, so I had time to check on my stash. I reached beneath the juniper, removed the box, and examined the contents. The can openers, still impossibly new, no longer had any power. But I felt they should stay. I shut the lid on the typewriter case and slid it back beneath the bush. I guess I wanted the objects to remain as they were, just in case I died or something. Some kid could find it in one hundred years, a trailer park archaeologist, open my time capsule and bring it to school for show-and-tell, the strange hoard of a long-dead teenage girl. Maybe he would write a play about it.

When I went inside, David wasn't there, even though I was right on time. Unfortunately, Lou Ann was. We sat in silence for fifteen minutes, at separate tables, and the Laundromat was uncomfortably hot. Between us, a fishing tackle box, tubes of acrylic paint instead of shiny lures.

"He did my taxes," she said. "Your dad. They were really complicated. Artists have the most complicated taxes."

"I'm sure," I said.

"I don't sell much," she said. "I mean, it's not like I make a living from selling art."

"You work here," I said. "This is a real job. Some people don't have any jobs. You've got two."

She nodded, and we continued to sit there in silence until she pushed her chair back, emptied lint traps, pulling out the giant trays from the dryers; even though they were empty, she made a show of tapping them into the garbage can. Some of the dryers had been broken for years. I watched Lou Ann spray the doorknob of the bathroom with Windex and stand back to inspect her work, no idea that a foot of concrete wall separated her from a box that contained her portrait of my father.

"I don't think they're coming," I said. David had promised to arrive at ten with two of the cheerleaders, a meeting of the "scenic department," but the cursed wicker picnic basket had been waiting for us, perfectly staged on the counter that people were supposed to use to fold clothes. Nobody folded clothes here. People rarely even matched socks. When I saw the basket, I should have known.

"Lou Ann?"

"Yes?" She spun around to face me, the paper towel wadded in her hand, tinted barely blue, far from the colors she had chosen for my father's body.

"I'm pretty sure he left that for us." I pointed at the basket, which she regarded with nonchalance, as if people left wicker picnic baskets at the laundromat all the time. Maybe this had happened before, and some other delinquent teenage girl had left her baby in a basket for Lou Ann to find, like baby Moses or something, and crazy Lou Ann just took it to the river and launched it from the reeds.

Lou Ann gingerly opened the basket. Inside, two cans of spray starch, four crisp white top sheets, bleached and ironed. Underneath the sheets, a fleur-de-lis stencil cut carefully into an index card, the edges scotch-taped. According to his directions, written on another index card, two of the sheets would be hung on wires, simulating walls. The other sheets would be stapled around wooden frames, a perfect rectangle cut in the middle of each, where the window would be. Lou Ann removed yet another index card, the rough sketch of what he was looking for.

"This is going to be hard for me," said Lou Ann. "I don't work like this."

I knew exactly how she worked. I said nothing, but pushed the tables against the wall. Four king-size top sheets would not fit on the linoleum floor of the Laundromat, and Lou Ann helped me heft the tables on top of each other, drag the plastic chairs outside.

Maybe it was the fumes from the spray starch, or maybe it was the unspoken secrets between us, but Lou Ann was chatty, made hyperactive small talk. She babbled as she shook a can and tried to apply an even coat.

"I always got a refund," she said. "He was like a magician, I swear."

"Everybody gets refunds," I said. The Bad Check List shrunk in February and March, as people made good. "All poor people get refunds."

We continued in silence, save for the rattling of the ball bearing inside the spray cans. Three sheets coated, and Lou Ann finally decided to squint at the directions on the back of an empty can. "Twenty minutes to dry," she said. "Oh. Highly flammable. Contents under pressure." I almost laughed at the irony. That pressure caused her to jump up and bolt to the door, prop it open with a piece of shale. "I guess we aren't supposed to breathe the fumes." She leaned against the open door, and lit a cigarette, as I finished spraying the last sheet.

"Highly flammable," I said, reminding her.

"I'm an artist," she responded. She smoked three cigarettes, one after the other, and another twenty minutes passed, as she blurted out standardized deductions. "Canvases." Thirty seconds later: "All my paints, of course." A minute. "My power bill, because my house is also my studio." Two minutes. "Medications, even over the counter." Ten seconds. "Turpentine." Three full minutes. "Mileage."

"You don't even have a car."

She stubbed out the cigarette and winced. "He was a magician," she said. She brushed past me and began to dig through her tackle box.

"I'm pretty sure that's illegal," I said.

"I've said too much," she said, laughed nervously.

As I sketched out the squares for the windows, Lou Ann crawled up the length of the sheet. She tossed a brush at me, and then a tube of cerulean blue. Brand new, fat with the stuff. She could have chosen any other color in the rainbow. I sighed, and placed the index card in the upper left corner, squeezed a glob onto the end of my brush.

Before I finished stenciling the first fleur-de-lis, Lou Ann abandoned the directions and with a flourish of her hand, thick black lines appeared at the top of her sheet, and then curves that flicked away, curled up. Six, nearly identical. I stopped painting and watched her connect the lines. She was the real magician, had summoned a chandelier into being.

"David wanted us to stencil," I said.

"It's a brothel," said Lou Ann. "Every brothel should have a chandelier." I couldn't argue with that, and her wrists flashed again, a brush coated with dark gray, highlights traced the black lines, and now the chandelier appeared made from iron, and with a few quick dashes, a loop of chain to an imaginary ceiling.

"What year is this?"

"2018," I said. Jesus. Maybe she had squirreled pills just like Kaitlynn, learned nothing from her overdose.

"The play," she said.

"1911," I said.

"Thank god I asked," she said. "I was going to paint light-bulbs." With a flick of her wrist, and an ochre-colored paint, candles sprouted from each arm.

I tried to space the fleur-de-lis evenly, but it took an entire hour to cover the first king-size sheet. In that time, Lou Ann had painted a mahogany side table, topped with a red vase stuffed with forget-me-nots. A skinny bureau, also mahogany, but furnished with elaborate iron fixtures. On the bureau, a series of tiny paintings in silver frames, each containing the outline of a woman.

"They are called cameos," she said. "David will appreciate the historical accuracy."

I resumed stenciling, patterning the empty expanse beneath the first window, claiming that space before Lou Ann could conjure a spittoon.

"I'd like to paint a fern," she said, but her voice was shrill. I think it was time for her to take her medications. Babbling, a paint-splattered menace, she stood and yanked at the tail of her giant white T-shirt, emblazoned with stains of her art, layers bursting through like fireworks.

"Whatever," I said, and adjusted the index card, began another fleur, the tube of paint halfway gone.

Before I knew it, she stood at the top of my sheet, just as I had slid the index card into the corner, the final fleur-de-lis.

"I loved him." Her hands flew up to her mouth, as if she could push the words back in.

I couldn't look at her. I slapped the index card down, rattled, and I squeezed the rest of the paint directly into the cutout. I didn't know how I would fix this, how I could put all the paint back in the tube. A pile of blue.

"He loved me," she said. "We loved each other." I refused to look up, but I could hear her shuddering breath, an exhalation, jagged with crying.

"Fuck you," I said. I stood to face her. Tough Tiff, full height.

Eye to eye. "I'm not sorry," she said, and that was her mistake. I lunged for her, but she darted to the left, skidded across the enormous glob of paint on my sheet, and tracked cerulean all the way out the door. She ran, but I didn't chase her. I don't know why. The linoleum was marked with only one shoe, and the tracks she left were strange but seemed right. Just the left shoe, bright blue, probably all the way to her house.

Cleaning the Laundromat was her job. Lou Ann would have to clean up her own crime scene.

I didn't chase her. Instead, I raided her box for another blue. I didn't care if the wallpaper was two different shades.

I placed the index card on the last of the sheets, and I began. I had an entire blank space to cover, and I moved the index card, and I moved it again and kept going until I was done.

This was something I could control.

"FOURTEEN BODIES IN TWENTY-FOUR HOURS," said David. "That sounds like a play you would write, Tiffany."

The Rocky Mountain Roller had filled with corpses, and then filled again.

Four cheerleaders and I circled David's bed, where he was stretched out on his immaculately white comforter. He called us for a meeting, and I guess it was a testament to his power that nobody dared sit.

"Tiffany, there's something else you need to know."

I sighed. "Okay."

"I got these girls to go to the library again. That's twice now."

"Ugh," said Becky. That's when I noticed her hair, the color of a traffic cone.

"They checked out every book on witchcraft and Satan worship," he said.

"What?" I was pissed. "We aren't even allowed to have *The Catcher in the Rye*. We have books on Satan worship?"

He reclined against his pillows, staring up at the ceiling, purposefully ignoring me. "I sent them to Shopko, and they bought nine boxes of kosher salt."

"And blonde in a box on clearance," said Kaitlynn. She pointed at Becky's hair.

"She didn't use toner," said David. "Believe me, she's been warned before." At this, Becky dropped her head in shame, which made her hair even more visible, as well as a rash on the back of her neck from the peroxide. "How hard is it to read a goddamn box of hair dye, Becky?"

She didn't respond. Kaitlynn rolled her eyes and grabbed my arm. "The Geo is full of dead pack rats and kosher salt," she said. "You have to carry the pack rats."

"Becky should be punished," I said, in hopes that David would see the justice in that. I looked at him, waiting for him to agree.

"Team spirit," said David. "You need some. Do what they say." He wasn't even wearing socks or shoes, while his cheerleaders wore camouflage, and Becky's hair was a flame against the greens and browns of her shirt. "I can't leave my house tonight," explained David. "My mother is going to attempt astral projection, and I promised that I would keep an eye on her. The last thing we need around here is another disappearing parent."

AS WE DROVE UP THE forest service road, I occasionally glanced behind me, studying the lumpy burlap bag crammed into the trunk of the Geo. I watched for any movement, concerned about survivors. It would be a big mistake to open a burlap bag with an angry pack rat inside.

We left the Geo in a drainage ditch. Stepping out into the darkness, I thought that Kaitlynn might help lift the bag of rats, as she was the strongest. Instead, she carried a plastic bag from Shopko, and disappeared into the woods immediately. Her flashlight was just a wink in the trees by the time I hoisted the bag onto the ground. Victoria and Caitlyn followed their captain, leaving me with Becky and the weak beam of her flashlight.

"I hope you brought extra batteries," I said. I thought about really getting lost, wandering around until morning. A helicopter from Search and Rescue would be able to spot Becky's hair from at least a mile away.

I wasn't going to hoist it over my shoulder, so I kind of dragged it along beside me, and the burlap snagged on the underbrush. I swore it was hot to the touch. It definitely had a particular smell.

It took twenty minutes for Becky and me to reach the clearing, but the cheerleaders had nearly finished. I could see the Meatloaf's tent, thirty yards away, but his snoring echoed along the tree line.

Kaitlynn and Victoria stood back and admired their work, empty boxes crumpled in Shopko bags, plastic handles tied in knots. Becky's flashlight, nearly spent, still revealed the pentagrams that dotted the meadow, circles nearly ten feet in diameter. The angles were sloppy, but I was relieved that the girls had indeed done their homework. I had worried they would make the same rookie move from every horror movie, but Kaitlynn and Victoria had not poured out a Star of David inside the rings. I doubt Ronnie would have expected Jews in the night. The salt glittered in the low beam, the five points of fire, earth, metal, water, and wood.

I stepped carefully over their work and crept closer to Ronnie's tent. I nearly gagged when I yanked the bow of twine that cinched the burlap bag and tried to be as quiet as possible as I dumped the pile of rats at the base of a tree. A sickening noise as they landed.

Ronnie's tent was set among the roots of the National Christmas Tree. Even in Becky's low beam, the tree didn't seem that impressive, really. I had heard about its perfect symmetry, but it looked like every other part of the forest. Not worth a one-man war. I followed Becky's flashlight as it trained all the way to the top; I guess I expected there to be a star or an angel or something.

As we walked back through the clearing, I saw Caitlyn, pouring a ring of salt around Ronnie's ATV. The girls might have looked up pentagrams, but obviously they read no further. I knew from Janelle that a ring of salt was a Wiccan spell for protection.

At least nobody would steal Ronnie's ATV.

Chapter Twenty-Eight

"WE'VE GOT LESS THAN A month before opening night," said David. "I'm not liking our chances."

"Your mathematics are terrible," responded Irene Vanek. "We have thirty-seven days left. I'm sure you have mastered addition and subtraction. You are sixteen years old." I knew that David would like to subtract Irene, permanently.

"I apologize," said David. "I keep forgetting who I'm dealing with. I'm sure you keep a close eye on the calendar. I would, too. You only have so many days left."

"Jesus Christ," said Irene. "I will probably outlive you."

"It's true," said Diana Whipple. "She does yoga every day."

"I only take a calcium supplement," said Irene. "I don't even take multivitamins. Just looking at you, I can predict a lifetime of antidepressants and pills for your blood pressure."

Enraged, David swiveled away from the stage, addressed me in his terrible whisper. "Are all feminists like that?"

I shrugged. I didn't bother to whisper. "I don't know. I've never met one."

David gathered himself and clapped his hands together. "Act two, first scene. I need the frostbite victims to stop stumbling over their lines."

The actresses assembled in their places. Miss Julie pretended to do paperwork with a quill pen, a giant red ledger spread across her lap. Of course, there was no ink in the quill, it was just an extra-long ostrich feather. At least we had props. Ruby, Beatrice, and Diana Whipple, all in identical blonde wigs, sat together on the fainting couch. We hadn't done a dress rehearsal yet, so I prayed that their voluminous costumes would fit across such a short space.

"Okay," said David. "I want the three of you to sit with your ankles crossed. I did research, and that was how a proper lady composed herself."

Ruby raised her hand. "I'm not supposed to have feeling in my legs."

"Right," said David. "Beatrice, I want you to reach down, and cross your sister's ankles for her. It will show the audience the depth of your shared trauma."

Beatrice was nearly blind, but she eased forward, and felt around for Ruby's feet. David was satisfied. To me, the three blonde women seemed to be perching on the upholstery like unfortunate birds that forgot to fly south for the winter.

Miss Neva had the first line. Beatrice squinted and wiggled her nose. "I smell smoke," she said.

"Sound more alarmed," said David. "Try it again."

"I smell smoke!"

"Good," said David.

As usual, Betty Gabrian was ready. She pointed her quill pen at Miss Neva. "That's impossible. Your nose was lost to frostbite."

"Miss Leslie is upstairs with a gentleman caller," said Ruby, attempting to calm Beatrice. "He smokes a pipe. That must be the odor that you are detecting, my dear sister."

"Does she have whiskey?" Betty was concerned. "That terrible scullery maid could find none in town. She claims the whole of Gabardine has been evacuated."

"I'm standing right here," said Erika Hickey. The character of Judith was in the corner of the stage, pretending to sweep. We still didn't have an antique broom that David approved of, so Erika did her best to pantomime. Her wig was brown and boring, but I hoped Bitsy could make a fantastic cleft lip. "I never tell a lie, Miss Julie. I would admit to being offended by your accusation, but I treasure my employment."

"Did you hear that, my gorgeous creatures? Finding a vocation in Gabardine is like finding a man who bathes regularly. It's rare, and you all need to appreciate what you have, and all I have given you."

"I have a whiskey stash in the forest," said Judith. "It was supposed to be a secret. I know how useless Miss Leslie is when she gets the tremors."

"Nobody likes a whore with tremors," said Miss Julie. Again, she pointed at the three blondes on the couch. "The three of you should be the most grateful. If Inga hadn't rescued you from the Indians, you would have died of exposure."

"She has wicked aim," said Miss Joanna. "We are forever thankful." Miss Joanna was supposed to be missing two fingers, and even in rehearsal, she clenched her fist to pretend. David had transformed her into a method actress.

"Uff-da," said Inga, and shot an imaginary rifle out of an imaginary window.

"I will never understand why those savages always want blondes," said Miss Julie. "I thought they stopped scalping people many years ago."

Chapter Twenty-Nine

MY MOTHER HAD TAKEN TO her bed, maybe for good.

The week before, I heard a crash in the bathroom. I didn't bother getting out of bed. My mom didn't fall down. My mother controlled everything, even things she shouldn't be able to, like gravity.

But when I heard her drive away, I found the bathroom scale on the kitchen counter, in pieces.

My mother gained four pounds, for no reason at all. She read her food journal to me, to prove it.

She hit 160, and for the first week the number was a mystery to be solved, and she busied herself with the investigation, calling her surgeon, even digging through last week's garbage, just in case she had devoured an extra Lean Cuisine in the middle of the night, sleepwalking or something. She kept a close count of every frozen entrée, so this was unnecessary.

After that first week, she stopped weighing herself hourly, the needle stuck at 160. She stopped being suspicious and frantic, and became something worse, because I had never seen it before. My mother became depressed. My mother got in her bed, and stayed there. The look in her eyes scared me, the shocked stare of a woman who swallowed her primal scream.

My mother would not surrender the gas station, would not

allow another soul to unlock those doors. There would be no gas in Gabardine. She would not surrender the keys, but she surrendered to her bed. I saw it coming, I think. The courtship of Waterbed Fred had made her jittery, and I think the very idea of dating was so alien, so frightening, that her blood pumped faster, and I'm no scientist, but maybe her body tried to protect her, in the only way it had ever known. I think it grew something inside her, a layer, a shield, and it weighed four pounds and even though it was a tiny amount, it was enough to break her completely.

ON THE SECOND DAY OF the gas crisis, my mother told me to take the keys to her new car and sent me to the grocery store. She scribbled a list on her forearm with a marker, and I transcribed it dutifully. I didn't want to screw this up. I wanted to drive the new car, and at the grocery store, I wheeled the cart and piled it full, plucked things from the shelves that only stoned frat boys would eat. During the real fuel crisis, Americans blamed the Middle East. During this fuel crisis, my mother was happy to be the enemy. She would win this war with Doritos and gummy bears.

I was concerned about money. I forged the checks for the grocery store, no problem. I forged checks at the gas station in Fortune, feeling like a traitor as I filled the tank of my mother's new car. But sooner or later, I was going to get popped for check fraud, and I read the newspaper, I knew that the bad girls in Montana were now being shipped to Texas, and the idea of Texas horrified me, not to mention that I was sixteen now and could be charged as an adult. I didn't want to forge checks, and I was afraid Mr. Francine would shut off our power just out of spite.

Every morning, I checked in on her. I knew she left the nest at night and pulled food inside her bedroom. Wrappers and cellophane stuck into the blankets piled around her, the kind of nest a pack rat would make, if a pack rat only had access to things full of trans fats and high fructose corn syrup. I peeked in, and if she was still sleeping, or even if she was just pretending, I plucked the wrappers and the detritus and piled it in my arms, dumped it in the garbage.

I couldn't believe this person was my mother, who shook the toaster out every other day, who rinsed out the stupid Lean Cuisine packages before tossing them away.

"The last thing we need is goddamn ants," she declared.

HALLOWEEN WAS TWO WEEKS AWAY, and Mr. Francine's normally fastidious desk was decorated with a ceramic pumpkin, almost the same color as Becky's hair mistake. The ceramic pumpkin was pushed as close to the edge of the desk as possible, as if it disgusted him, as if this nod to the holiday had been enforced by supervisors. The pumpkin was filled with the cheapest Halloween candy, so against his will, he must have filled it on his own dime. Tootsie Rolls, and not even the normal kind, but the type that nobody ever wanted: vanilla and fruit.

"Don't touch," he said, before I even had a chance to sit down. Apparently, these terrible candies were meant for people only on official business, but nobody ever came to see Mr. Francine under happy circumstances. I doubt that somebody paying a delinquent power bill would think to grab, nor that Mr. Francine would offer. The pumpkin was completely full, and I had no idea how long it had been perched on his desk, but I swear the top layer of candy had dust.

I'm supposed to be working on my self-control. I'm supposed to be conscious when things rise up inside of me, name them, shake their hands. I know the pilot light is always lit, will always be inside me. The second the door closed behind Rufus, the second that it was just me and Mr. Francine, a compulsion burst into my head, and I swear I could feel it, really feel it, right behind my eyes like some kind of migraine. Like anger, it was a need for release, but this time it was a confession. I've learned that making things right can be like unleashing a punch, the consequences just as painful.

"Mr. Francine?"

"No talking. You know that." Mr. Francine didn't even look up at me. He was involved in his own obsessive thoughts and peeling Post-it notes, one by one, and placing them in the center of a page full of lists of numbers. He didn't trust the adhesive, rubbed his finger across over and over until he was sure the Post-it note was secure. Official business, important business, even though each yellow square was blank. I watched his process, centering the yellow square, moving that page to the left side of his desk, before moving to the next.

"I need to tell you something."

"No, you don't." He returned to his ritual, center, stick, rub, stack. What would be written? What tiny message needed to be expressed, so exactly, so immaculately? Most people wrote something first, then stuck it, a note that could be a reminder of something forgotten, or a dashed-off comment, a critique, or even praise, unlikely in the case of Mr. Francine.

"I took all of your can openers. Three of them. I stole them out of your secret bunker." As soon as the words flew from my mouth, I regretted them.

He looked up, a Post-it note stuck on the end of his finger. "I take an inventory every week," he said. "A very, very careful inventory. I would have noticed."

"It's been over a year," I said. "I'm sorry."

"You have made me doubt my accounting," he said. "Even worse, you jeopardized my survival."

"Yes," I said. "I did those things."

"I'm not surprised," he said. "People like you are the reason I have a shelter in the first place. A survival shelter. Not a secret bunker. Don't minimize this."

"I'm not," I said. "I'll bring them back tonight. I swear to god."

"I don't want your promises," he said. His voice had raised, an edge sharpened, the volume sliced like that pearl-handled knife. "You are a piece of filth. This is the same as attempted murder, as far as I'm concerned."

"I'm sure you would have found a way to open up the cans," I said. "You're a really smart guy. You would have figured something out."

"Some people plan for the apocalypse," he squawked. "And some people create it!"

I'd never heard Mr. Francine yell, but I figured I deserved it. His raised voice was enough to conjure Kelly, who pushed Rufus out the door and beckoned me inside.

She already knew what I'd done, but she gave me the speech I was expecting. "You know about consequences, Tiffany. I have to do my job." She leaned close to me, and in a quieter voice, reminded me of the conditions of my probation. "If he presses charges, things will change."

There was nothing I could say. I pushed my pages at her and

steeled myself to face the scene outside of her door.

Sheriff Schrader was waiting for me, but his gun was holstered. He must have broken speed limits to respond so quickly, and there was a look on his face of exasperation, but I wasn't sure if I had caused it or if he was annoyed by Mr. Francine.

"He wants to press charges," said the sheriff.

"Okay," I said. I sensed Kelly, standing behind me in the doorway. I didn't expect her to protest or offer up any kind of defense. These were consequences, and this was her job. She was silent, but the sheriff looked over my shoulder at my probation officer.

"I've got to take her in," he said. He sighed and pointed to the door. I moved toward him, and Mr. Francine stood up from behind his desk, flung himself against the wall as if I was truly a menace.

"I called 911," he said. "This is serious business, Sheriff. I would expect handcuffs, at the very least."

"Sit down and be quiet," said Sheriff Schrader, and Mr. Francine obeyed. As the sheriff passed Mr. Francine's desk, his holster brushed the ceramic pumpkin, and I didn't flinch as it hit the floor and shattered. It's almost like I was expecting it to happen. The sheriff glanced at the broken pieces, and the unloved Tootsie Rolls, and offered no apology.

I followed behind, wondering if it would help if I stopped to clean up the mess. The sheriff moved too quickly for me to even consider it. My head was full of noise as I tried to remember the piece of paper that listed the rules of my probation, the exact language, and I was sure I had crossed yet another line. I was just glad that it was the sheriff who knocked over the pumpkin, that property destruction would not be added to the charges. I had done the work, I had made things right, and I had been so careful not to get knocked down. I breathed through my nose and out through my mouth, and I knew that I would be okay. I would put myself back together again. I would not stay broken. I took a glance over my shoulder, and Kelly stared back at me sadly, and I took one last look at that stupid pumpkin.

That's not me.

Pushed to the edge, precarious.

I'm not that girl anymore.

SHERIFF SCHRADER DROVE LESS THAN three blocks, and without a word, stopped his car in the empty parking lot of my mother's gas station. I expected a speech or for him to write a ticket, but he just leaned over and opened the passenger door.

The gas station had been closed for days, and maybe he was trying to make a point by dropping me off here. Like I was responsible for the gas crisis of Gabardine. He sighed, and I unbuckled my seatbelt and watched as he drove away.

The last time the gas station was closed, my mother had bariatric surgery. The doors were locked for exactly eleven days, the orders from her surgeon. But she had warned the regulars in advance, and they stocked up on snack foods and gasoline. They suffered through it.

I didn't want to go home. As soon as his car disappeared from sight, I left the empty parking lot. I was pretty sure he would not approve of me walking the streets of the town, as I had just committed another crime, and I was a threat to public safety once again. I took my chances. I felt the need to walk through Gabardine, because I was most likely going to be shipped off to Texas. I turned off the highway and tried to really look at the stores and the streets, to commit them to memory. You stop seeing things after a while, not blindness, but seeing things for what they are. Never what they could be; that's not this type of town. Off the highway, just blocks away from the gas station, I walked past the thrift store, another abandoned thing, and today, I finally paid attention.

In the window, written on the back of a cardboard box, white paint that dripped in places. A sign that had been in that window every single day I ever walked past: Everything Must Go.

Today, it struck me as the truest thing I'd ever heard.

FROM THE DESK OF TIFFANY TEMPLETON

I told you there were two secrets about Dogwood.

On my eighty-second night, I woke to an alarm, the first and only alarm I heard, amazing for a locked-down institution. Bleary-eyed, we were ordered to stand in the halls.

The girl who cried all night, the girl who was afraid of the dark. The girl who was never tough enough. I knew it was her, even before I saw the body.

She ate a handful of the blue salt.

The staff sprinkled it across the icy sidewalks, but the girl who was afraid of the dark had filled her pockets when nobody was watching.

When they carried her out, I stared at the blue stains around her mouth. I couldn't bear to look at her eyes.

The next morning, a bus took us to Billings. The thirteen girls that remained were all sent back to the counties we came from. We left with our belongings, and a week's worth of Seroquel, shaken into an ordinary envelope, left unsealed.

We were rushed away, because the school had been

shut down for good. The blue-mouthed girl was the eighth suicide in five years, and somebody finally took action.

I know things now. I know the blue mouth. I know the truth about desperation.

The girl should have been allowed to sleep with the lights on. She should have been offered some kindness, some grace. In order to clean up my mess, I need to do the same. I'm going to turn the lights on.

Chapter Thirty

ON THE FIFTH DAY OF the gas crisis, Waterbed Fred came to our door. I don't know if he had given up on courtship, but he didn't bring flowers. He didn't even bring potato chips, even though his truck was parked outside.

"This isn't my idea," he said, apologizing on our front porch before I could say a word. "I was sent here. They took a vote, and everything."

I assumed he was referring to the city council, and stared at his boots as he stepped around the screen door. Maybe someday Bitsy would fill out like this, maybe someday Bitsy would grow a mustache that I should hate on principle, but swoon over secretly.

I didn't speak, just pointed to my mother's bedroom. I didn't know if he had been in my mother's bedroom before. Even though they'd been dating for a month, I was basically under house arrest and would have noticed the delivery truck, or a smear of mustache dye on my mother's face.

He knocked, and then knocked louder. "She's dead," he said, stepping back slowly from the door. "She's gone and done it." He looked at me, and I swear he was on the verge of tears.

I knew my mother wasn't dead. She was not the suicide type. She would want to make a big speech first, issue proclamations, rip up the deed to the gas station just like she promised.

I sighed and pushed past him. I didn't bother knocking. I turned the knob, and in the gloom of her bedroom, I could still see her white face, jaw clenched, furious. She was wide awake, and her nest had grown in size; her head the only thing visible in a mountain of quilts, afghans, even winter jackets. I didn't recognize the newest parts of her nest. I had a suspicion David was smuggling these things to her, shoving them through her bedroom window. The gas crisis meant nothing to him. He lived for this kind of drama, and I knew he had a stockpile of medication from his allergist. Even if the town dried up and died from a lack of gasoline and snack foods, David would continue to mule blankets across the trailer court in the dark of night.

I didn't want to hear any of it, didn't want to bear witness to the assassination of Waterbed Fred. Walls in trailer houses are thin, and I sat on the steps of the front porch and waited. Less than five minutes later, Waterbed Fred joined me.

"I tried to be helpful," he said. "Compliments don't work. I kept reminding her that she was two-thirds the size she used to be."

"I don't think you can help," I said. "Unless you can figure out a way to rig all the scales in Carney County."

"Two-thirds," he said. "I mean, that's amazing. She won't hear it. Her head just poking out of all those blankets, glowing in the dark. Just that head, like a horror movie, insulting me. Even when we switched to Crystal Pepsi, she wasn't that mean."

"I'm sorry," I said. "I'm sorry that they sent you here. Four pounds and the entire town shuts down."

His whole body seemed to collapse right there on the top step, muscle and bone no use for this battle. His posture melted, and he dropped his chin to his chest, exhausted. "She's two-thirds the size, but six times more terrifying. I guess that balances out."

"I don't think your math is right," I said.

"It never is," he said. "I just drive the truck, and somebody else does the invoices."

BITSY AND I MADE OUT in the front seat of my mother's car several times a day. I didn't want to go all the way, and he respected that but respected the virginity of my mother's new car even more. I don't know if it was the make and model, but he bought Armor All and wiped down the dash, sprayed Scotchgard on all the carpeting. New cars were a rarity in Gabardine.

The women arrived for play practice in the white van; there was no gas crisis in Fortune. Betty witnessed Bitsy polishing my mother's side mirror, and as she walked inside the theater, she cast a knowing glance over her shoulder.

Today, David blocked a scene from the first act, and the ladies could not get it right. He'd even begged me to rewrite it, to add characters, a haughty reverend and a gang of pious women.

"This play is a feminist statement," I said. "Eight women and only eight women. Irene Vanek says that it's revolutionary."

"What about *The Vagina Monologues*, Tiffany? That's all women, and there's like a hundred different vaginas." Once again, that free month of HBO proved invaluable.

"I refuse to add a male character just because you can't accommodate Miss Connie's walker. She can't sit on the couch during the entire play." Truthfully, I probably could have rewritten the scene, but I had a lot going on, between my mother's hibernation and Bitsy's constant presence.

I thought that the scene was fine. Just referring to the visit from a squad of Bible-thumpers worked—just like the fire, some things had to take place offstage.

Betty Gabrian stared stage left, where a window would be. Supposedly, she was watching the reverend and his flock walk away. "I've been threatened with damnation for ten years but never by a man cursed with a birthmark on his face. There is irony there, my dears. We are not women of ill repute."

"We have no illnesses," said Miss Connie. Eileen Lambert shuffled forward with her walker to pat Betty on the back, offering consolation. "We are in the spring of our youth."

"No," said Betty. "Only our repute is ill. I will forgive your atrocious vocabulary. The reverend was referring to our salacious reputations."

"I am unusually limber," declared Miss Leslie. "My reputation is gold."

"Uff-da," said Irene Vanek, rolling her eyes. She still had not mastered a Hungarian accent, but David was terrified of her.

"And those women," continued Betty. "That flock of pious creatures. Hatchet-faced, every single one of them."

"Their husbands are regular customers," said Judith. "I've seen them with their wives in town, at the mercantile. As the only woman in this brothel who purchases dry goods, I can assure you that I am correct."

"Hypocrites," declared Betty Gabrian. "The only thing I hate more than hypocrisy is tuberculosis. May God spare us from both."

"Where is the whiskey?" Loretta's file had been accurate. The wig had created a patch of hives above her eyebrows. David kept Benadryl in his pockets for this very reason.

Chapter Thirty-One

WHEN YOU HAVE A BOX filled with twenty thousand dollars stashed behind a Laundromat, it feels like you are in a completely different movie, the kind of movie I usually hate. If I knew the twenty thousand belonged to Bitsy and his mother, I would have left in on their porch, anonymously. Everybody in Gabardine needed money. There was a depth to love, but also a depth to amends. It's simply not enough to throw cash at the surface of a problem and watch as it takes on water, until it sinks entirely. I knew what happened when adults came into sudden money. I've seen what they do with their tax returns.

I stopped Betty before she could climb into the passenger seat of the van. She now claimed the best seat in the van. She had made the right moves, ascended the hierarchy of the nursing home. Betty played the game, and she played it hard.

I knew I had made the right choice.

"I need to tell you something," I said and pulled her to the back of the van, the exhaust pipe pumping out steam in the cold air. "I need you to keep it a secret."

"Oh, dear. Aren't you using protection?" Betty grabbed my arm, and I thought she was going to try to shake some sense into me. "I can tell from looking at him that his genes are no good. No good at all." She paused. "We can take care of this."

"We don't have very much time, so I need you to listen to me." Inside the van, the women had craned their heads to watch our encounter, and I spoke as quietly and quickly as possible. "I've got twenty thousand dollars in cash. It's in a box behind the Laundromat."

"That doesn't surprise me one bit," said Betty. "But I don't think the procedure is going to cost that much."

"I need you to spend it."

Betty looked at me suspiciously. "I know what you're capable of, and you know that it fills me with joy. If there was ever a fifteen-year-old girl with twenty thousand dollars that needed to be laundered, it would be you."

"Sixteen," I said. "I'm sixteen now."

"I missed your birthday," said Betty. "I missed your sweet sixteen."

"Here's your chance to make it up to me," I said, conscious of Irene Vanek, who was attempting to open the van window to eavesdrop. Thankfully, her elderly hands did not have the strength. "I've got to remain anonymous."

Betty gasped. "A hitman? Your brother is odious, but you already stabbed him once. You'd be the first suspect."

"There's a city council meeting next Tuesday. I'll pick you up, and I need you to look as powerful and glamorous as possible."

"I shall wear my wig." She stood up a little straighter, newly empowered.

THE BEST SALESPERSON IN GABARDINE had taken to her bed, and besides, she could never know about the money. Betty Gabrian was the second-best choice. I prayed that Betty could make a successful pitch, could intimidate the city council with her posture and her eloquence. Posture and eloquence were things my mother didn't have, but she was a magician at the gas station.

Like a good writer, I did my research. I drove to Fortune on Tuesday, as soon as school was over. I got the numbers I needed, and picked up Betty. As promised, she wore a slim velvet suit, black, no blouse. Her impressive cleavage was covered by ropes of pearls. Her wig was crooked, but we would adjust that before we got out of the car.

"This should be an emergency meeting," declared Mr. Francine, after the Pledge of Allegiance.

"There needs to be public notice for emergency meetings," muttered one of the old men. "It's in the bylaws." The three old men sat in their usual chairs, and I was growing quite fond of them.

"We've got a gas crisis," said Mr. Francine. "And I see Vy's daughter is in the audience. Maybe she's shown up with some sort of ransom."

I shook my head.

Betty stood, wig straightened, and she smoothed her velvet trousers. "This is poppycock. Call for new business, and stop wasting our time."

"New business," stated Mr. Francine.

Betty remained standing. She popped open her black velvet purse with a pearl clasp. She was definitely the right choice for the job. She stepped forward, bulging envelope in hand, and thwacked it down in front of Mr. Francine.

"I want to buy a streetlight," she said.

"This isn't Monopoly," he said. "You can't just buy utilities."

"I checked," she said. "Yes, I can. There is twenty thousand dollars in that envelope."

"Cash?"

"Yes," she said. "I want a receipt for every goddamn dollar. It hasn't started snowing, so your city maintenance workers are free, unless they are day drinkers. If you can't get it done in two weeks, I've got a contractor and an electrician in Fortune just waiting for my call."

"We should keep it local," said the secretary. "We can't have an outsourcing scandal on top of a gas crisis. Gabardine will become a ghost town."

"It already is," said Betty. "Right now, I'm haunting you. Two weeks. I want your answer right now."

"Hold on a minute," said Mr. Francine. "I need some more details."

Betty fished the Post-it note from the bottom of her purse. I had itemized everything, thanks to the city planner in Fortune, who was intrigued by my questions, and recognized my leather jacket as belonging to his brother-in-law, who pawned it to pay to have his front teeth capped. She read aloud, in the voice she had learned from David. She projected to the back of the room, unnecessary in such small quarters. The city council flinched. "The lighting rig is $5,432. A twenty-foot pole is $595.95, unless you want me to buy it from Fortune, but I know what strange pride you people have in your trees. It's going to cost around $3,000 to set a new foundation, and $1,150 for the electrician, and you'd better not hire that dipshit that cheated on our best nurse. Grand total, $10,177.95, but I expect there to be problems, because I'm dealing with lazy cusses. I want the remainder to go to the food bank."

"This is a list of demands," said Mr. Francine. "This is just like something Vy would do."

"Public safety," said Betty Gabrian. "And you shall have the legacy of being the first city council to bring a streetlight to Gabardine."

Mr. Francine leapt from his folding chair and to his feet. Next to Betty, his suit looked shabby. "Who's going to pay for the electricity?"

"The City of Gabardine," stated Betty. "Public safety." At this, the old men applauded.

"It's not in our budget," said Mr. Francine. "That's a damn fact."

"I can do math as well as you," declared Betty. "You can pass it on to the taxpayers. It comes out to fifty-four cents per year."

"Fine," said Mr. Francine. "But if this is about public safety, I want that damn light to be installed outside this building. I'm the only person who has to deal with the criminal element."

"Teenagers on probation sit in your office once per month," said Betty. "During daylight hours. You're more at risk to catch hantavirus."

"There are no rats in my office," said Mr. Francine.

"Just one," said Betty. "The streetlight will be installed in the center of the trailer court. Right next to the dumpster."

I guess this amends was a guarantee that my spying days were finished. Let some other kid sneak around the other parts of Gabardine, let some other kid peek in the windows of real houses built on concrete foundations. In my neighborhood, we would have no teenage spies. In our trailer court, no girl would ever be afraid of the dark.

Chapter Thirty-Two

MY MOTHER NEVER DID ANYTHING small. I think she was incapable of it. She gained four pounds and created a fuel crisis.

It was the topic of every conversation I stumbled upon as I walked through town, or overheard at the grocery store, and even in the halls of our high school, the fuel embargo was bigger news than any forest fire.

I wanted to tell everybody to relax. They could still get gas, less than twenty miles away. Betty Gabrian predicted that the gas station in Fortune would raise their prices by a dollar, but that didn't happen.

I walked with my head down, avoiding eyes, but as I passed the gas station on Friday, I looked up. The panel that usually held my mother's current weight had been covered by a dangling flag. I do not know the flags of the world, but thankfully, the flag maker had used a Magic Marker to scrawl "Saudi Arabia" across the bottom. It was made of cloth, which was impressive. Someone had really committed to this project; I doubted that any Gabardinians had Saudi flags in their attics. This level of arts and crafts suggested David, of course, but my mother was the center of his universe, so I ruled him out. Goddamn the Ben Franklin and their well-stocked arts and crafts section.

My social studies teacher decided that this was a teachable

moment, so all of a sudden, we were learning about OPEC in 1973. Admittedly, our textbooks were out of date and pretty racist and sexist, but they'd been published in the '90s. Even with a thirty-year-old textbook, the historians had not thought the real fuel crisis was something worth including.

"Your mother is basically an Arab," said Kaitlynn, and this was so lame that I knew she thought of it herself.

"My mother is clinically depressed. She is not an oil cartel."

"My parents said there is going to be a riot. The first thing I'm going to burn is your stupid leather jacket." I reconsidered. Perhaps David had fed her this line after all.

The most common question, the one I couldn't answer: What is wrong with your mother?

I had been asking myself this same question for sixteen years.

I FELT BAD TAKING SUCH a nice car over such disastrous roads, but I drove slowly, and every time I heard the undercarriage bottom out I reminded myself that this was a life-saving mission, or at the very least, a chance to spy on the Meatloaf.

I left the car parked on the road—I wasn't going to risk dipping two wheels into a ditch. If there were any vehicles that needed to pass, they could attempt that maneuver.

It was already bitterly cold by the end of October, but the hike made me sweat, and I removed my leather jacket. The problem with a giant vintage leather jacket is that you can't just tie it around your waist or drape it over your shoulders. I hung it from a tree on the trail. My jacket was one of a kind. If somebody tried to swipe it, they would have to drive across state lines to wear it.

Daylight, and the Meatloaf was at full vigil. In a milk crate beside him, his gun poked out, and I could see pepper spray, three cans of energy drinks, and a box of Kleenex. He was serious; he had Kleenex within arm's reach for his seasonal allergies. Without the jacket, I moved silently. I sat fifty yards away and watched. He might have been taking his vigil seriously, but I could have easily executed an act of terrorism. This was day sixty-eight of his mission. I was expecting him to have stubble or something, but his face was hairless. Maybe the threat of Satan-worshipping terrorists had traumatized the follicles in his face. I've learned from Kelly that we all process trauma differently.

After ten minutes, I grew bored of watching the Meatloaf watching the tree line. I called out his name, but he still leapt for the milk crate.

"I'm unarmed," I announced.

He stared at me as I approached—maybe he didn't recognize me without the leather jacket. "I'd still like to check your pockets," he said.

Whatever. I stood still and let the Meatloaf pat me down. All I had in my jeans were the keys to the new car. Day sixty-eight, and he was slipping, for sure. He didn't even ask why I had unfamiliar car keys, let alone a set that held a fob that could lock and unlock and remote defrost. Christ, there was even a panic button, which I thought was kind of cool, but probably useless in Gabardine. Who would respond to the panic button? Would Toyota send a plane? Would mechanics leap out with toolboxes, connected to parachutes?

"Did you bring me supplies?"

"Um, no."

"Did you come to relieve me?" If the Meatloaf thought I would care about the National Christmas Tree, or could be trusted to protect such a treasure, he was definitely losing his edge.

"No. It's Mom."

"If she's dead, I can't handle that right now. I'm sorry for your loss. Come back in December and tell me again. I've been prepared to be an orphan for a few years now."

"Jesus, Ronnie. She's depressed. She shut down the gas station."

He ignored this. "Last week, I woke up, and somebody left me a meatloaf. I was so excited. In a casserole dish and everything. Tinfoil on top. I almost stuck a fork right in it, but I have better training than that."

"You don't have any kind of training," I said.

"My suspicions were right. My suspicions are always right. Some motherfucker had baked a pack rat inside."

Wow. That was some next-level revenge. I didn't think David would have gone that dark. It had to be Kaitlynn. And that was impressive. I'd witnessed her incompetence in home ec.

"I need your help with Mom. We've got a fuel crisis."

"No," he said. "I have a job to do." He paused. "Wait. A fuel crisis? Did we get invaded?" The Meatloaf obviously did not have many visitors or keep up on current events.

"She gained four pounds. She shut the gas station down."

"Four pounds?" He popped open an energy drink, and I knew it was warm, so I gagged a little bit when he took a deep swallow. "I've got Satan worshippers and people trying to poison me. Those are real problems."

"I just want you to talk to her," I said. "We both know that you are her favorite."

"No," he said. "I'm not leaving. Maybe I'll write her a note or something. Maybe you could come back with a Get Well Soon card for me to sign. Just don't stab anybody to get it." He took another slug from his energy drink. "Four pounds?" I watched him consider this, his hairless face scrunched with the math. "Maybe it's menopause."

I recoiled. I had not thought about that. How in the hell did my knucklehead brother come up with a legitimate answer? How did he even know about menopause? Maybe it was the energy drink.

"I will suggest that," I said. "But I'm not coming back here. If you want to write her a note, you're going to need to give it to me now."

"It's not worth it," he said. "I need to save every milligram of ink. I only brought three pens, and documentation comes first."

"What are you documenting? Seriously. What are you waiting for?"

"How's Lorraine?"

"Fine," I said, and this was true. I didn't tell him that she had gone back to the Sweet compound at the end of September. He would return to his trailer without a job, a family, or a flat screen. Maybe he would crawl inside my mother's nest. I watched him pound the rest of his energy drink, and then crush the can with his bare hand. He belched, and I stood up to leave. "Thanks for nothing, Ronnie. As usual."

"Someday you will get a calling," he said. "Someday you will understand. When you get a calling, you don't have a choice."

"I'm not expecting a calling," I said. "I still can't use the phone."

Chapter Thirty-Three

"THIS TRAILER PARK IS LIKE the Bermuda Triangle," said Bitsy. "I don't get it. All these dads just disappear." We sat on the top of the sand hill and looked down on the lights of the trailer court.

I considered this. Twenty-two houses, but only one father. The McGurtys had the only dad in the entire loop, but he was still just a kid himself. Six kids, starting at age fifteen, and I was there the day he brought in his driver's license and waved it in my mother's face, finally legal to buy beer. (Of course, the minute he drove away, triumphantly, with a cheap six-pack of Miller, my mother told me that it was Mrs. McGurty who really deserved the beer, six kids in six years, and who cares if she was breastfeeding. Her womb could really use a drink.)

"My dad didn't disappear," I finally said. "He died. That's different."

"I just think it's weird," he said. The sand was cold against my jeans, the last days of October, and the moon rising just after dinner. It was only eight o'clock, but dark like the middle of the night, the hours when people finally slept deeply. I rarely spied at three o'clock in the morning, but when I did, the stars were so sharp that I wanted to wake everybody up, just to take a look. Come see what you're missing. Take a look at that sky. Come with me in your pajamas and watch Lou Ann paint throughout the dead hours.

Bitsy pointed at the trailer park, the windows lit all along that sloppy loop, the black sky broken only by the moon on the mountains, by the windows of single mothers. I lay on my back on the cold sand and looked at Bitsy's finger, silhouetted against the moon. "Statistically, I mean. There shouldn't be that many single mothers in one place."

"Economics. All trailer parks are full of single mothers. It's what they can afford." I closed my eyes, and I stretched out, but the sand was unyielding, my body so rigid I swore I could feel every individual grain of sand. In the summer, you could surf on this hill, but in the winter, it clumped together. The sand never froze, not even in the most frigid stretches of winter.

I kept my eyes closed, and it was so quiet that I could hear him breathing.

"My dad was going to buy a house," he said, and I heard his breathing change. "He was a man with a plan."

"I know," I said.

"No," he said. "You don't know." I squeezed my eyes as tight as I could. I did know his dad, the worst parts of him, the secret parts. "My dad made things happen. Like football. He created a whole football team."

"I'm sorry," I said.

Tell the truth. Be the toughest Tiffany, for real this time.

"He ran away," said Bitsy. "You're the first person I've ever been able to say that to. Nothing bad happened to him. That's why we didn't look for him. We only pretended."

"It's my fault," I said.

"Whatever," he said. "He took off because he was selfish. You don't get to take credit for this one. You can't wreck people. You're not your mom. The only person you're good at wrecking is yourself."

I didn't respond, and once again, his breathing changed, quicker, the hyper boy I'd grown up with, body galloping ahead without him. I swear the heat inside him traveled through the frozen sand. I heard the flick of the lighter, and then I could smell the smoke from his cigarette. I straightened my back, just to make the sand dig a little deeper, just to feel it all.

"My dad couldn't handle being an adult. He didn't want to be a husband or a dad. He just wanted to coach football."

"Listen to me," I said. "He didn't run away to get away from you. He ran away because he got caught."

"What are you talking about?"

"You know what I'm talking about. I watched you, Bitsy. Just like I watched everyone. You didn't think it was weird that random people just walked into your house all the time?"

"Stop," he said.

"Your dad sold drugs," I said. "You knew. You and your mother knew the whole time."

He was silent, and I watched his face illuminate from a deep draw on his cigarette, a sizzle I could actually hear, the glow revealing a stare I had never seen before. Almost an X-ray, like he was seeing through things. He exhaled, and the smoke covered his face, and those eyes, lost in a cloud of his own making.

At that moment, I knew he would always find a way to hide the truth. He would keep this secret forever, no matter the cost. I knew the real expense of secrets, all too well. He stubbed his cigarette into the sand, and the stillness was broken as it hissed, extinguished. I wanted to know the truth about us, and on that sand hill, looking out at the twinkling lights of all those homes and all their secrets, I knew I had nothing to lose. "Why did you go out with me?"

He didn't answer my question. He had been caught, and I

knew what desperation did to people. Finally, he spoke. "You can't tell anybody."

"He used my brother as a drug mule," I said. "He nearly killed Lou Ann Holland."

"That's not my fault," he said.

"I didn't turn him in to the police. I broke into your house and took all of his money and all of his drugs. He took off that night."

I couldn't bear to look at him. I clenched my entire body, just waiting for him to hit me. That's what I would have done.

"Don't ever talk to me again," he said.

I listened as the sand crunched as he stood. I waited to hear him walk away, waited to hear him run, dash down the hill to jump in his truck and crash it into something.

Finally, I heard him march down the hill, and I knew he meant it. He would not talk to me. Consequences. He would keep my secret, because he had to. I was a thief, but his father was much, much worse.

I listened to his descent, until I couldn't hear him anymore, and finally, I opened my eyes. Things had changed. Tough Tiff upset another universe.

Above me, the stars remained fixed in place.

FROM THE DESK OF TIFFANY TEMPLETON

I put everything in its right place. Except this. This has been stuck inside me, lodged in my throat. Dangerous. I could choke or I could cough it out.

This is my last confession.

I went back. Something at the Bitzches' called me, told me I wasn't finished. In September, I returned.

Coach Bitzche sat on a stripped mattress, no pillowcases. It must have been laundry day, and Bitsy and his mom were in the living room, not folding or sorting, but watching some beefcake in a hot tub with four women, another dating show. I watched Coach Bitzche check his watch, tug on the whistle around his neck, a ritual. He crouched down beside the bed and slid out one of Ronnie's boxes and a gray metal toolbox. Cross-legged, he pried at the shipping tape and peeled, until the flaps of the cardboard box were free. I expected him to pull out Bibles, honestly. Instead, a stack of white envelopes wrapped with a rubber band, and a manila envelope folded around a brick of something. More prying and peeling of tape, and when he finally just ripped it apart, I watched the cash fall all around him. The Bitzches were poor enough to live in a trailer court, but I watched for ten minutes, as he carefully smoothed each bill, organized and stacked the denominations into piles, at least an inch tall. He removed binder clips from the toolbox, and arranged the cash in a semicircle around him. The white envelopes were arranged in another semicircle, eight envelopes, evenly spaced, like he was doing a tarot reading. A fear rushed, and it seemed to come from my stomach, and I knew right then and there that everything had changed. I could see that far ahead, without the King of Swords.

I ducked when I heard a car, and the headlights nearly caught me as I tucked myself farther in between the dumpsters. A station wagon parked in front of the Bitzches' house, and I was fascinated when the interior light flashed on as the doors opened. Nurses, in hospital scrubs imprinted with balloons, terrible plastic shoes. The passenger swung a new loaf of Wonder Bread as she approached the front door, the balloons seemed to match the primary colors, the dots on every package of Wonder Bread.

I swear that I nearly puked, as acid continued to boil up through my throat, and my mouth filled with saliva as I watched the nurses enter the house without knocking, walk right through the living room without even acknowledging Bitsy or his mother.

He didn't seem to be surprised when they entered his bedroom. I guess this wasn't a house call. They gave him the loaf of bread, which he cradled under his left arm like a football. With his right hand, he plucked the two envelopes at the very end of the semicircle, and each woman tucked one in a pocket of her scrubs. Wordlessly, they left the room, and I watched Coach Bitzche immediately readjust the envelopes on the bed, evenly spacing them once again. It all seemed like witchcraft, and when he tugged on his whistle once more, I knew I was hexed.

The nurses in the station wagon drove away from the trailer court, but Coach Bitzche remained sitting, staring at the ring of assembled objects, as if daring them to move. After another twenty minutes, I was the object cursed into action, as I'd seen enough. I walked the short distance home and took the hottest shower I could stand.

The next Monday, I skipped fourth period. I knew Mrs. Bitzche was on her route, and it was strange to be spying in the middle of the day. My black clothes were conspicuous, but the trailer park was empty.

Like most people, the Bitzches didn't lock their door.

In the bedroom, I reached for the familiar toolbox. The bed was freshly made, but the room still smelled like something dirty.

Inside the box, another stack of cash and five Ziploc bags stuffed with sandwiches. This made no sense. Coach Bitzche seemed to run an expensive picnic operation. I unzipped a plastic bag and slid out the bread, and suddenly, pills escaped in all directions, scattered across the floor of the master bedroom. In my lap and rolling across the carpet, white ovals, yellow capsules, and fat circles speckled with blue. Always blue.

As quickly as possible, I bent down to the floor, and on my knees, I picked up every pill that had rolled away. I could see under the bed, and there were no dust bunnies. Mrs. Bitzche was a fastidious housekeeper. She had seen this toolbox. She had seen the Wonder Bread. She had let strangers into her house without a word. She knew.

I left the toolbox behind, crammed the sandwiches into the pockets of my leather jacket, the pills and the cash into a felonious lump in my jeans. I took everything, even the empty envelopes.

At the Laundromat, I crammed myself into the tiny bathroom, and I counted the money. I was the daughter of a tax man and a woman obsessed with invoices, so I counted it twice. Twenty thousand, one hundred and thirty-seven dollars. Carefully, I disassembled each sandwich and dumped the pills into one of the Ziploc bags. I zipped the top, clicked the blue strip over and over again. Again I had that fear, an unreasonable feeling that two hundred pills could escape. I dumped the bread and the remaining sandwich bags into the bathroom garbage, but even that made me paranoid. I removed the garbage bag and twisted it and tied it in a knot. I buried it in the dumpster in the middle of the trailer court, underneath a stained rug and a clattering assemblage of empty wine cooler bottles.

Coach Bitzche was absent on Tuesday. On Wednesday, Principal Beaudin made an announcement in gym class, declared it a study hall until further notice. Bitsy stayed at home, maybe to make coffee for the Search and Rescue team. On Monday, Mrs. Bitzche claimed to discover a missing suitcase, and the search was called off. In Idaho, I'm sure parishioners were mystified by the sudden disappearance of their pastor, but they had experience in accepting things without explanation. I knew the reason, and it was not metaphysical. Even the police didn't find it odd that two men vanished at exactly the same time. I guess they were used to the hazards of living in the wilderness. The coach and the pastor were not in the stomachs of grizzly bears, and I kept that secret to myself.

That's the story. If you want me to testify in court, let me know. I have experience now. Just promise to leave Bitsy out of it. We can't help who we are born to. I wish Bitsy had been like a stray dog that I found in the trailer park, and we could have just loved each other like that, both of us unclaimed, and untethered to horrible owners.

Chapter Thirty-Four

WE COULD CALL IT A theater now, but from the outside, it still looked like a garage. David and I stood outside, plugging outdoor lights into an extension cord. One on each side of the stage, our floodlights. They were strictly utility lights, 1000 watts, and the stands and the cages around the lightbulbs were that utility-yellow color that only straight men seem to find satisfying.

"We could spray-paint them," said David.

"You and your spray paint," I said. "It's a sickness. I'm afraid you're going to spray-paint the actresses, too."

"I bet it would look better than Bitsy's makeup," he said.

"Bitsy won't be doing the makeup," I said.

"I'm not surprised," he said. "I knew you would find some way to destroy it." David paused, and turned to look at me. I could tell he was sorry. It was a rare thing. "He was terrible at it. No big loss."

A rumble up the street, and Waterbed Fred's truck pulled up in front of us. In the passenger seat, Janelle waved madly, and even from twenty feet away, I could tell she was wearing false eyelashes. David had been begging her to do this for years, but apparently only Waterbed Fred was worthy of the effort. Interesting.

Waterbed Fred honked his horn. This was the first time I had ever heard him do such a thing. Apparently, he was smitten.

The actresses responded to the noise, and made their way out into the parking lot. We watched as Janelle leapt from the passenger seat, wearing a fringed baby doll dress, even though it was barely thirty degrees outside. She winked at us, and I wished David had given her a better tutorial, because the lash stuck, and she had to tuck it into place with one finger.

We heard the door swing open at the back of the truck, and then Waterbed Fred was carrying folding chairs, three in each arm, and I think I heard Mrs. McQuilkin gasp as his biceps flexed.

David was delighted, of course, but as soon as he saw them up close, his brow furrowed.

"They're padded," he said.

"Of course," said Betty Gabrian. "I paid extra."

"Did you get a lot of your friends to come to the show?"

"I've invited them all. Except for the locked ward. Dementia is one thing, but those people bite. I don't think that would be a good thing." Sixty seats, ten rows, three on each side of the aisle. After we hauled them all inside, David fussed with the arrangement until he was satisfied.

"I'm concerned about continence," said David.

"Especially Africa," said Ruby.

WHEN I RETURNED TO MR. Francine's office, he sighed deeply, and pointed at the calendar on his wall. "You have the wrong day, Miss Templeton."

"I know. I need to leave something for Kelly." He stared at me as I thrust the envelope in his direction. I knew how organized he was and imagined he had a system for incoming mail. I wanted to stay on his good side. "Do I need to sign anything?"

"A confession would be nice," he said. "You can just bring that straight to the courthouse."

"It's important," I insisted. It was a confession, just not for his eyes.

"I'm not a post office," he said. "And I know how little respect you have for the mail."

"Can you please just leave it in her office?"

Mr. Francine looked at me as if I had finally brought the apocalypse. I was the end of the world. At least he was prepared for it. When he took my pages, he had no idea that I had included another explosion in Gabardine, a letter to Kelly that would change everything.

I was glad I had sealed it shut.

FROM THE DESK OF TIFFANY TEMPLETON

November 6, 2018

Dear Kelly:

I'm probably going back to the detention center, and I'm pretty sure it's in Texas now, which would give me something to write about, but I think I'm done with writing. When I confess, things explode. I think I'm done with all of it. I deserve this. I told Bitsy everything, and my mom is still in her nest, and there is no gasoline in Gabardine. I ruined an entire town, I think.

I don't want to be that girl.

Behind the Laundromat, there is a juniper bush. If you put some heavy gloves on, you can reach a typewriter case. I've left it unlocked. Inside you will find all the evidence. I don't care if you return any of the things, but I want you to have proof that you did your best.

I could not be fixed.

Get out of Gabardine.

Sincerely,

Tiffany Templeton

Chapter Thirty-Five

WHEN I HEARD THE NOISES in the kitchen, I was shocked.

My mother sat at the table, bleary-eyed in a bathrobe.

This was like a great bear, emerging from hibernation, shaking off the winter.

The gold foil from a piece of chocolate stuck in the folds of her sleeve. She pointed her unlit cigarette at me as I walked through the door.

"I dreamed of your father. He was wearing that trench coat I hated so much, the black one that looked like a goddamn couch cover. He didn't say a word. But this light surrounded him, until it filled up the entire room. I swear to you, Tiffany. The light was the exact color of the popcorn butter."

I had been so wrapped up in making things right that I didn't notice the construction. The streetlight had been erected within a day. My role was a secret, so I wouldn't have been invited to a ribbon-cutting ceremony.

The light had been switched on while I was in the shower, and at first I had not noticed the yellow cast of the arc sodium light, but she was right. The color of popcorn butter. The trailer court was flooded with it. We'd never had shadows, not unless the moon was especially bright. Now, everything doubled in another shade, a brownish orange. The light that struck every immoveable object left a twin on the ground, stretched out and taller. David was paralyzed by the thought of overhead light, and he was going to hate the glow.

"That's weird," I said. "The trench coat, I mean. Maybe it's like Groundhog Day, and he appeared to warn you that we are going to have a really bad winter."

She stared at me. "I tell you about something beautiful, and you compare your father to a rodent."

"He was an angel," I said. "Let's just call him an angel."

"I don't believe in that nonsense," she said. She sighed and lit her cigarette, but her face still looked dreamy, the most at peace I'd ever seen. I leaned across the table and pulled open the only curtains in the trailer park. The streetlight filled the dirty window, and my mother recoiled from the blast of incandescence.

"What in the hell?"

"We got a streetlight. It's not in the street, really. It's next to the dumpster."

"Who approved of such a thing?"

"Mr. Francine." This was kind of true, so I didn't feel bad. "I just wanted to show you, so you could stop thinking that light was from an angel."

"A ghost," she confessed. "I don't believe in angels, but I do believe in ghosts."

"I won't tell anyone," I said. "I believe in them, too."

"Twenty days was enough," she declared. "Please tell me the entire town fell apart." I wanted to tell her about Bitsy, about Lou Ann, about the can openers. The only undoing of the last twenty days happened to me, and I had pulled the string.

"Of course," I said. "No riots or anything, but you got people talking."

She looked around the kitchen, like she was seeing it for the first time. I followed her eyes as they fell on unopened bags of potato chips on top of the refrigerator. "Get rid of all of this food," she said.

"I could start cooking," I said. "We don't have to live on Lean Cuisines. I could cook healthy meals."

"That's ridiculous," she said. "You're still on probation. No knives in this house. Unless you learned how to chop vegetables with that sharp tongue of yours." She stopped herself. "I'm sorry," she said. "Let me think about it."

"Okay," I said. I moved across the kitchen and reached for the potato chips, tossed them in the garbage. I could always fish them out later and hide them under my bed.

"It caught up with me," she said.

"What?"

"I forgot to grieve for your father," she said. "I figured it out this morning." My mother went straight back to work after my father died, and straight back to chasing the magic number, ran toward a number on a scale. I guess she didn't know that something was chasing her until it finally caught up.

"I miss him, too." We had never really talked about our grief, we had never really talked about any sort of feelings. My dad held all the feelings in the house, I think, absorbed them, so we didn't have to.

"I'm sorry, Tiffany." My mother looked up at me, and jabbed her cigarette out in the glass ashtray. "I really mean that."

"I know," I said and began to open the cupboards, pulling out the contraband.

"Back to work," she announced and stood up from the kitchen table. "You better not have fucked up my car."

Chapter Thirty-Six

SHOWTIME WAS AT SEVEN, BUT David wanted me there at four. This was unsurprising. When I pushed through the doors, he was sitting on a folding chair, front row, staring at the stage. He rose when he heard my footsteps and turned to face me, holding out a carefully wrapped box.

"For you," he said, and this was, in fact, surprising.

I didn't want to take the box from him, but he forced it into my hands, cringed when I began tearing at the paper. I stopped and peeled back the scotch-taped corners carefully. This made him happy.

"I don't need any gifts," I said.

"You earned it," he said. "This is something you need. It fits."

Christ. I was sure the box held a pair of sparkly butt jeans, and David was doing what David was always doing, cultivating.

Instead, inside layers of thin tissue, a brand-new black leather jacket.

"Like I said, it fits. Try it on."

I didn't know what to say, just followed his orders, and it did fit, perfectly.

"Jackets should have sleeves that end just at your wrist, and shoulders that are cut and don't come out somewhere near your elbows."

"Thank you."

"There," he said. "If you zip it up all the way, nobody will see your dirty T-shirt."

AT SIX, THE OLD MEN set up their card table, offered up the programs, folded exactly, each one prepared by David. There were no tickets to collect, no hands to stamp, no change to count back. The sets, the costumes, the chairs, the complete overhaul of a building. The days and nights of worrying, the hours of rehearsal, the minutes we had stolen from elderly women who had none to spare. Despite all it had cost, we would not charge admission.

The programs were printed on expensive paper, and I wondered where David found the money in the budget. On the cover, a decent photoshop attempt—David had clipped an old-timey photo of a woman who looked like Annie Oakley, even though our characters were not flinty-eyed sharpshooters. He didn't bother removing her shotgun or her dirty cowboy hat. The sepia-toned woman had been carefully clipped with scissors, and behind her, in vivid color, a collage of fire. Admittedly, some of the flames in the collage had been stolen from our local forest service fire season pamphlet, some were not photos but cut from oil paintings that probably depicted the devil in hell, and the remainder seemed ripped from fireplace scenes in one of his *Martha Stewart Living* magazines. At the tip of a corner, he had missed a tiny piece of red fabric, a tiny bit of a Christmas stocking.

Satisfied, I opened the program, and my jaw dropped. After all those months, after my copious notes, David still hadn't bothered to learn the real first names of his actresses. I knew if I questioned him, he would claim it was an artistic decision.

The Soiled Doves of Gabardine:
A Play in Three Acts
Written by Tiffany Templeton
Directed by David Alexander Muscarella
Produced by Vy Templeton

MISS JULIE . . . MRS. GABRIAN

MISS JOANNA . . . MRS. WHIPPLE

MISS LESLIE . . . MRS. MCQUILKIN

JUDITH . . . MRS. HICKEY

INGA LISZAK . . . MRS. VANEK

MISS NEVA . . . MRS. SMETANKA

MISS CONNIE . . . MRS. LAMBERT

MISS AIMEE . . . MRS. BARDSLEY

Featuring the singing of "Waterbed" Fred Hakes

By six forty-five, almost every seat was taken. From backstage, I squinted as something sparkled and caught my eye, something shiny, so out of place among the beaten-up folding chairs and the sawdust-covered floor. Peering closer, I saw a small cluster of empty folding chairs, second row, right on the aisle. A silver ribbon tied the chairs together, and I had spent enough time suffering through David's gift wrap station that I recognized it immediately.

I wish I could say the entire crowd gasped at the appearance of my mother, but I think they were all still pissed about the gas station. Regally, she paused at the top of the aisle, and the silver ribbon suddenly made sense. A shiny blouse, smooth as aluminum foil, the collar and the long tails flared with detail work. From this distance, I couldn't tell if it was beaded, but it didn't look cheap. Underneath, a familiar black skirt, the usual jersey material, but ending just above a pair of high-heeled ankle boots, and I couldn't help but think of David Bowie, or an astronaut. Her hair, her achingly practical hair, was sprayed in waves that flew from her forehead and snaked around her neck. Long necklaces, three in total, different lengths, all silver chain. The blouse did not billow, did not blow around her body like a cape or a curtain. It actually fit her, and I could see that it clung to what used to be love handles and now were just small mounds of loose skin. I'm not sure why she decided that this was the night to debut what David called "body conscious." We made eye contact from one hundred feet, and I don't know what kind of reaction she was expecting. I was just happy she was out of her goddamn nest. Her eyes met mine, and there was some kind of pride there. Not sure if it was pride for her outfit, or pride for finally leaving her bedroom, or pride for the new theater. I don't think it was pride that her daughter wrote a play. My mother detested the arts, because for a Libertarian, spending that much time engaging in self-indulgent creation was the same as smoking three packs of cigarettes, an addiction for weak minds. She didn't read books or watch movies, didn't have the time, and I think she had decided long ago that artists deserved consequences for smoking their minds away, not cancer, but a life of poverty and social alienation.

I realized my mother was not alone. Kelly stood beside her. I was pretty sure that Kelly hanging out with my mother was some kind of conflict of interest, but before I could get indignant, the air above the middle section of seats began to flicker, as a thin shower of dust descended slowly, reflected in the lights. The audience stilled, quieted, and we could hear a commotion on the roof. My mother, sensible as always, placed a protective arm in front of Kelly; they would wait to take a seat until the danger had passed. The dust came down in waves, and hair and faces were covered by T-shirts raised over heads. It was Gabardine, so nobody except my mother, my probation officer, and David got dressed up for the theater. No clothes would be ruined. The commotion continued, and I could see the galvanized metal buckle in places. A few seconds passed as we all craned our necks, then the metal snapped back into place. The dust dissipated until it was just a few motes, the usual ambient sawdust that David and the shop vacuum could never eradicate, despite his daily attempts.

Reluctantly, I left backstage and moved onto the floor of the auditorium. Although I had never been given the official title, I knew David considered me to be the stage manager. I stopped a few feet away from my mother, but close enough to smell Kelly's familiar perfume.

"Pack rats," called out an old man at the card table stacked with programs. "Sounds like a whole crew."

"On the roof?" Kelly was clearly alarmed, perhaps imagining an attack from above, like the rats were paratroopers.

"You're safe, lady. Pack rats won't eat you. They'll eat fiberglass, but they ain't going to eat someone like you."

"Are you being racist?"

The old man stammered. "That's not what I meant."

Another old man came to his rescue. "Your people make great pie crusts," he said.

"Jesus," said Kelly, and she and my mother began their descent toward me, to the specially marked seats. I ignored them both and bolted for backstage. There really wasn't anything for me to do, but I wanted to look important.

* * *

AT TEN AFTER SEVEN, DAVID was satisfied with the attendance. Three empty chairs, but still kind of standing room only, because a group gathered against the far wall, refusing to sit close to my mother.

The curtains parted, and Waterbed Fred stood in the center of the stage. People applauded before he even did anything, because Waterbed Fred had a fan club. Because he was handsome, and because he carried snack foods.

He looked nervous, but stared off into the distance, opened his mouth, and sang.

"Abilene" filled the entire room, and it was absolutely gorgeous. David feared a copyright lawsuit, as if the crowd contained entertainment lawyers or some Hollywood star whose car had broken down in our town and who just happened to stumble across an amateur theater production. The lyrics were not changed, but I think the crowd was just entranced and didn't really question why Waterbed Fred was singing about a town in Texas.

In the second act, a special guest star. It began with a titter, really. That's the best way to describe the sound. The audience was too polite to laugh out loud, but they made enough sound for me to poke my head out from backstage.

I followed their eyes and a few pointed fingers. A pack rat had stopped center stage, apparently soaking up the limelight. The actresses continued, ignoring the creature, which probably weighed eight pounds. Most pack rats would scurry around, looking for food or anything to chew on, really. They made their nests out of the weirdest stuff, and right now, I just hoped the pack rat would not choose to pull at the cord of an oxygen tank or make a dash for the bullets we had carefully scattered across the credenza. David had actually done the careful scattering, and

I mean really careful, arranged them for close to ten minutes.

Pack rats are like regular rats, except they have freakishly human hands, like a tiny baby. I cringed, hoping the old men in the front row would not start tossing candy. Miss Julie continued her lines, but Judith, always the most capable of the women, ignored the script, lifted her dragging skirt, and made her way to center stage. The pack rat stared at her, made no move. And now the audience couldn't hold it back. They cackled at the standoff, and Judith's eye contact was not enough to frighten the animal, maybe because she was developing glaucoma. The laughter had caused the entire cast to pause, and I knew that Betty Gabrian had the next line, and I just hoped she would continue, and eventually the pack rat would lose interest, and dash back up into the rafters.

No such luck. Judith did not like being laughed at. With one practical shoe, she kicked the rat, thankfully not into the audience. Instead it flew stage right, where David stood with his clipboard and his copy of the script, ready to feed lines to any of the actresses with dementia. I watched the trajectory of the rat, as it sailed across the set of the brothel and into the curtains.

David shrieked. Rightfully so. The curtains buckled and shook, and over the laughter, I heard the clatter of the clipboard falling, followed by a series of exclamations, and to his credit, he did not use one profane word. He never did. Even the shock of a pack rat flying at his face would not excuse tackiness.

"I refuse to burn to death," said Miss Julie. "I was destined for a bigger demise. I was destined for a showstopper. Maybe a guillotine."

"Uff-da," said Inga, and drew a finger across her neck. In Hungary, they had guillotines. I was pretty sure.

The three blonde sisters removed folding fans from a side table, and their wigs barely moved, no matter how much they fluttered.

Backstage, David threw a garbage bag of empty tin cans against the metal wall. It was supposed to be thunder, but it sounded like a raccoon in a dumpster.

"Calamity!" Judith leapt to her feet. "That noise! Gunfire! This brothel cannot withstand a gunfight. We've only got one gun and little hope to create a tactical defense!"

"We're surrounded by flames," Betty Gabrian reminded her. "A literal wall of flames."

"It must be Indians," said Judith. "They are the only enemies brave enough to attack at a time like this!"

"Native Americans," muttered Eileen Lambert. This was not in the script.

Again, David hoisted the garbage bag over his head and threw it against the wall with all his might.

"It can only be our lord and savior," said Judith. "He has sent a message. We will die, but we will die as pious women."

David rushed behind the hanging set, yanked the blind behind the window, replacing the painted flames with a gray blind bought at Shopko that nobody had bothered to paint. The factory color was turgid enough.

"A storm!" Miss Julie rushed to the window, and pretended to peer out. Backstage, I began pouring jugs of water into a metal tub. It sounded like somebody running a bath, but we hoped the audience would be so enraptured that they could mistake it for rain. Thank god, I had nine gallons of water, all lined up.

"As usual, I will be the bravest whore in Gabardine!" Eileen Lambert exited stage left, slowly, her walker pushed toward backstage, where I was waiting. I dumped an entire gallon of water over her head, and she was not pleased. Dripping, miserable, she whispered to me: "You little asshole." I pointed back to the stage, and she returned to the scene. "A deluge from the sky! A sudden summer storm!"

Miss Julie craned her neck, taking stock of the imaginary yard and the cord from the blind caught on her necklace, and the blind snapped upward, taking Miss Julie's neck with it. This is what you get for buying crap from Shopko. Thankfully, Miss Julie remained calm, yanked her necklace apart, beads scattering across the stage. The blind hung crooked, and I'm sure the audience could see the metal wall backstage. As long as they didn't see David, I was okay with this. "It's a miracle!" Miss Julie stepped back from the crooked blind and addressed her employees. "I've never seen so much precipitation!"

"What about that really fat gunslinger? He sweated so much that he slipped right off me."

"The rain!" Miss Julie clasped her hands together. "God has saved our unfortunate souls. God is good!"

"Where is the whiskey?" Miss Leslie searched behind a throw pillow on the couch.

"We shall live on in history," declared Miss Julie. "This shall forever be known as The Last Stand in Gabardine!" Backstage, I choked up a bit, knowing this was untrue. The real last stand of Gabardine happened three weeks ago, when my mother turned off the fuel pumps.

Miss Julie stepped to the center of the stage, and Kaitlynn lit her petticoats with four plastic flashlights, two held in each hand. It was supposed to seem like a spotlight, and it had worked in rehearsals, but today, the beams shone through the lace and revealed her panties and fresh tubing, a recent colostomy bag.

"This town shall forever persevere," declared Miss Julie, center stage, addressing the audience directly, and then there was applause, especially hearty from the front row, the old men overwhelmed by either civic pride or Miss Julie's panties. We had expected some applause, and David instructed Miss Julie to milk it, wait for it to die down so her next line would not be lost. She waited a little too long, and the audience began to shift in their seats, looking at each other, wondering if this was the ending. Finally, Miss Julie raised her fist in the air. A thump from backstage, as Kaitlynn dropped one of the flashlights, and the beam shot across the dirty stage floor, but picked up the glitter on all of the scattered beads. Maybe this was better.

The audience was enraptured once more, as Miss Julie pumped her fist, something that was not in the script. "This town shall rebuild! This town shall always rebuild! We shall not fear flood, nor famine, nor fire!"

"Only venereal diseases," muttered Eileen Lambert.

Undaunted, Miss Julie conjured up her best stage tears. "Gabardine shall survive!"

At this, Kaitlynn and Caitlyn unhooked the bungee cords, and the red curtains swept across the stage but did not close entirely. An oxygen tank stuck out too far.

Applause, even some shrill whistles. I peeked around the curtain, and the entire audience had risen to their feet.

I knew what to expect. The actresses gathered in a group, nearly identical to the same lineup David had commanded months earlier, minus the stars and the stripes. From backstage, I watched as they reached to each other, grasped hands and bowed in unison. Normally, the actresses would take a step backward and pretend to beckon the director onto the stage, but David strode to the center without being asked, and he bowed so deeply that his shellacked hair broke free from the carefully combed part, and a hunk of hair fell across his sweaty forehead. I knew he was overwhelmed with his success, because he didn't bother tucking it back into place when he stood. I think he was expecting somebody to rush up to the stage with roses.

This was not that type of town.

I heard my name, heard Betty Gabrian call out for me, trying to get me to join David at center stage. I shook my head, refused.

I was not that type of girl.

From backstage, I could see the entire audience, as the old men flicked on the fluorescent lights that never were replaced, but even that harsh blue light was beautiful to me, and all of those people did not look garish, but beautiful. I knew Ronnie would not show up to such a thing, but my breath caught in my chest when I examined the crowd and did not see Bitsy. This was not surprising, either. What blew me away were the people I didn't expect: TJ, the two men from the garage, Sheriff Schrader, and Lionel from the Ben Franklin.

A familiar refrain, a thought that had haunted every single day I left our trailer house and encountered people who knew my family, knew my reputation, knew exactly what I did. That litany, the roster I could not shake, no matter how I tried. I know all of your names.

It was a familiar refrain, but tonight it felt different.

I know all of your names, and I am thankful for it.

Chapter Thirty-Seven

THE NEXT MORNING, I KNOCKED. I had precious cargo in my hand, and by precious, I mean dangerous. Who could know how this would turn out? Inside the house, I could hear Janelle call for David. Answering the door would be his job, even though Janelle was most likely sitting on the couch. David probably insisted on this—I'm sure he was the one that dealt with salesmen, bill collectors, the errant Jehovah's Witness.

Even though it was a weekend morning, David was fully dressed, and well. Like he was waiting.

He stared at the answering machine in my hands, cord wrapped around it again and again.

"I knew it," he said. "I knew you stole it."

"Yes," I said.

"You should have gift wrapped it," he said. "Have I taught you nothing?" He grabbed it out of my hands, and I waited for him to invite me inside. He didn't. This was how amends worked, I guess.

Through the open door, I could see Janelle on the couch, in a haze of incense and steam from a giant mug of tea.

"I'm sorry," I said, and Janelle only offered me a sad little smile. David stood in the doorway, clutching the answering machine.

"I know it by heart," said Janelle. "And I don't need it

anymore." I'm not sure if she had finally become self-actualized, if her books and spells had worked, or if Waterbed Fred had his own kind of magic.

"You are a spoiled brat, Tiffany Templeton. That's your problem. Do you know how lucky you are to have a walk-in closet?"

"Change your furnace filters," I said. Janelle flashed me a thumbs-up and drank her tea, while David continued to stand there, glaring at me.

"Do you want some sort of medal?" David began to push the door shut, but something stopped him. "I've been a good friend to you. For the most part. You're just a goddamn pack rat. Stealing and scurrying around and being filthy."

I nodded in agreement, turned on my heel, and left the porch. I owed him, and I also owed him the last word. For once, he earned it.

I HAD ONE MORE ERRAND that morning, but I barely made any distance in the trailer court before the sheriff pulled up next to me.

I could handle whatever he threw at me, but just in case, I hid the painting under my jacket. He rolled down his window, and I could feel the heat blasting from inside his patrol car.

He was stern-faced, but he was always stern-faced. I waited for the worst, but instead he addressed me like a normal person. "You wrote that play last night?"

"Yes, sir."

"Fantastic. Loved every minute of it. Especially the pack rats. Don't tell anybody, but you're now my favorite juvenile delinquent. The rest of them are useless."

Before I could thank him, he drove away, and I followed his taillights to Lou Ann's house.

LOU ANN'S FRONT STEPS WERE still splattered with cerulean footprints, just the one shoe. The paint in the Laundromat had been scraped, but the stain remained, a blur of blue that soaked into the linoleum. She hadn't bothered cleaning up this trail, and I didn't blame her one bit. Even though she was a painter, cleaning the front steps of oil paint would require sanding. And then repainting, and then maybe polyurethane. Maybe it wasn't the work that stopped her. Maybe she decided to live as a marked woman.

Unlike I had done with the answering machine, I wrapped the painting in a towel from the lost and found box in the Laundromat. I still could not look at it, could not acknowledge the shape of my father, and especially the expression she had captured on his face.

Lou Ann did not answer her door. She was clearly terrified and slid open the kitchen window.

"Did you tell your mother? Is she hiding somewhere?"

"My mother is incapable of hiding," I said. "You know that."

"I found somebody to do my taxes," she said. "It's a big relief."

"I want to keep this," I said. "I stole it last year."

"The nude," she said. "Oh my."

I fished in my pocket and withdrew $137. The last of Coach Bitzche's money. I pushed the wad of cash into her hand. "I think artists should get paid. I learned that this year."

"Thank you," she said.

"I've got one question," I said. "Why did you paint him that color?"

"He chose it." Through the screen of the window, I could see tears beginning in her eyes. "He went through the entire box of paints. I think he was trying to find the color of his soul." I didn't have much sympathy, but since she wouldn't open the door, it's not like I could comfort her.

"If you ever paint my soul, make sure you paint it black."

"Red," she said. "Red like fire. A girl who isn't afraid of the flames."

"Whatever," I said. I didn't know how to respond. "I'm not going to tell my mom. I'm not going to tell anybody." I rubbed my foot on her dirty welcome mat, slid my shoe back and forth on the remnants of a cerulean footprint.

"You never really know somebody," she said. "That's the problem with spying, Tiffany. You only see the window. You only see part of the picture and only part of the time."

"You knew I was watching?"

"Your dad warned me," she said.

At this, tears sprang up in my own eyes, and I hated it. I hated her to see this. I began to walk away but stopped on the top step. When I turned around, she was still watching through her screen.

"Thank you for loving him," I said.

And I meant it.

A NEW KID SAT ON a folding chair in Mr. Francine's office. He looked like he'd been crying. The pimples on his face were fiery, like he'd been wiping away his tears with sandpaper. I think he was in junior high, because I didn't recognize him. The criminals in this town kept getting younger.

I wanted to offer him some encouragement, but I was extra careful around Mr. Francine.

Kelly smiled when I entered the room. I was expecting a speech about teen suicide, maybe even a referral to a counselor. My letter had been so melodramatic, and I was embarrassed.

Instead, Kelly clapped her hands. "Bravo," she said. "It was amazing. And your mother was so nervous. It was adorable."

"I don't think anybody has used that word to describe my mother before."

"And that man who sang at the beginning! I have to admit I have a bit of a crush."

I rolled my eyes. "That's Waterbed Fred. From all my letters."

"Wow," she said. "I get it now. I couldn't wait to talk to you today." Here it comes. She's going to give me the same questionnaire we took the first day at Dogwood. Ten questions to determine suicidal ideation.

"I hope my letter didn't freak you out."

"What letter?"

"Never mind." Goddamn that Mr. Francine. Actually, I'm glad he stole it. I had it coming.

"The sheriff was in here this morning. He brought Mr. Francine some can openers. He bought them with his own money. You don't need to worry about any charges, Tiffany. I think the sheriff hates Mr. Francine. And I think he kind of likes you."

"Really?"

"Tiffany, I know you find it hard to believe, but there are people who care about you."

I sighed. "Bitsy isn't talking to me anymore. Consequences."

"Boys are stupid. Trust me on this. Most of them grow up and just get dumber."

"Okay," I said.

"Your mother was beaming," she said. "I'm serious. She was the first person to jump up and applaud."

"Really?"

"Your play was amazing," she said. "I'm proud of you. You are a natural writer, and you proved it. Now put all of your letters together, and you'll have a book."

"I wasn't trying to write a book. I was just trying to tell the truth."

"I want you to keep in touch with me. Regular letters, please. No more confessions." She stood up and pointed at the door. "You're done."

"I've still got four months."

"I'm not worried about you," she said. "And now the county won't be worried about you, either."

"I'm off probation?"

"Yes," said Kelly. "You're free. Join a circus. Follow a cult. Whatever you choose, I support you. Just keep writing."

"How do you know I'm not going to stay in Gabardine?"

"The world needs you, Tiffany. Tough Tiff is destined for greatness."

"Thanks, I guess."

"You made my student debt worthwhile," she said. "Hopefully, that won't be the last time I say those words."

"There's still a bunch of Sweets in grade school," I said.

"Get out of here," she said. Before I left, I made sure to give her one last envelope.

Inside, a Thank You card. Paid for and everything. I signed it, and that was all. Important things need to be typewritten.

No more confessions.

FROM THE DESK OF TIFFANY TEMPLETON

Dear Kelly:

I've only got eleven pages of stationery left, but now it's an even number. Ten. You deserve it. Enclosed is a gift certificate for my mother's gas station. She actually gave it to me without a fight. She likes you. It's only for fifty bucks, but that should get you a full tank, and you can spend the rest on Kleenex or whatever. I hope you fill up your car and keep driving. I'm not scared of a new probation officer. I've got nothing to hide. I'm no good at secrets. Someday, I hope to be as loud and proud as David. I don't think anybody in the trailer park is ever going to get curtains, but they don't need to worry. My days of being a juvenile delinquent are over. And if I can help somebody else, I will. Just like you helped me. I don't think I can stop kids from making pipe bombs. Sorry about that. I know what it's like to blow things up, and I know that sometimes it's necessary. You just have to admit what you did, and then pick up the pieces. Thanks for everything.

Sincerely,

Tiffany Templeton

Chapter Thirty-Eight

THE NEXT DAY, I WOKE to a dusting of snow. Winter had crept up without us noticing, as sneaky as a girl spy.

At the Laundromat, I kneeled in the powder to pull out the typewriter case. I knew my jeans were going to soak through, but this was worth it. I was not going to leave a time capsule. I would leave an empty box for the next bad girl to fill. There would always be another bad girl. I had blazed a trail in the trailer park for those who did not belong, who took things too far, and now I was leaving her a space to put those things. I burned the entire envelope and took the can openers home with me. We still didn't have silverware, but we would be prepared for the apocalypse.

I thought the painting would be harder to burn, that I might have to return with lighter fluid or build some sort of pyre. But as soon as I flicked my lighter and lit the corner, the entire surface spread with blue flame. I thought the oil paint would have shed all those chemicals after a year, but like most things, it would always remain highly flammable, just waiting for a spark. I dropped it in the juniper bush and watched for ten minutes, until all that remained were black ashes skittering among the gusts of wind and snow. I scooped up as many of the ashes as I could and entered the Laundromat with sooty hands and left the mess in the garbage can. Lou Ann could deal with the aftermath.

I would survive without Bitsy. I would survive without David.

This is what a feminist looks like.

Chapter Thirty-Nine

IN THE HALLWAYS AT SCHOOL, I was a ghost once more. If Dogwood hadn't been shut down, I would consider committing a crime just to go back, but an ethical crime this time, like blowing up a laboratory that experimented on monkeys. I knew where I could get a pipe bomb.

One day I saw TJ, wearing his winter jacket, a new model but just as puffy. I saw him hang back near the drinking fountain.

I watched the NyQuil bottle raise to his lips, and he guzzled twice as much. We did have social studies in two minutes, so the extra dosage was warranted. None of the kids in the hallway seemed to notice, but they didn't know what to look for.

I couldn't help myself. Months ago, we were in the same gang. When I approached him, he was dazed, but when he recognized me, his face twisted in confusion.

"Are you okay?" I whispered this, even though the traffic in the hallways was nearly deafening.

He stood taller, corrected his normally sloppy posture. He knew we were being watched. The NyQuil bottle disappeared into his pocket. "Why are you talking to me?"

"I'm concerned," I said.

"I have a cold," he said. "Fuck off."

* * *

LATER THAT AFTERNOON, I FINALLY walked out the front door, free from a place that seemed more of a prison than the one I had been remanded to. Kaitlynn waited for me by the flagpole. Since a freak windstorm my freshman year, only the halyards remained.

I tried to walk past her, but she called out my name.

She leaned against the barren flagpole. I knew it must have been ice-cold, but she wanted to look tough, or nonchalant, or something. All these poses. We all have all these poses.

She reached into her jeans pocket, removed a receipt. It was crisp, folded in half. She placed it into her palm, and blew it toward me, into the air. We both watched as it landed on the slushy sidewalk between us. Neither of us made a move to pick it up.

"It's from David," she said. "He wants you to pay him for that jacket." I was wearing the new jacket at that very moment. I knew David was mad, but not enough to take back a makeover.

"Fuck that," I said. "I'll just give it back." I began to pull the jacket from my shoulders, even though it was probably twenty degrees outside.

"Stop," she said. "He won't want it back. It's tainted."

"Jesus," I said. I began to walk away. I would pay him back for the jacket, and I could be free of these girls for the rest of high school.

"You are a psycho," she said. "I can't believe you stole from poor people."

"It was an answering machine," I said, and the receipt twitched a bit in the wind, just like the boy I missed so terribly. I reached down before the wind could catch it, send it scurrying across the parking lot like a dead leaf.

"You'd better pay him back," she said. "He said he would get a restraining order."

I stared at the receipt. He'd bought the jacket at a store in Spokane, and how he did that would have to remain a mystery. "I will leave forty dollars on their porch."

"Unless he gets the restraining order," she said. "I don't think you'd be allowed to go on their property." She stared at me, and all the fake aggression had disappeared from her face. "You really should wear lipstick. I think it would help."

Satisfied, she stomped away. She knew how to hurt, had learned from the best.

I stood in the parking lot, still clutching the receipt. I knew how to hurt people, too. I lost Bitsy, and there would be no receipt, no exchange. I paid the price.

Chapter Forty

ON THE FIRST DAY OF December, we got our first heavy snow of the season. The streets were still clogged with the storm, but in Gabardine, the parade would go on. We had no main street, just the highway, so the sheriff and his deputies parked at each end of town, lights flashing, apologizing to the reverse snowbirds from Canada. We had no detour. That describes Gabardine perfectly.

In the gas station, my mother grumbled at all of the purchases, kids gathered for the parade, carefully counting out pennies and nickels to buy candy. She was used to pennies and nickels, and she was also used to kids, but not a hundred in two hours, and the floor of the gas station was flooded with snow from tiny boots. The first kid slipped and fell without incident, but the second landed hard and crushed a bag of Doritos. At that point, my mother stopped grumbling, and began to issue commands. I had a job, and that was to mop.

"The last thing I need is a damn lawsuit," she said. "I don't even have a wet floor sign."

Too late. The door swung open, and before I could warn him, David rushed into the store in his usual fashion. This time, there was nothing fashionable about his quick descent to the floor. I stood there with the mop in my hand and examined him as he lay still on the wet linoleum. He said nothing, and my mother peered over the counter. David was never silent, so she probably thought he was dead.

From the floor, he reached into the pocket of his beloved cashmere jacket and removed a familiar envelope.

"Here," he said. "This is awkward enough. Don't make me beg."

Still on his back, I took the envelope out of his hand.

"Get up," said my mother. "You'll ruin that coat."

David eased himself to standing, and for the first time I could remember, he looked embarrassed. "There was no Thank You card," he said. "Typical."

Inside the envelope, I knew there were three ten-dollar bills and two fives.

My mother watched without a word. For once, she could not control the dynamic in the room, and even she could sense the weight between us.

"I don't believe in Thank You cards anymore," I said. "And you're lucky Mrs. Bitzche even delivered it." I had made sure to write my return address as clearly as possible.

"It was never about the jacket," he said. He stared down at the floor, and I saw the back of his neck flush red. "My mother told me that. My mother forgave you, and she told me my karma would be bad until I did the same."

"Smart woman," said my mother.

"Please don't write about this," said David. His eyes remained trained on the spot where he had fallen. "I have a reputation."

"You're my friend," I said. "You'll always be my friend."

He looked up then and offered a sad smile. "It's an honor to be stuck with you, Tiffany Templeton." He bowed to my mother and exited into the frigid air, and I watched through the window as he popped up his collar against the cold.

As the clock ticked closer to eleven, the traffic in the store died down, as the kids joined their parents, teachers, and the most patriotic of townies. I carried my mop outside, and it was so cold that it froze immediately. We had no sidewalks, and down the length of the highway, I could see groups in winter coats clinging to each other for warmth. If you didn't know better, you would think Gabardine was full of lovers.

When I returned inside the store, my mother had a stricken look on her face. At first, I thought she figured out who bought the streetlight.

"We didn't have a fire season this year," she said. "I can't remember a year without a fire season."

"That's a good thing," I said.

Wide-eyed, she grasped the cash register drawer. "What if your brother was right? What if he really did have a mission?"

"Seriously?" I nearly dropped the mop handle. "He's a brain-washed idiot."

"That's true," she said. "Maybe it was just good luck. We were due."

"Ghosts," I said. "You admitted that you believed in ghosts."

"If you tell anybody I said that, I'll kill you."

"I can keep your secret," I said. Promises would be kept. "But I know why we didn't have a fire season."

She rolled her eyes. "Don't talk to me about meteorology," she said. "I'm sorry if you've got an interest, but you don't have the looks to be a weather girl."

"I think it was ghosts," I said. "Eight of them."

She considered this. "Maybe you're right." She shut the cash register softly, but the bell still rang out, an incomplete sale. "I'm okay with eight dead prostitutes. This town needs all the strong women it can get."

I guess it was wrong to call it a parade. There was only one vehicle, only one attraction that drew people out into the bitter cold: the National Christmas Tree.

The sawyer had taken it down yesterday, and I heard there was a crowd for that, too. A crane swung the tree onto the back of a logging truck, a local sawyer and a local logging truck, so I knew the newspaper had a worthy headline. Pride in the sawyer who was the son of another sawyer, and pride in the logging truck, also passed down from a father to a son.

As far as my own familial relations, my mother was unimpressed with the hoopla, but I wouldn't have been surprised to see my brother clinging to the tree as it passed through town, refusing to let go. That would have at least made the parade interesting. Most likely, he was standing in front of the stump, waving an American flag, maybe crying.

I'm not an environmentalist, but it did seem weird for an entire town to celebrate the death of something, a murder that measured seventy-nine feet.

Ten minutes before the parade, the gas station was completely empty, and I heard my mother swear as she ejected the drawer from the cash register. All that change had piled beyond the capacity, and the drawer was stuck, probably pennies. She yanked, but it would not budge. In the last eight months, I had discovered where my mother's strength truly resided. It wasn't in her forearms. Even though she would never admit it, my mother had something inside her that would not allow her to give up on me, even when she said otherwise. My mother would not give up on anything she really cared about, and this included the cash register drawer, and with one loud grunt, she finally dislodged it. Unfortunately, it dislodged past its springs and flew onto the floor. She didn't ask me to pick up all the loose change. I think she was still relishing her new body, and her ability to crouch, and she took to the floor and began to pluck the errant coins. In her particular way, of course. Instead of scooping all of the change together, she picked up all the pennies first.

She was still crouched down on the floor when the door of the gas station swung open, and Kaitlynn burst through, silver ski jacket and a purple-and-black scarf, the stripes so close together that it seemed to be the color of bruises.

I stood in front of the deadly popcorn machine, mop still in hand. Tough Tiff would have used it as a weapon.

She marched straight up to me. I could tell by her intensity that she was following orders, just like always. Unfortunately, she didn't know that David had just left and made things right.

"We know the truth about you. We know you're a lesbian." She squared her shoulders and tossed her hair. I'd seen this pose a thousand times since kindergarten.

"That's the best you've got?" I dipped the mop into the bucket, and when I shoved it into the wringer, I cranked as hard as I could. I hoped she could see my muscles flex. "That's not even an insult."

"Nobody likes a freak. You're going to die alone."

At this, my mother suddenly sprung up from behind the counter, her fist full of pennies, and startled Kaitlynn. Wisely, she took a step back from me.

"What did you just say?"

"Nothing," said Kaitlynn. "No big deal."

"I heard you," said my mother. "Who in the hell do you think you are?"

"Kaitlynn," she said. "The one with the K." Clearly, she did not grasp my mother's tone.

"I know exactly which Kaitlynn you are. I know everything in this town. Your current stepfather has hepatitis C because he used to be a meth head. Next time you see Sheriff Schrader, ask him about your real dad, and the time he got busted in the bowling alley parking lot. He tried to sell you to some Canadians."

Kaitlynn's face blotched purple as her scarf, and she took another step backward.

"That's not true," she said.

"Of course, you don't remember, because you were just a baby. But the rest of this town will never forget that he couldn't even get ten dollars." My mother smirked. "Canadian dollars."

As usual, my mother knew everything, and Kaitlynn's jaw dropped open, so I knew it was the truth. I would hold on to this information, just in case I needed it later. My mother slammed the fistful of pennies on the countertop, and the crack made Kaitlynn jump backward into the candy aisle.

"I don't ever want to see your rat face or your cheap clothes in my store. Got it? You're no longer allowed here."

Kaitlynn nodded her head and backed toward the exit. Of course, my mother was not finished.

"I would ask you to apologize, but I never want to hear you open your mouth again."

A cold blast of air from outside as Kaitlynn swung open the door and fled out toward the highway. I watched her silver jacket pass several groups gathered in front of the garage, including two of her fellow cheerleaders. Kaitlynn kept walking. She was the type of girl who didn't need a parade, because she lived inside one her entire life. At this moment, she walked so fast that nobody could shower her with compliments, a silver blur getting smaller and smaller, until she ducked down a side street, and I lost sight of her entirely.

"Thank you," I said.

"My pleasure," she said. "You're not going to die alone. I'm pretty sure your brother won't find anyone, either."

It had taken some work, and a lot of time, but I had accepted that these words from my mother were her version of kindness. This was who she was, and I never expected her to change. Things were right, things had been forgiven. When she asked me to make popcorn, I knew for sure.

The rumble of the truck approached, louder than the hissing and spitting as the kettle spun. My mother and I both watched out the window, and that was enough. We would not join the crowd along the highway. The cab of the truck appeared, and behind it, a tree so massive that it filled the entire window, and for a few moments, all we could see was green.

Acknowledgments

THIS BOOK WOULD NOT BE possible without the grace and kindness of my friends and family. They kept me going, and they caught me every time I fell, and picked up the pieces when I broke apart. My mother was lifted up by the love of Gary Jones, Lisa Cooper, Launa Baas, Dana Wallace, and the rest of my biological family. Special thanks to my aunt, Mary Baker Johnson, who reminds me every single day to live ferociously, and love fearlessly. I'm fortunate to have a family of friends that never left my side: Julie Janj, Hunter Thomas, Adam Muscarella, Lucy Hansen, Patrick Ryan, Kelley Provost, Rashid Abdel Ghafur, Renee Tost, Robin O'Day, Jeff Orchard, Erinn Ackley, Paula Miskuly Tripp, Frank Casciato, Kia Liszak, Sharma Shields, Vasa Parsons, Kelly Plotz, Jenna Blum, Mark and Pam Gibbons, Alison Callahan, and Amber Boyce.

Thank you to John Runkle and Dallas Wilson, and Jane Peterson and Eileen McGurty, who offered me places to write, and to Book Club for Mayor and the Missoula Group, who offered me a place to be loved. Thank you to Dr. Laura Wharton, and the nurses at Cabinet Peaks Medical Center in Libby, Montana, for taking care of my mother, and for holding my hand through the end. We were blessed by your presence, and the dignity you provided.

I have a great team of cheerleaders and advisors, and I am indebted to Jenny Bent, Andrea Peskind Katz and Great Thoughts Great Readers, Kathy Murphy and the Pulpwood Queens, J. Ryan Stradal, Barbara Theroux, Gwen Florio, Gretchen Durning and Ben Schrank. Mara Panich, Aimee McQuilkin, and Quinn McQuilkin were extraordinary beta readers, and Mike Malament was an exceptional (and patient) photographer. Big love to all my students, past and present, and the Zootown Arts Community Center for hosting us. Thank you to Fact & Fiction, Shakespeare & Co, and all the independent bookstores that hosted me, as well as every book club brave enough to have me in their homes. When I got lost, Pete Fromm and Deirdre McNamer rescued me, and reminded me of how damn lucky I am to be able to share my words. I am incredibly grateful to each and every reader out there; none of this would be possible without your continued support of authors and books.

Sometimes, real life can take away the best parts of you, and leave behind a blank page.

Don't give up. When you are loved, and are brave enough to love somebody else, the stories will always be there.

XOXO,
Richard